THE REGENCY
HIGH-SOCIETY AFFAIRS
COLLECTION

**Passion, Scandal and Romance
from your favourite historical authors.**

THE REGENCY
HIGH-SOCIETY AFFAIRS
COLLECTION

Available from the Regency High-Society Affairs
Large Print Collection

THE SOCIETY CATCH

Louise Allen

First published in Great Britain 2004
Large Print edition 2010
Harlequin Mills & Boon Limited,
Eton House, 18-24 Paradise Road, Richmond, Surrey TW9 1SR

© Louise Allen 2004

ISBN: 978 0 263 21602 8

Harlequin Mills & Boon policy is to use papers that are natural,
renewable and recyclable products and made from wood grown in
sustainable forests. The logging and manufacturing process conform
to the legal environmental regulations of the country of origin.

Printed and bound in Great Britain
by CPI Antony Rowe, Chippenham, Wiltshire

Chapter One

The encounter that led directly to Colonel Gregory being disinherited by his father and to Miss Joanna Fulgrave running away from home in disgrace took place at the Duchess of Bridlington's dress ball on the sixth of June.

It was a very splendid occasion. As her Grace fully intended, it succeeded in both marking the approaching end of the Season and ensuring that any other function held between then and the dispersal of the *ton* from town seemed sadly flat in comparison.

Joanna progressed as gracefully to the receiving line outside the ballroom at Bridlington House as the necessity to halt on every step and to guard her skirts from being trodden upon allowed. Beside her Mrs Fulgrave mounted the famous double staircase with equal patience. The Fulgrave ladies had ample opportunity to exchange smiles and bows with friends and acquaintances, caught up as they all were in the slow-moving crush.

As always, mothers of less satisfactory débutantes observed her progress, and in undertones reminded their daughters to observe Miss Fulgrave's impeccable deportment, her exquisitely correct appearance and her perfectly modulated and charming manner.

If Joanna had not combined these enviable virtues with a natural warmth and friendliness, the young ladies so addressed would have long since begun to dislike her heartily. As it was, they forgave her for her perfections while their mothers poured balm upon each other's wounds with reminders that this was Miss Fulgrave's second Season now drawing to a close and she was still unattached.

That was a matter very much upon her fond mama's mind. No one, Mrs Fulgrave knew, could hope for a more dutiful, lovely, conformable daughter as Joanna. Yet not one, but seven, eligible gentlemen had presented themselves to Mr Fulgrave, were permitted to pay their addresses to

Joanna and went away, their pretensions dismissed kindly but firmly. In every case Miss Joanna was unable, or unwilling, to provide her harassed parent with any explanation, other than to say she did not think the gentleman would suit.

However, that very morning Joanna had refused to receive the son of her mama's dearest school friend, a gentleman of such excellent endowments of birth, fortune and looks that her father had rapidly moved from astonishment to incredulous displeasure and Joanna discovered the limits of parental tolerance at last.

'How can you say you will refuse Rufus?' her mother had demanded. 'What can I say to Elizabeth when she discovers you have spurned her son out of hand?'

'I hardly know him,' Joanna had said placatingly, only to meet with a snort from her parent. '*You* hardly know him: why, you said yourself that you had not met his mama for over ten years.'

'You met Rufus Carstairs when you were six.'

'He pulled my pigtails and took my ball.'

'When he was ten! Really Joanna, to turn down the Earl of Clifton because of some childish squabble is beyond everything foolish.'

Joanna had bitten her lip, her eyes downcast as she

searched for some acceptable excuse. To tell the truth, the reason why she would have turned down anyone from a Duke to the richest nabob, was quite out of the question, but she was hesitant to wound her mama with the specific reason why she would not have considered Rufus Carstairs in any case.

'Well?'

'I do not like him, Mama, really I do not. There is something in his eyes when he looks at me…' Her voice trailed off. Those penetrating blue eyes were the only clue to something burning inside the polite, elegant exterior that filled her with a profound mistrust. 'It is as though I have no clothes on,' she finally blurted out.

'Joanna! Of all the improper things…I can only hope that your natural innocence has led you to mistake the perfectly understandable ardour of a young man in love for something which I sincerely trust you know nothing about!' Mrs Fulgrave had broken off to compose herself. 'Has he said anything to put you to the blush? No. Has he acted in any improper manner? No, I thought not. This is another of your whims and your papa and I are reaching the end of our patience with you.'

Pausing yet again on the stairs, Joanna closed her eyes momentarily at the memory of her mother's voice, normally so calm and indulgent. 'You could not hope for a more eligible or flattering offer. I suggest you think very seriously indeed about your position. If you think that your papa can afford to support you in an endless round of dances and parties and new dresses while you amuse yourself toying with the affections of decent young men, you are much mistaken.'

'Mama, I am not toying with Lord Clifton's affections,' she had protested. 'I hardly know him—he cannot love me! I have not seen him since we were children…' But her mama had swept out, throwing back over her shoulder the observation that it was fortunate that the earl would not be able to attend the ball that evening and risk a rebuff before Joanna had a chance to come to her senses.

They climbed another two steps and came to a halt again. Mrs Fulgrave exchanged bows with Lady Bulstrode, taking the opportunity to study her daughter's calm profile. What a countess she would make, if only she would come to her senses!

Long straight black hair coiled at the back of her head and held by pearl-headed pins; elegantly arched brows, which only she knew were the result of painful work with the tweezers; wide hazel eyes, which magically changed from brown to green in extremes of unhappiness or joy, and a tall, slender figure. Mrs Fulgrave could never decide whether Joanna's white shoulders or her pretty bosom were the best features of her figure, but both were a joy to her *modiste*.

Madame de Montaigne, as the *modiste* in question styled herself, had excelled with tonight's gown. An underskirt of a pale almond green was covered by a creamy gauze with the hem thickly worked with *faux* pearls. The bodice crossed in front in a mass of intricate pleating, which was carried through to the full puffed sleeves, and the back dipped to a deep V-shape, which showed off Joanna's white skin to perfection. Her papa had presented her with pearl earrings, necklace and bracelets for her recent twentieth birthday and those completed an ensemble that, in Mrs Fulgrave's eyes, combined simple elegance with the restraint necessary for an unmarried lady.

It was no wonder that the earl, who could hope to engage the interest of any young lady who took his fancy, should be so taken with the daughter of his mother's old friend. He had seen her again for the first time as adults on his return from a continental tour where he had been acquiring classical statuary for what was already becoming known as a superb art collection. Joanna might not be a brilliant match, but she was well bred, well connected, adequately dowered and lovely enough to turn any man's head.

Joanna herself was engaged, not in wondering how her gown compared with anyone else's, nor in dwelling on that morning's unpleasantness, but in discreetly scanning the throng on both wings of the staircase for one particular man. She had no idea whether he would be there tonight, or even if he was in the country, yet she hoped that he would be, as she had at every function she had attended since her come-out more than two years ago.

The man Joanna was looking for was her future husband, Colonel Giles Gregory, and for his sake she had spent almost three years preparing herself to be the ideal wife for a career soldier. A career soldier, moreover, who would one day become a general, would be elevated far above his own father's barony and would doubtless, like the Duke of Wellington, become a diplomat and statesman of renown.

She had fallen in love with Giles Gregory when she was only seventeen and just out of the school-room. She was already causing her anxious mother to worry that when she came out she would prove to be a flirt and a handful. Unlike her calm, biddable sister Grace, who had become engaged to Sir Frederick Willington in her first Season, Joanna showed every inclination to throw herself into any scrape that presented itself.

Then their cousin Hebe had arrived from Malta to plunge the family headlong into her incredible and improbable romance with the Earl of Tasborough. As the earl was in deep mourning and had just inherited his title and estates, yet insisted that his Hebe marry him within three weeks, preparations were hurried and unconventional. As groomsman, the earl's friend Major Gregory found himself thrown into the role of go-between and supporter of the Fulgrave family as they coped with the marriage preparations.

Much of his time had been taken up amusing young William Fulgrave, freeing William's mama from at least one concern as she made her preparations. Army-mad William had plagued the tall major for stories and neither appeared to take much notice of sister Joanna, who would quietly come into the room in her brother's turbulent wake and listen silently from a corner.

Joanna moved up a few more steps, her eyes on

the black-clad shoulders of the gentleman in front of her, her mind back in the tranquil front room of the house in Charles Street. The sedate parlour had become full of vivid and exciting pictures as Giles held William spellbound with his stories of life on campaign. She had soon realised that, whatever William's blandishments, his hero never talked about himself but always about his soldiers or his friends. Insidiously the qualities that meant that his men would follow their major into hell and back, and then go again if he asked, drew Joanna deeper and deeper into love with him.

She understood very clearly that she was too young and that he would not even think of the gauche schoolroom miss that she was now in any other light than as a little sister. But she would be out that Season and then she could begin to learn. And there was so much to learn if she was going to be the perfect wife that Giles deserved. And the wife she knew with blind faith he would recognise as perfect the moment he saw her again.

Almost overnight Mrs Fulgrave's younger daughter became biddable, attentive and well behaved. From plucking her dark brows into submission to mastering the precise depth of a curtsy to a duchess or a rural dean, Joanna applied herself. Her parents were too delighted in the transformation in their harum-scarum child to question what had provoked this miracle, and no probing questions disturbed Joanna's single-minded quest for perfection.

And month after month the army kept Major, then Colonel, Gregory abroad. Joanna never gave up her calm expectation that they would meet again soon, although every day, as soon as her father put down his *Times*, she would scan the announcements with care, searching anxiously for the one thing that would have shattered her world. It never occurred to her that Giles might be wounded, let alone killed, for she believed that no such fate would intervene in his predestined path to greatness. But there was another danger always present and each morning Joanna breathed again when the announcement of Colonel Gregory's engagement to some eligible lady failed to appear.

Mother and daughter finally reached the top of the stairs and Joanna sought diligently for something appropriate to say to the duchess. It would be important as the wife of a senior officer to say the right things to all manner of people. The Duchess of Bridlington, Joanna recalled, liked to be in the forefront of fashion, setting it, not following. She eyed the unusual floral decorations thoughtfully.

'Mrs Fulgrave, Miss Fulgrave.' Her Grace was gracious. She liked pretty girls who would enjoy themselves, flirt with the men and make her parties a success, and Miss Fulgrave, although not a flirt, was certainly a pretty girl who was never above being pleased with her company. 'A dreadful squeeze, is it not, my dear?' She smiled at Joanna.

'Not at all, your Grace.' Joanna smiled back, dropping a perfectly judged curtsy. 'It was delightful to have the opportunity to admire the floral decorations as we came up the stairs. How wonderful those palms and pineapples look, and how original: why, I have never seen anything like it.'

'Dear child,' the duchess responded, patting her cheek, highly pleased at the compliment. Her gardeners had grumbled about stripping out the succession houses, but she had insisted and indeed the exotic look had succeeded to admiration.

Joanna and Mrs Fulgrave passed on into the ballroom, its pillared, mirrored walls already reverberating with the hum of conversation, the laughter of nervous débutantes and the faint sounds of the orchestra playing light airs before the dancing began.

As she always did, Joanna began to scan the room, her heart almost stopping at the sight of each red coat before passing on. She must not let her anxiety show, she knew. An officer's wife must be calm and not reveal her feelings whatever the circumstances. A small knot of officers was surveyed and dismissed and then, suddenly, half a head above those surrounding him, was a man with hair the colour of dark honey. A man whose scarlet coat sat across broad shoulders strapped with muscle and whose crimson sash crossed a chest decorated with medal ribbons on the left breast.

'Giles!' Joanna had no idea she spoke aloud, and indeed her voice was only a whisper. It was he, and three years of waiting, of loving, of hard work and passionate belief were at an end.

He was making his way slowly up the opposite side of the dance floor, stopping to talk to friends here and there, bowing to young ladies and now and again, she could see, asking for a dance. Joanna's hand closed hard over her unfilled dance card, which dangled from her wrist on its satin ribbon. As it did so a voice beside her said, 'Miss Fulgrave! May I beg the honour of the first waltz?'

It was a round-faced young man with red hair. Joanna smiled but shook her head. 'I am so sorry,

Lord Sutton, I will not be waltzing this evening. Would you excuse me? I have to speak to someone at the other end of the room.'

She began to move slowly but purposefully through the crowd, her eyes on Giles's head, trying to catch a glimpse of his face. Why was he in London? She had seen no mention of it in the *Gazette*. Anxiously she studied the tall figure. Her heart was pounding frantically and she did not know that all the colour had ebbed from her face. She felt no doubts: this was her destiny. This was Giles's destiny.

He had almost reached the head of the room now. Joanna fended off three more requests for dances. Her entire card had to be free for whenever Giles wanted to dance. Or would they just sit and talk? Would he recognise her immediately or would she have to contrive an introduction?

She was almost there. She calmed her breathing. It was essential that his first impression was entirely favourable. She could see his face clearly now. He was very tanned, white lines showing round his eyes where laughter had creased the skin. He looked harder, fitter, even more exciting than she remembered him. Ten more steps…

Giles Gregory turned his head as though

someone had spoken to him, hesitated and stepped back. Joanna saw him push aside the curtain that was partly draped over an archway and enter the room beyond.

The crowd was thick at that end of the room where circulating guests from both directions met and spoke before moving on their way. She was held up by the crush and it took her perhaps three minutes to reach the same archway.

When she finally lifted the curtain she found herself alone in a little lobby and looked around, confused for a moment. Then she heard his voice, unmistakably Giles's voice. Deep, lazily amused, caressing her senses like warm honey over a spoon. She stepped forward and saw into the next room where Giles was standing…smiling down into the upturned face of the exquisite young lady clasped in his arms.

'So you will talk to Papa, Giles darling? Promise?' she was saying, her blue eyes wide on his face.

'Yes, Suzy, my angel, I promise I will talk to him tomorrow.' Giles's voice was indulgent, warm, loving. Joanna's hand grasped the curtain without her realising it; her eyes, her every sense, were fixed on the couple in the candlelit chamber.

'Oh, Giles, I do love you.' The young lady suddenly laughed up at him and Joanna's numbed mind realised who she was. Lady Suzanne Hall was the loveliest, the most eligible, the wealthiest débutante of that Season. Niece of her Grace the Duchess of Bridlington, eldest and most indulged daughter of the Marquis of Olney, blonde, petite, spirited and the most outrageous flirt, she had a fortune that turned heads, but, even penniless, she would have drawn men after her like iron filings to a magnet.

Why does she want Giles? Joanna screamed inwardly. *He is mine!*

'Oh, it is such an age since I have seen you! Do you truly love me, Giles, my darling?' Suzanne said, her arms entwined round his neck, his hands linked behind her tiny waist.

'You know I do, Suzy,' he replied, smiling down at her. 'You are my first, my only, my special love.' And then he bent his head and kissed her.

The world went black, yet Joanna found she was still on her feet, clutching the curtain. Vision closed in until all she could see was a tiny image of the entwined lovers as though spied down the wrong end of a telescope. Blindly she turned and walked out. By some miracle she was still on her feet although she could see nothing now: it was as though she had fainted, yet retained every sense but sight.

Outside the archway she remembered there had been chairs, fragile affairs of gilt wood. Joanna put out a hand and found one, thankfully unoccupied. She sat, clasped her hands in her lap and managed to smile brightly. Would anyone notice?

Gradually sight returned, although her head spun. No one was sitting next to her, no one had noticed. She tried to make sense of what had happened. Giles was here, and Giles was in love with Lady Suzanne.

She had read—for she read everything that she could find on military matters—that it was possible to receive a mortal wound and yet feel no pain, to continue for some time until suddenly one dropped dead of it. Shock, the doctors called it, a far more serious and deadly thing than the everyday shocks of ordinary life. Perhaps that was what she was feeling: shock.

Joanna was conscious of a swirl of bluebell skirts by her shoulder and Lady Suzanne appeared, hesitated for a moment and plunged into the throng. Her voice came back clearly. 'Freddie! I would love to waltz with you, but I have not got a single dance on my card left. No, I am not teasing you, look…'

Joanna found she could not manage to keep the smile on her lips. Her hands began to tremble and she clasped them together in her lap. Any minute now someone was going to notice her and start to fuss. She *had* to get herself under control.

'Madam, are you unwell?' The deep voice came from close beside her. Joanna started violently, dropping her fan, and instantly Colonel Gregory was on one knee before her. 'Here, I do not think it is damaged.'

She began to stammer a word of thanks, then their eyes met and he exclaimed, 'But it is Miss Joanna Fulgrave, is it not?' Joanna nodded mutely, taking the fan from his outstretched fingers, using exaggerated care not to touch him. 'May I sit down?' Taking her silence for assent, he took the chair next to her, his big frame absurdly out of place on the fragile-looking object.

'Thank you, Colonel.' She had managed a coherent sentence, but it was not enough to convince him that all was well with her. Joanna fixed her gaze on her clasped hands, yet she utterly aware of him beside her, his body turned to her, his eyes on her face.

'You are not well, Miss Fulgrave. May I fetch someone to you? Is your mother here, perhaps?'

'I need no one, I thank you,' she managed to whisper. 'I am quite well, Colonel.'

'I beg leave to differ, Miss Fulgrave. You are as white as a sheet.'

'I...I have had an unexpected and unwelcome encounter, that is all.' Her voice sounded a little stronger, and emboldened she added, 'It was a shock: I will be better presently, Colonel.' *Please leave me,* she prayed, *please go before I break down and turn sobbing into your arms in front of all these people.*

Giles Gregory was on his feet, but not in answer to her silent pleas. 'Has a gentleman here offered you some insult?' he asked, keeping his voice low and his body between her and the throng around the dance floor.

'Oh, no, nothing like that,' Joanna assured him. She forced herself to look up. The grey eyes with their intriguing black flecks regarded her seriously, and, she realised, with some disbelief at her protestations.

'I will fetch you something to drink Miss Fulgrave; I will not be long, just try and rest quietly.'

Joanna sat back in the chair, wishing she had the

strength to get up and hide herself away, but her legs felt as though they were made out of *blanc manger.* Her mind would not let her think about the disaster that had befallen her; she tried to make herself realise what had happened, but somehow she just could not concentrate.

'Here. Now, sip this and do not try to talk.' He was back already, two glasses in his hands. How had he managed to get through the press of people? she wondered hazily, not having observed the Colonel striding straight across the dance floor between the couples performing a boulanger to accost the footmen who were setting out the champagne glasses.

The liquid fizzed down her throat, making her cough. She had expected orgeat or lemonade and had taken far too deep a draught.

'I would have given you brandy, but I do not have a hip flask on me. Go on, drink it, Miss Fulgrave. You have obviously had a shock, even if you are not prepared to tell me about it. The wine will help calm your nerves.' He sat down again, turning the chair slightly so his broad shoulders shielded her. He watched her face and apparently was reassured by what he saw.

'That is better. Now, let us talk of other things.

How are your parents? Well, I trust? And your sister is married by now, I expect?' He seemed happy to continue in the face of her silent nods. 'And William—how old is he? Twelve, I should imagine. And still army mad?'

'No.' Joanna managed a wan smile. 'Not any longer. He is resolved to become a natural philosopher.'

Giles Gregory's eyebrows rose, but he did not seem offended that his disciple had abandoned his military enthusiasms. 'Indeed? Well, I do recall he always had an unfortunate frog or snail in his pocket.'

'That is nothing to the things he keeps in his room.' Joanna began to relax. It was like having the old Major Gregory back again: she could not feel self-conscious with him and the last few minutes seemed increasingly unreal. She took another long sip of champagne. 'And he conducts experiments which cause Mama to worry that the house will burn down. Papa even takes him to occasional lectures if they are not too late in the evening.'

'And your father is not anxious about this choice of career?'

'I think he is resigned.' Despite herself Joanna smiled, fondly recalling her father's expression at the sight of the kitchen when Cook had indignantly summoned him to view the results of Master William's experiment with the kettle, some yards of piping and a heavy weight. She took another sip and realised her glass was empty.

Giles removed it from her hand and gave her his untouched glass. 'Very small glasses, Miss Fulgrave,' he murmured.

'Have you heard from the Earl of Tasborough lately?' she asked. It must be the shock still, for she was feeling even more light-headed, although the awful numbness was receding to be replaced by a sense of unreality. She was having this conversation with Giles as though the past three years had not been and as though she had not just seen him kissing Lady Suzanne and declaring his love for her.

'Not for a week or so. My correspondence is probably chasing me around the continent.' He looked at her sharply. 'Why do you ask? Is Hebe well?'

'Oh, yes,' Joanna hastened to reassure him. 'You know she is…er…in an—'

'Interesting condition?' the Colonel finished for her. 'Yes, I did know. I had a letter from Alex some months ago, unbearably pleased with himself over the prospect of another little

Beresford to join Hugh in the nursery. I will visit them this week, I hope.'

Joanna drank some more champagne to cover her confusion at his frank reference to Hebe's pregnancy. Mama always managed to ignore entirely the fact that ladies of her acquaintance were expecting. Joanna had wondered if everyone secretly felt as she did, that it was ridiculous to pretend in the face of ever-expanding waistlines that nothing was occurring. The Colonel obviously shared her opinion. 'You are home on leave, then?'

'Yes.' He frowned. 'It is a long time since I was in England.'

'Almost a year, and then it was only for a week or two, was it not?' Joanna supplied, then realised from his expression that this revealed remarkable knowledge about his activities. 'I think Lord Tasborough said something to that effect,' she added, crossing her fingers.

'I am a little concerned about my father. My mother's letters have expressed anxiety about his health, so when the chance arose to come home I took it.' He hesitated, 'I have many decisions to make on this furlough: one at least will entail a vast change to my life.'

His marriage, Joanna thought bleakly. That

would certainly be a vast change to a man who had lived a single life up to the age of thirty, and a life moreover which had sent him around the continent with only himself to worry about.

'Shall I take your glass?' Joanna realised with surprise that the second champagne glass was empty. Goodness, what a fuss people made about it! She had only ever had a sip or two before and Mama was always warning about the dangers of it, but now she had drunk two entire glasses, and was really feeling much better. She gave Giles the glass, aware that he was studying her face.

'You seem a little restored, Miss Fulgrave. Would you care to dance? There is a waltz next if I am not mistaken.'

Joanna took a shaky breath. Mama did not like her to waltz at large balls and permitted it only reluctantly at Almack's or smaller dancing parties. But the temptation of being in Giles's arms, perhaps for the first and only time, was too much.

'Yes, please, Colonel Gregory. I would very much like to waltz.'

Chapter Two

Joanna let Giles take her hand and lead her out on to the dance floor, trying not to remember what had just happened, forcing herself not to think about how she would feel when this dance was over and he was gone. Time must stand still: this was all there was.

She let her hand rest lightly on his shoulder and shut her eyes briefly as his fingers touched her waist. This was another memory to be added to the precious store of recollections of Giles, the most vivid being the fleeting kiss which she had snatched in the flurry of farewells when Hebe and her new husband had driven off after the wedding. Everyone had been kissing the bride and groom: what more natural in the confusion than that she should accidentally kiss the groomsman? Giles had laughed at her blushes and returned the kiss with a swift pressure of his lips on hers: Joanna could still close her eyes and conjure up the exact sensation, the scent of Russian leather cologne…

'Miss Fulgrave?'

'Oh, I am sorry! I was daydreaming, thinking about my steps,' she improvised hurriedly to cover up her complete abstraction. She must not waste a moment in his arms by thinking of the past: only this moment mattered.

The music struck up and they were dancing, dancing, Joanna realised, as if they had been practising together for years. Giles Gregory was a tall man, but her height made them well-matched partners and his strength and co-ordination meant that their bodies moved together with an easy elegance which took her breath away.

'You dance very well, Miss Fulgrave,' he remarked, looking down and meeting browny-green, sparkling eyes. He had thought her much improved on the bouncing schoolroom miss he remembered; in fact, he had hardly recognised her at first sight, but now with the colour back in her face and animation enhancing those unusual eyes, he realised that he had a very lovely young woman in his arms. Who or what had so overset her? he wondered, conscious of a chivalrous urge to land whoever it was a facer for his pains.

'Thank you, Colonel, but I think I must owe that to you. Do you have the opportunity to attend many dances whilst you are with the army?' Joanna realised she must take every opportunity to converse, as while they were talking she could be expected to look into his face. She tried to garner every impression, commit each detail to memory: the darkness of his lashes, the small mole just in front of his left ear, the way his mouth quirked when he was amused, that scent of Russian Leather again…

He swept her round a tight corner, catching her in close to avoid another couple who were making erratic progress down the floor. Joanna was very aware of the heat of his body as she was suddenly pressed against him, then they were dancing once more with the conventional distance between them.

'Dances?' He had been considering her question. 'Surprisingly, yes. We take whatever opportunities present themselves, and as not a few officers have their wives with them whenever circumstances allow—and certainly when we were wintering in Portugal—there is often an im-promptu ball.'

'And the Duke encourages such activities, I believe?' Joanna asked. As they whirled through another ambitious turn she caught a glimpse of her mama's face, a look of surprise upon it. She felt wonderfully light-headed. *This* was reality, the music would never stop. Giles would never leave her.

'Yes. Wellington enjoys a party and he thinks it does us good,' Giles smiled reminiscently.

'*His family*, he calls his officers, does he not?'

'You know a lot about old Nosey, Miss Fulgrave. Are you another of his ardent admirers? I have never known such a man—unless it were that fellow Byron—for attracting the adulation of the ladies. None of the rest of us ever stood a chance of the lightest flirtation while Wellington was around.'

'Why, no, not in that way, for I have never seen him.' Better not to think of Giles wanting to flirt. 'But he is a fine tactician, is he not?'

She saw she had taken Giles aback, for he gave her a quizzical look. 'Indeed, yes, but that is a question I would have expected from Master William, not from a young lady.'

'I take an interest, that is all,' she said lightly, wishing she dared ask about his life with his regiment, but knowing she could never keep the conversation impersonal.

And then, with a flourish of strings, the music came to an end, Giles released her and they were clapping politely and walking off the floor. Joanna felt as though the places where his hands had touched her must be branded on her skin, it felt so sensitive. Her hands began to tremble again.

'Miss Fulgrave, might I hope that the next dance is free on your card?' It was Freddie Sutton looking hopeful. 'And now that I know you have changed your mind about waltzing tonight, may I also hope for one a little later?'

'Miss Fulgrave.' Giles Gregory was bowing to her, nodding to Freddie. 'Sutton.' He smiled at her, and she read a look of reassurance in his eyes and guessed that she must be looking better. 'Thank you for the dance.'

Then he was gone, swallowed up in the crowd. She looked after him, catching a glimpse of the back of his head and slowly realising that with the ending of that dance the entire purpose for which she had been living for the past three years, and her every hope for the future, had crumbled into dust.

'Thank you, Lord Sutton.' She turned back to him, her smile glittering. 'I would love to dance the next waltz with you, but just now what I would really like is a glass of champagne.'

To the chagrin and rising dismay of her mama, to the censure of the flock of chaperons and to the horrified and jealous admiration of her friends, Joanna proceeded to stand up for every waltz and most of the other dances as well. She did refuse some, but only to drink three more glasses of champagne, to be escorted into supper by Lord Maxton, a hardened rake and fortune hunter, and to crown the evening by being discovered by the Dowager Countess of Wigham alone with Mr Paul Hadrell on the terrace.

'I felt I must tell you at once,' that formidable matron informed an appalled Mrs Fulgrave, who had been looking anxiously for her daughter for the past fifteen minutes. 'I could not believe my eyes at first,' she continued, barely managing to conceal her enjoyment at having found the paragon of deportment engaged in such an activity with one of the worst male flirts in town. 'I am sure I do not have to tell *you*, Mrs Fulgrave, that Mr Hadrell is the last man I would want a daughter of mine to be alone with!'

This final observation was addressed to Mrs Fulgrave's retreating back, for Joanna's harassed mother lost no time in hurrying to the doors that led to the terrace. It had never occurred to her for a moment that Joanna might be out there, but there indeed she was, leaning against the balustrade in the moonlight, laughing up at the saturnine Mr Hadrell, who was standing far too close and, even as Mrs Fulgrave approached, was leaning down to—

'Joanna!' Her errant daughter moved away from her beau with her usual grace and no appearance of guilt. He, however, took one look at her chaperon's expression and took himself off with a bow and an insouciant,

'Your servant, Miss Fulgrave. Mrs Fulgrave, ma'am!'

'Joanna!' Emily Fulgrave repeated, in the voice of a woman who could not believe what she was seeing. 'What is the meaning of this? You have been flirting, waltzing—and, to crown it all, I find you out here with such a man! And to make things even worse, I was told where I could find you, and with whom, by Lady Wigham.'

Joanna shrugged, a pretty movement of her white shoulders. 'I was bored.'

'*Bored!*' Mrs Fulgrave peered at her in the half-light. 'Are you sickening for something, Joanna? First your obstinacy this morning, now this…'

'Sickening? Oh, yes, I expect I am, but there's no cure for it,' she said lightly. She did indeed feel very odd. The aching pain of Giles's loss was there somewhere, deep down where she did not have to look at it yet, but on top of the pain was a rather queasy sense of excitement, the beginnings of a dreadful headache and the feeling that absolutely nothing would ever matter again.

Her mother took her arm in a less than sympathetic grip and began to walk firmly towards the door. 'We are going home this minute.'

'I cannot, Mama,' Joanna said. 'I am dancing the next waltz with—'

'No one. Home, my girl,' Emily said grimly, 'and straight to bed.'

The dreadful headache was there, waiting for her the next morning when she awoke, as was the hideous emptiness where all her plans had once been. It was as though the walls of a house had vanished, leaving the furniture standing around pointlessly in space.

Joanna rubbed her aching head, realising

shakily that she must be suffering from the after-effects of too much champagne. How much had she drunk? Hazily she counted five glasses. Could she have possibly drunk that much? She could recall being marched firmly from the ball with her mama's excuses to their friends ringing in her ears. 'The heat, I am afraid, it has brought on such a migraine.' But the carriage ride home was a blur, with only the faintest memory of being lectured, scolded and sent upstairs the moment they arrived home.

Oh, her head hurt so! Where was Mary with her morning chocolate? The door opened to reveal her mama, a tea cup in her hand.

'So you are awake, are you?' she observed grimly as her heavy-eyed daughter struggled to sit up against the pillows. 'I have brought you some tea, I thought it might be better for you than chocolate.' She put the cup into Joanna's hands and went to fling the curtains wide, ignoring the yelp of anguish from the bed as the light flooded into the room. 'Well, what have you got to say for yourself, Joanna?'

'Have you said anything to Papa?' Joanna drank the tea gratefully. Her mouth felt like the soles of her shoes and her stomach revolted at the faint smell of breakfast cooking that the opening door had allowed into the room. Surely she could not have a hangover?

'No,' Emily conceded. 'Your papa is very busy at the moment and I do not want to add another worry for him on top of your refusal yesterday to receive dear Rufus. Unless, that is, I do not receive a satisfactory explanation for last night.'

'Champagne, Mama,' Joanna said reluctantly. 'I had no idea it was so strong.' She eyed her fulminating parent and added, 'It tasted so innocuous.'

'*Champagne!* No wonder you were behaving in such a manner. Have I not warned you time and again to drink nothing except orgeat and lemonade?'

'Yes, Mama. I am sorry, Mama.' *I am sorry I drank so much*, her new, rebellious inner voice said. *I will know better next time, just a glass or two for that lovely fizzing feeling...*

'I had thought,' Emily continued, 'of forbidding you any further parties until we go down to Brighton for the summer, but I am reluctant to cause more talk by having you vanish from the scene, especially as I know the earl will be in town for at least another fortnight. Fortunately there are only minor entertainments for the rest of the month. I hope the headache you undoubtedly have will be a lesson to you, my girl.'

She got up and walked to the door. 'I must say, Joanna, this has proved greatly disappointing to me. I had been so proud of you. I can only hope it is a momentary aberration. As for Rufus Carstairs, I will have to tell him you are indisposed and will not be able to receive him for a day or two.'

On that ominous announcement the door closed firmly behind her and Joanna curled up in a tight ball of misery and had a good weep. Finally she emerged, feeling chastened and ashamed of herself. It was very good of Mama not to punish her for what had happened, she fully appreciated that. And dissipation only made one feel ill, it appeared. Perhaps she should return to normal, if only to prevent her mother ever speaking to her in that hurt tone of voice again.

It was all hopeless, of course: she was twenty years old and as good as on the shelf. How could she bear to marry another man when she would always be in love with Giles? Still, spinsters had to behave with modesty and decorum, so she might as well continue like that and become used to it.

* * *

This pious resolve lasted precisely two days; in fact, until the rout party at Mrs Jameson's and her next encounter with the Earl of Clifton. Mrs Jameson's parties were always popular although, as she admitted to Mrs Fulgrave when the ladies were standing talking halfway through the evening, it did seem rather flat after the Duchess's grand ball. Emily, who could still not think of the ball without a shudder, agreed but pointed out that anything on such a scale must induce a sense of let-down afterwards.

Her daughter was certainly feeling that sensation, for the combination of being on her best behaviour, and knowing that many of those present this evening had observed her behaving in quite the opposite way, was oppressive. She tried hard not to imagine that people were talking about her behind her back, but could not convince herself. It became much worse when she realised that Lady Suzanne Hall was amongst the young ladies present.

Joanna had never had more than a passing acquaintanceship with Suzanne, who was at the centre of a group of her friends, all talking and giggling together. Knowing that she was going to regret it, but quite unable to resist, Joanna strolled across and attached herself to a neighbouring group so she could hear what was being said behind her.

There was a lot of giggling, several gasps of surprise and then one young lady said, 'Colonel Gregory? Why, Suzy, you cunning thing! What does your papa say?'

'As it is Giles, why, what could he say? He has always been against it, but darling Giles is *so* persuasive.'

'Oh, you lucky thing! I saw him at the Duchess's ball and I thought he was so dashing and handsome…'

Joanna moved abruptly away. So, he had asked Lord Olney for Suzanne's hand in marriage and the Marquis had agreed. Now all she could look forward to was the announcement. Joanna scooped a glass of champagne from the tray carried by a passing footman and drank it defiantly before she realised that the Earl of Clifton had entered the room and was being greeted by his hostess. Joanna took a careful step backwards towards a screen but was too late: he must have enquired after her, for Mrs Jameson was scanning the room and nodding in her direction.

Regretting her height, which made her so

visible, Joanna slipped her empty glass on to a side table and prepared to make the best of it. He could hardly ask her to marry him in the middle of a crowded reception, after all.

She watched him make his way across the room, critically comparing him to Giles. Rufus was slightly above medium height with an elegant figure and a handsome, slightly aquiline, face. His hair was very blond, his eyes a distinctive shade of blue, and Joanna suspected he knew exactly how attractive he was to look at. He was also always immaculately dressed in an austere fashion.

But compared to Giles's tall, muscular figure, his air of confident command and the quiet humour in his face, Rufus Carstairs cut a poor figure to her eyes, and, although she could not quite decide why, a sinister one at that. His eyes flickered over her rapidly as he approached and once again she had that disconcerting feeling that he was paying more attention to her figure than was proper.

'My lord.' She curtsied slightly as he reached her side.

'So formal, Miss Fulgrave.' He took her hand in his and bent to kiss it. Joanna snatched it away, hoping that this unconventional greeting would go unnoticed.

'My lord!'

'Oh, come now, Joanna.' He tucked his hand under her elbow and began to stroll down the length of the room. 'How can you stand so on ceremony with an old friend even if we have only recently been reunited?'

'We were hardly friends, my lord,' she retorted tartly, wondering if she could extricate her elbow and deciding it would create an unseemly struggle. 'As I recall, you considered me a pestilential brat and I thought you were a bully.'

'But now you are a beautiful young lady and I am but an ardent admirer at your feet.'

'Please, Lord Clifton, do not flirt, I am not in the mood.' She looked around the room for rescue. 'Look, there is Mr Higham. Have you met him? I am sure he would wish to meet you.'

'I have no wish to meet him, however.' Rufus's hand was touching her side, she could feel its heat through the thin gauze of her bodice. Only a few days before Giles's hand had rested there. 'Joanna, when are you going to permit me to speak to you?'

'You are speaking to me now. Oh, good evening, Miss Doughty. How is your mama?'

With a faint hiss of irritation Lord Clifton steered

Joanna away from her friend. 'That is not what I mean and you know it, Joanna. Your parents are more than willing for me to address you.'

Joanna wondered if she had the courage to refuse him there and then and risk a scene, but those blue eyes were glittering dangerously and she was suddenly afraid of what he might do. 'Yes, I know, but it is too soon, my lord, we are hardly acquainted again.'

He smiled suddenly, but the attractive expression did not reach his eyes. 'Such maidenly modesty! I know what I want, Joanna, and what I want, I get. I have a fondness for beautiful things and my collection is notable. And I do not think I am going to be fighting off many rivals, am I? I have heard the whisperings since I returned to London. Miss Fulgrave, it seems, is very picky and turns down every offer. Do you expect men to keep offering and risking a rebuff?'

'I am surprised that *you* risk it, then,' she retorted, trampling down the mortifying thought that people were gossiping about her.

'But I told you, I get what I want and I want you, Joanna. Just think of the triumph of carrying off the Perfect Débutante, the young lady who has refused so many. How lovely you will look installed as chatelaine of Clifton Hall. I will be calling very soon. Now, I am expected at Rochester's for cards. Goodnight, my dear.'

Watching him saunter back across the room and take his smiling leave of his hostess, she wanted to throw the glass at the wall, scream, do something utterly outrageous, but only the dark glitter of her eyes betrayed her innermost feelings. Somewhere, deep inside, the girl she had once been before she had met Giles was reawakening: older, more socially adept, polished, but still that rebellious, adventurous spirit burned, and now it roused itself and stared out at a hostile world through new and defiant eyes.

The next day while walking in Hyde Park with her maid, she saw a smart curricle bowling along the tan surface towards her. At the reins was the petite figure of Lady Suzanne, a dashing tricorne and veil on her blonde head, her figure clad to perfection in a deep blue walking dress. She was laughing with delight as she controlled the two high-stepping bays at a brisk trot and, with a wrench, Joanna realised that not only was the man beside her Giles Gregory but his right hand was over Suzanne's on the reins and he was laughing too at her un-inhibited enjoyment.

They swept past Joanna and for a moment she thought he had not noticed her, then the team was reined in and began to back. Joanna could hear Giles's voice, 'Keep your hands lower, Suzy, for goodness' sake, you are trying to make a team back up, not encourage a hunter over a fence!'

The curricle drew level with her again just as he said, with unmistakable pride in his voice, 'Good girl! There, I told you you could do it. Good morning, Miss Fulgrave, I do beg your pardon, we were past before I recognised you. I hope your family is well?' His eyes asked something else, and Joanna felt a surge of warmth that not only had he remembered her distress, but that he had the tact not to mention it in front of Lady Suzanne.

'Quite well, I thank you, Colonel,' she replied, wondering at her own composure. 'All of us are in good health.'

'Excellent. Are you ladies acquainted?'

'Oh, yes,' Lady Suzanne said with a light laugh. 'We know each other by sight, do we not, Miss Fulgrave? And, of course, I saw you at my aunt's ball.' As did most of the *ton*, her expression said, as her pretty blue eyes rested on Joanna's face.

She did not like another woman drawing her Colonel's attention, that was plain.

'Indeed.' Joanna could feel the seams of her gloves creaking as she clenched her fists. 'And I saw you. Such a lovely gown. Good day, Lady Suzanne, Colonel. Enjoy your drive.'

She forced herself to smile as she turned on her heel and began to walk home. Nothing mattered any more, the only thing left was to immerse herself in whatever diversions presented themselves so that she did not have the opportunity to even think about Giles.

Her mother noted with concern her silence and set face when she came in but within days she found that her daughter's uncommunicativeness was the least of her problems.

At the end of two weeks the list of outrages committed by her lovely, obedient, perfect daughter included flirting heavily with every rake who came within her orbit, being found playing dice with three young gentlemen in a back room at a party, galloping on Rotten Row and eating ice cream in Gunther's with Lord Sutton, having 'lost' her maid. This was on top of her managing, by what stratagems her mama could not establish, to avoid Lord Clifton on every occasion he called. The final straw was to walk up St James's because—as she told her speechless mother— she 'wanted to know what all the fuss was about'.

That exploit led to Mr Fulgrave's involvement, resulting in a painful interview. Joanna was forbidden any parties until they went to Brighton in two weeks' time and had to suffer the ignominy of not being allowed out at all without her mother's escort.

'I do not understand it, I really do not,' Mr Fulgrave said, more in sorrow than in anger. 'At your age dear Grace was married with her first child and was mistress of a large household, while you are behaving like a hoyden of seventeen who knows no better. Lord Clifton will not contain his impatience for much longer my girl, and if these disgraceful exploits come to his attention he will withdraw his suit in disgust.'

Alone in her bedroom Joanna considered these strictures with little sense of remorse. She felt too numb to really care, although the hope that she would drive away Rufus Carstairs gave her a glimmer of pleasure. But disappointingly a course of dissipation did not seem to provide the distraction from the circling thoughts of Giles that she had hoped. Still, it was at least more stimulating than meekly withering into an old maid, which seemed the only alternative to an unwanted marriage.

Nothing, therefore, deterred Joanna from her plans for that evening, which involved leaving the house by the back door after she was supposed to be asleep and meeting her old acquaintance Catherine Marcus. Mrs Marcus, once plain Kate Hampton and now a rich young matron, had informed Joanna three evenings before when they met at a reception that she was getting up a party to attend the masquerade at Vauxhall Gardens. Her dear Joanna, she was sure, would thoroughly enjoy it.

Mama did not approve of Mrs Marcus, whom she considered to be fast and flighty, but, as far as she knew, she and Joanna had never been close at and she was therefore unlikely to lead her daughter astray. The thought that their reacquaintance would involve an expedition to Vauxhall for a masquerade, an activity entirely beyond the pale as far as Mrs Fulgrave was concerned, was inconceivable.

Her mask dangling from its ribbons in one hand, the other clutching her blue domino tightly around her, Joanna made her escape and was picked up by the Marcuses' coach without mishap at the appointed place. No one, she congratulated herself, would know and she had always wanted to experience a masquerade. In the flickering light her friend did not notice the shadows under her eyes and the party set off full of high spirits.

Chapter Three

Vauxhall Gardens seemed an enchanted dream to Joanna. Lights in their thousand twinkled amid the branches and framed pavilions and kiosks in a magical glow. Every twist and turn in the paths opened on to new vistas crowded with party-goers; music and laughter filled the air and Mrs Marcus's party spent the first hour simply strolling, watching the passing throng and revelling in the strange feeling of safety their masks produced.

Mrs Marcus had invited a large group of friends and, although all the young ladies seemed to Joanna to be startling free and easy and the men escorting them more than a little inclined to take advantage of whatever flirtation was on offer, she felt quite comfortable in the company. Everyone seemed to behave towards her as befitted her unmarried status and she rather suspected that Kate had had a quiet word with her friends about their inexperienced new acquaintance.

Joanna firmly refused the offer of a glass of champagne when they retired to a kiosk for shaved ham and other trifles before joining the dancing; as everyone else became gayer and more light-headed, she retained a perfectly level-headed awareness of everything going on around her. Things were certainly becoming a trifle warm but, although she realised her mama would faint away at the sights her younger daughter was coolly ob-serving, she felt only an amused curiosity.

However, she rapidly regretted allowing herself to be taken out on to the dance floor by one young gentleman who proved to be either a very inept dancer or perhaps simply an inebriated one.

'No, no, it is quite all right,' she protested lightly for the third time as he trod on her toe during the boulanger. 'So crowded, is it not? Oh!' His foot found her hem and half dragged the domino from her shoulder. Joanna pulled it back, found she had lost the ties securing it at her neck and that she could not see to untangle the ribbons whilst wearing her mask. 'Oh dear, can we just go to the side of the dance floor?' Her partner, apologising

profusely at his carelessness, guided her out of
the throng and stood by, helpfully holding her
mask while Joanna adjusted her cloak.

'Would you like to dance again?' he asked as
he handed back the black satin mask.

'And have her toes completely bruised? I think
not, young man.' Lord Clifton appeared at her
side, masked, but with his unmistakable blue eyes
glittering through the slits. 'May I offer you my
escort home, Miss Fulgrave?' He turned abruptly
to her partner, who took a step back. 'We need
keep you no longer, sir.'

'Yes, thank you for the dance, sir,' Joanna said
hastily. He seemed inclined to square up bellig-
erently to the interloper and she added pacifically, 'It is quite all right, I know this gentlemen.'

The young man took himself off with an af-
fronted bow. 'Would you be so good as to escort
me back to my hostess, my lord? She is over
there.' Joanna forced herself to speak calmly and
pleasantly, although her mind was racing. She
could hardly make a scene here.

'The fast young lady in the pink domino? Not,
I am sure, a hostess your mama would approve
of, Joanna.' He took her arm and began to steer
her away from the Marcus party. 'And where

exactly does your mama believe you to be at this moment?' Joanna knew she was colouring, but could not help it. 'Ah, blamelessly in your bed. I think we had better return you there.'

'No! I cannot simply walk away from Mrs Marcus like that.' But from the set of his mouth and the very firm grip on her arm she knew that, short of screaming and struggling, she was going to do just as Rufus told her. 'I must at least thank her and say goodbye or she will worry.'

'Very well.' She could feel his eyes on her set face and she tried to look as happy as possible before they reached her party. 'Do not sulk, Joanna, it does not suit you. Think what a disillusion it is for me to find my perfect bride-to-be in such company.'

'I am *not* your bride-to-be!' She broke off abruptly at the appearance in front of them of a tall figure in a black domino, a petite blue-clad figure on his arm.

'Joanna!' It was unmistakably Giles, and she realised with a shock that she had not replaced her mask. She fumbled it back into place, unable to meet his eyes. 'Are you in any difficulties, Miss Fulgrave?'

'No! No, none at all, just rather flustered by the crowd, Colonel, thank you. I was just about to leave. Goodnight.' From being his captive, she almost towed Rufus after her towards Mrs Marcus, leaving Giles Gregory staring at their retreating backs.

'What the…who was that she was with, I wonder?'

'Oh, that was Rufus Carstairs,' his companion said confidently. 'Lord Clifton, you know. I would know those eyes anywhere. Frightfully eligible, but he makes my flesh creep. Well, the perfect Miss Fulgrave *is* behaving badly, is she not?'

Giles Gregory looked down at her. 'Just as badly as you, Suzy, you little witch. Now, come along and let us get home or your papa will cut off your dress allowance and take a horsewhip to me.'

She laughed. 'Not when I tell him you came to rescue me, Giles darling.'

'As well you knew I would, you baggage, considering you left me a note!' he said affectionately. 'Now, do any of your errant girlfriends need an escort as well?' He firmly walked her away from the dancing, but his eyes were scanning the crowd for the tall girl in the blue domino.

Joanna sat in the furthest corner of the earl's carriage apprehensively expecting him to try and kiss her, but to her relief he made no attempt to do so as they rattled over the cobbles and through the night-time streets.

Flambeaux outside town houses cast a flickering light into the interior and she saw he appeared to be thinking. Eventually, unable to stand the silence any more, she said, 'I hope I do not take you away from your own party this evening?'

'Hmm? No, not at all. I was just thinking what best to say to your parents: I would not wish them to be out of reason cross with you.'

'Say to them? Why, nothing! I will let myself in and they will be none the wiser.'

'You shock me, Joanna, you really do! Naturally I cannot be so deceitful, nor can I let you. I will have to tell them for, after all, we are alone in a closed carriage.'

'You mean you…that you think I should…'

'Your parents are, I know, in favour of my suit. Now I imagine they will be only too anxious for the engagement.'

Joanna stared at him speechlessly, then found her voice. 'I would not marry you, Rufus Carstairs, if you were the last man on earth.'

'Hardly an original sentiment, my dear. Now, here is your street. Ah, no need for any surprises,

I see, they must already be aware of your absence.' And, indeed, the lights were blazing downstairs as the carriage pulled up. Numbly Joanna allowed herself to be handed down out of the carriage and into the house.

Her mother took one look at her and said, 'Wait in the drawing room please, Joanna,' before vanishing with the earl into the front salon.

How her absence had been discovered she never knew. It seemed hours that she sat in the chilly room, exhaustion dragging at her eyelids, her mind tormented by the thought that Giles had seen her apparently happy to be with Rufus Carstairs.

At last her parents appeared, grim-faced, yet with a subdued air of triumph. 'Well, Joanna,' her father said heavily, 'you are fortunate indeed to so escape the results of your wicked folly. The earl, against all reason, still wishes to make you his wife. He has agreed to wait until the end of the week to allow you to recover from this ill-advised romp but he will be coming then to make you an offer and you, Joanna, are going to accept it.'

'No!' Joanna sprang to her feet, her hands clenched, her voice trembling. 'No! I will never marry him.'

'Then I wash my hands of you,' her father

declared, also on his feet. 'You will go to your Great-aunt Clara in Bath. She needs a new companion and, as we cannot trust you to take part in Society, let alone in the more relaxed atmosphere of Brighton, that is the best place for you.'

'To Great-aunt Clara?' Joanna's tired, sore mind wrestled with the shock. 'But she never goes out.'

'Indeed,' Mrs Fulgrave said repressively. 'I am sure she will appreciate your company. You can read to her, assist with her needlework, help entertain her friends when they call. I shall tell the earl that her ill health has meant that we felt we had no choice but to send you. We must just hope that in a few months, when you have come to your senses, he is still interested in making you an offer.'

Joanna contemplated her sentence. Banishment to Bath, to a household of old age and illness, to the care of a formidable relative who, if she were truthful, rather scared her, and no diversion whatsoever to distract her mind from Giles. And at the end of months of incarceration, the only hope held out to her was that Rufus Carstairs might still want to marry her. And she had a dreadful apprehension that he would. He did not seem like a man who tolerated being thwarted. He was a man who would chase the length of Europe to beat a rival to a choice statue.

'Please do not send me away, Mama,' she said, her voice wavering on the edge of tears. 'I will be so miserable.'

'You should have thought of that before plunging into these wild scrapes,' her father said severely. 'Your mother will write to your great-aunt tomorrow. I only hope she is prepared to countenance your presence, considering what she will learn of your recent behaviour.'

He stood up, gathering his dressing gown around himself. As he picked up his chamber candle he remarked with unconscious cruelty, 'Perhaps the contemplation of the loneliness of a single old age will convince you that the rewards of truly happy domestic life with a devoted husband are worth more than the transitory plea-sures you have been indulging in.'

Joanna walked slowly up to her bedchamber, well aware that, however late the hour, she could not possibly sleep now. What was she to do? She stood, her forehead pressed against the glass of the window, her eyes unfocused on the darkness outside. Where did she belong now? Probably, she thought bitterly, her role in life would be as the spinster aunt, or cousin or devoted niece. *Dear Joanna, always so good with the children, always available to help with the old ladies...* It wasn't that she did not like old ladies, or children, come to that, it was just that she had hoped to have her own children—Giles's children.

Suddenly she whirled away from the window, propelled by a determination not to be crushed, not to be dictated to. Her life was in ruins: well, no one else was going to rebuild it but she. 'Strategy and tactics,' she said out loud. 'Strategy and tactics.' Then the burst of energy left her and she sank down on the bed. Strategy was no good without an objective.

Resolutely she straightened her spine. She had trained herself to be a soldier's wife—now she had to use the courage she had prided herself she possessed. Her short-term objective must be to decide what to do with the rest of her life, and her strategy would be to go somewhere she could think about this in peace. And that was not Bath, where she would be the disgraced niece to be watched and lectured.

So...Joanna bit her lip and thought. Who could she run away to? Not Hebe and Alex at Tasborough Hall: not when Hebe's confinement was so close. There were Uncle and Aunt Pulborough in Exeter—but they would be scandalised by the arrival of an errant niece—a second cousin in Wales, but he had been recently widowed. One after another Joanna passed her relatives under review and came to the conclusion that the only one who might have helped her, if circumstances had been different, was Hebe. Or, her own sister.

Thoughtfully Joanna picked up a notebook from the night table and wrote, *Grace, Lincoln.* She had no idea how Lady Willington would react, let alone her brother-in-law, Sir Frederick, but perhaps they might serve as a diversion. Her dearest friend from Miss Faversham's Seminary for Young Ladies in Bath had been Georgiana Schofield; Georgy was now Lady Brandon and living in Wisbech, from where she wrote frequently to say she was utterly bored and was dying for darling Joanna to visit her.

'If I set out on the stage for Lincoln,' Joanna reasoned out loud, 'there is sure to be a point where I can change and go to Wisbech, and everyone will think I am with Grace. And when they realise I am not, I will have vanished into East Anglia without a trace.' She added, *Georgy, Wisbech,* to her list.

Or would her mama suspect she was with Georgy? No, for Mama never asked to see her letters from her school friends and Joanna doubted she even knew Georgy's married name. Something she had just thought touched a chord of memory. East Anglia... Aunt Caroline, of course! Her father's youngest sister, the sister no one was allowed to mention, the one who had made a scandalous marriage.

But Joanna had once overheard a conversation between her parents that she had not dared ask about, yet had never forgotten.

'I am sorry, my dear,' her mother had said firmly. 'But she is your sister when all is said and done, and despite the scandal I will continue to write once a year at Christmas to enquire after her health and to tell her news of the family.'

'The affair nearly killed Papa,' her own father had replied harshly. 'Is she the sort of woman you wish our Grace and Joanna to associate with?'

'Nonsense,' Mama had replied calmly. 'Writing to offer Christmas wishes will not expose our girls to scandal or bad influences. You must do Caro justice, my dear. Has she ever attempted to return to London from East Anglia or to call here?'

Her father's muttered response was inaudible

and Joanna, guiltily aware that she had been eavesdropping, had left the study door and had walked on. But somewhere in East Anglia she had a disgraced and scandalous aunt. Would she understand? Could Joanna talk to her and find someone who could counsel her?

But how to find her? Joanna thought hard, then realised that if her mother was writing to Aunt Caroline, then she probably had her direction in her remembrancer where she noted all her addresses, birthdays and other important lists. She got up, opened the door on to the dark and silent house, and went downstairs.

Chapter Four

Three days after Joanna's disastrous masquerade party, Giles Gregory turned his match greys neatly into Half Moon Street, sensing his spirits lift perceptibly as he saw the smart black front door of the Tasboroughs' town house in front of him.

He felt heartsore, anxious and hurt, and the thought of Hebe's warm common sense and Alex's astringent comradeship had seemed like a beacon on the journey from his family home in the Vale of Aylesbury. He had crossed with them journeying up to town from their Hertfordshire estate when he had made his painfully short visit to his parents and, instead of finding refuge at Tasborough, had had to drive back to London to seek out his friends.

He handed the reins to his groom and jumped down. 'Take them 'round to the mews, Mellors, and tell his lordship's man that I am expecting to stay for a day or two. If that is not convenient, come back and let me know and you can take them to the livery stables, but I do not expect the earl has brought more than his carriage horses and one hack up for a short stay.'

The man drove competently away down the street and Giles took the front steps in two long strides. The door was opened by Starling, the family butler, who permitted himself a small smile on seeing who was there.

'Colonel Gregory. It is a pleasure to see you again, sir, if I may be so bold. His lordship is out, but her ladyship is in the Blue Room. She is not generally receiving, but I will venture to say she will be at home to you, sir, if you would care to go up. Will you be staying? Your usual room is free.'

'Thank you, Starling.' Giles handed him his hat and gloves. 'I hope Lady Tasborough will not object to a house guest for a night or two.'

He made his way up to the elegant room on the first floor which was Hebe's favourite retiring room, and opened the door. 'May I come in?'

'Giles!' She was lying propped up against a pile of cushions on a *chaise longue*, a wide smile of delighted welcome on her face.

He strode across to her side, warmed by her delight. There were times when he wondered if he would ever find someone like his friend's wife, someone whom he could love as Alex loved Hebe, someone who would love him back with such passionate devotion.

'Good grief, Lady Tasborough!' He stopped in front of her, his mouth curving into a warm, teasing, smile. 'Just when is this child due? I give you fair warning, I have delivered one baby in my time, and it is not an experience I am willing to repeat.'

Hebe held out her arms to him, giggling as he attempted to kiss her across the bump. Sheets of notepaper scattered unregarded to the carpet. 'It isn't due for six weeks, Giles, so you need not be alarmed. Have you truly delivered a baby? Whose was it?'

'The wife of one of the men. The father fainted, the doctor was away cutting some poor man's leg off, there was not another woman in sight, so it was down to me.' He grinned at her affectionately. *This* felt like coming home. 'Six weeks? Are you sure it isn't twins?'

'Oh!' Hebe stared at him wide-eyed. 'Surely not? There are none in either family as far as I know, and it does follow, does it not?'

'I think so. I'm only teasing you. How are you, Hebe? I am surprised to find you in town just now.'

'I am well, only so tired of feeling like a whale. I cannot recall when I last saw my feet. But never mind me, what are you doing here? Can you stay until we go back to Tasborough? Please do, we would love that so much.'

'Are you sure? It won't be difficult at the moment?'

'Not at all, and you will distract Alex and stop him fretting about me. I am in disgrace because I will not see any of the fashionable *accoucheurs*, which is the excuse I gave for coming up the other day. Alex says if all I want to do is shop, then I must go straight back to the country and rest. But we are here for another two days at any rate.' She settled herself against her cushions and watched him with her wide grey eyes steady on his face. 'The decanters are over there. Pour yourself a drink, then come and sit down beside me.'

Giles did as he was bid, dropping on to a footstool beside the *chaise* and settling himself comfortably. 'Now, tell me what is wrong, Giles,' she commanded.

'Wrong?' He shifted so that he was sitting with

his back against the side of the *chaise*, his face turned from her.

'Yes, wrong.' Hebe rested her hand lightly on his shoulder. 'You look as though someone has been kicking you—spiritually, I mean.'

Giles put up his own hand and covered hers. 'Clever Hebe. That is exactly how I feel. I went home to Buckinghamshire two days ago because Mother has been writing to say that she is worried about Father. The doctor thinks he had some kind of seizure last month, now one side of his face is stiff and he is limping. Denies there is anything wrong, of course.'

'How old is the General?'

'Only sixty, but he's had a tough life. Wounded at least six times, broken bones, yellow fever. He was never the kind of officer who stayed back at headquarters in comfort. Now he's getting tired, but he will not admit it, and that's a big estate for one man to manage. If I had a younger brother…'

'So you came home to see him?' Hebe curled her fingers within his and gave an encouraging squeeze.

'Yes. I did not want to rush straight there as soon as I arrived in the country or he would suspect why I came home. My idea was to see for myself how he did, and, if he really looked bad, to sell out. I thought I'd try horse breeding and at the same time take over some of the estate management. Nothing too much at first, just the bits that really bore and tire him.'

'And gradually he would let you do more and more and he would never have to admit he couldn't cope?'

'Yes. At least, that was my plan.' He fell silent. The pain of his father's reaction was almost too raw to speak about yet. 'Where's Alex?'

Hebe laughed. 'At his club, taking refuge because I will not let him fuss over me, and if he stays at home he fidgets himself to death.' Hebe paused, then, 'How did your father react?'

'Badly.'

'Tell me,' she persisted gently.

'He demanded to know what had happened to make me lose my nerve and to want to sell out, like some coward of a Hyde-Park soldier,' Giles said harshly. Hebe gasped.

'He doesn't mean it.' Giles continued more easily now the shaming words had been said. 'He expects me to be a general too—and even younger than he had been. I think in his heart he knows why I am talking of selling out and he is railing against his own weakness, not mine.'

'I shouldn't think that makes it hurt any less,' Hebe said, lifting her hand to touch it softly to his face. Giles turned his cheek against her knuckles, comforted. Lucky, lucky Alex.

'No. And of course he knows he has been unjust and doesn't know how to put it right. So he managed to find yet another sin to throw at my head to justify his anger.'

'What else?'

'He wants to know what I think I'm about, flirting with Lady Suzanne Hall and not making her an offer. *Damn good catch*, the old boy says with considerable understatement, and he isn't going to stand by hearing stories about me trifling with her affections.'

'Are you?' Hebe asked.

'Flirting or trifling?'

'Intending to marry her,' Hebe said tartly.

'None of those things. I've known Suzy since I was ten and she was toddling. She's the sister I never had and I'd as soon marry a cage full of monkeys. I feel nothing but the deepest sympathy for whichever poor idiot marries her. That girl is the most outrageous minx I have ever come across.'

'So you are not in love with her?' Hebe persisted.

'I love the girl—but just as a sister—and she

and her parents know it. She has been practising flirting and wheedling on me since she was eleven because she knows I'm safe and her mother likes me to squire her about when I'm in town because *she* knows I'm safe. I scare off the bucks and the fortune hunters and Suzy can play the little madam to her heart's content.

'But she's probably the best catch of the Season, as my father is all too aware. Some old pussy has been telling him I was seen with her driving in the park and dancing with her rather too often and that's enough for him. And that's another thing,' he added bitterly. 'Her father didn't want her to learn to drive because his own sister was hurt in a bad accident, so what must she do but wheedle me into persuading the poor man that I can teach her.'

'Well, you *are* a very good whip, Giles,' Hebe pointed out.

'Yes, and I'm well known for not letting ladies drive my teams, so Father puts two and two together, gets six and then finds no sign of me doing the right thing. And, of course, as he points out, it's about time I was getting married and setting up my nursery and look at Lord Tasborough with one heir to his name already and that pretty little wife of his increasing again...'

'Oh, poor Giles,' Hebe said with indignant sympathy. 'You have been giving your head for a washing, haven't you? What are you going to do? Oh, listen, I think that's Alex.'

The door opened to reveal the Earl, his face breaking into a grin when he saw who was with his wife.

'Giles! No, don't get up, stay there.' He bent down and gave his friend a powerful buffet on the shoulder, wrung the hand that was held out to him, and dropped to the carpet by his side. 'Are you here to stay? Is that why I find you here flirting with my wife?'

'He isn't flirting,' Hebe said, half-anxious, half-laughing. 'He thinks I'm expecting twins.'

'Good God!' The Earl twisted round to regard both his wife and friend. 'Are you serious? And what do you know about it, might I ask?'

'He says he's delivered a baby.'

'But not twins,' Giles hastened to say. 'No, don't hit me! It is merely that kissing your delightful wife is like trying to reach her over a pile of sofa cushions and either someone's mathematics are out, or it's twins. Or triplets...' he added wickedly, ducking away from Alex's punch.

'Oh, stop it!' Hebe cried, slapping at black and

blond heads impartially. 'I might as well have two more small boys on my hands as you men. Giles is staying until we go back to Tasborough: he is having a perfectly horrible time at home. Giles, tell him.'

Giles recounted his story again. When he reached his father's reaction to his plan to sell out, Alex went quite still, then simply reached out and gripped his arm. Giles found his vision suddenly blurred and rapidly finished the rest of his tale.

'Just how angry is the General?' Alex asked. No one ever referred to Lord Gregory by his title.

'Angry enough to disinherit me.'

'Can he?' Alex enquired.

Giles shook his head with a rueful grin. The morning's final, painful, interview was beginning to seem less painful and more farcelike now he could talk about it. 'There's the entail, and the money I inherited from Grandmama Ingham—he can't do a thing about either of those. If he really puts his mind to it he can find about sixty acres and a couple of farms—and the furniture, of course— to leave elsewhere. But he doesn't mean it.'

'What will you do?' Hebe was still not reassured.

'I am under orders from Mama to come up to town and embark upon a life of reckless dissipation.' He twisted round to smile at Hebe. 'I'd already taken rooms at Albany as a *pied-à-terre*, but they aren't fitted out yet, which is why I had hoped you'd take me in.'

'*Dissipation?* But why?'

'She says he will soon hear all about it and order me back home to be lectured. At which point he will decide that the best thing for me is to rusticate on the estate for a while.'

Hebe laughed. 'How clever of your mama! Of course, if he thinks you don't want to do it and would rather be in London, then helping with the estate will be just the thing to punish the prodigal, and after a few weeks he'll be so used to it, and will enjoy having you there so much, that you will get exactly the result you want.'

'Has it ever occurred to you that your mother is a better strategist than your father?' Alex enquired.

'Frequently. She always outflanks him and the poor man can never understand how she has done it.' He shifted his position and one hand flattened a sheet of paper, which crackled. 'Sorry, I appear to be crushing the letter you were reading.'

'Oh, goodness!' Hebe exclaimed, taking the crumpled pages. 'I had quite forgotten in the excitement of Giles arriving. It is from Aunt Emily,' she explained to the two men. 'She sent a footman with it this morning, just after you had left, Alex. It is the most incredible thing. She says she is to send Joanna to stay with her great-aunt in Bath because she is in disgrace.'

'I will go into the library.' Giles started to get up. 'You will want to discuss this in private.'

'No, stay, please. You are one of the family, Giles, and besides, you are staying here and will have to know what is going on.' She started to re-read. 'And it is not as though it is anything actually, er, indelicate.'

'What, not an elopement with the apothecary or the unfortunate results of an amorous encounter with the footman?' Alex enquired, earning a look of burning reproach from his wife.

'I still think I had better leave,' Giles persisted. 'I can go to an hotel until my rooms are ready at Albany. Your aunt will want to call and discuss the problem, that is obvious, and she will not feel at ease if she knows I am staying here.'

'Nonsense, Giles. We need you to help us get to the bottom of this puzzle. Aunt Emily says it all began at the Duchess of Bridlington's ball. Joanna got drunk on champagne, flirted outrageously and then went on to commit just about every act in the list of things she could do to be labelled fast. And, to cap it all, she is wilfully refusing an offer from a highly eligible nobleman—discreetly unnamed.'

'*Joanna?* Drunk on champagne?' Alex looked incredulous. 'That girl is a pattern-book of re-spectability and correct behaviour.'

'The Duchess of Bridlington's ball?' Giles sat down again. 'Oh, lord.' His friends looked at him incredulously. 'Don't look at me like that! I haven't been seducing the girl! But I think I may have started her off on the wine—' He broke off, his eyes unfocussed, looking back into the past. 'You know, she had had a bad shock of some kind: that's why I gave her a couple of glasses of champagne.'

He had forgotten about his encounters with Joanna in the face of his estrangement with his father, but, looking back in the light of Mrs Fulgrave's letter, things began to make sense. 'At the ball I found her sitting outside one of the retiring rooms looking shocked,' he began.

'You mean someone might have said something *risqué* or unkind to her?' Hebe ventured.

'No, not that kind of shock.' He remembered the blank look in those wide hazel eyes and suddenly realised what it reminded him of. 'Alex, you know the effect their first battle had on some of the very young, very idealistic officers who came out to the Peninsula without any experience? The ones who thought that war was all glory and chivalry, bugles blowing and flags flying?'

'And found it was blood and mud and slaughter. Men dying in something that resembled a butcher's shambles, chaos and noise—' Alex broke off and Hebe could see they were both somewhere else, somewhere she could never follow. 'Yes, I remember. What are you saying?'

'Joanna had the same look in her eyes as those lads had after their first battle, as though an ideal had disintegrated before her and her world was in ruins. She was white, her hands were shaking. I asked her what was wrong, but she would not tell me. I assumed it was a man. We talked of neutral subjects for a while. After two glasses of champagne she was well enough to waltz, which helped, I think. Movement often does in cases of shock—' He broke off, remembering the supple, yielding figure in his arms, those wide hazel eyes that seemed to look trustingly into his soul, his instinct to find and hurt the man who had so obviously hurt her.

They discussed the matter a little more, speculating on the spurned suitor to no purpose and, after a while, left Hebe to rest.

Giles went up to his usual room. While Alex's valet unpacked for him he paced restlessly, fighting the urge to drive straight back home to see how his father was. To distract himself from his cantankerous parent, he thought about Joanna Fulgrave. To his surprise he found he was dwelling pleasurably on the memory. He frowned, trying to convince himself that he was merely intrigued by what had turned a previously biddable débutante into a fast young lady. But there was more than that, something that lay behind the desperate hurt in those lovely eyes, something which seemed to speak directly to him.

He shifted in the comfortable wing chair where he had finally come to rest. His body was responding to thoughts of Miss Fulgrave in a quite inappropriate way.

It was two months since he had parted from his Portuguese mistress. There were, of course, the ladies of negotiable virtue who flourished in town. They had not featured on his mother's list of dissipated activities that she had suggested to him. 'Cards, dearest, drink—I know you have a hard head for both, so they are safe. Be seen in all the most notorious places. Perhaps buy a racehorse? Flirt, of course, but no young débutantes, that goes without saying… Do you know any fast matrons?'

'Only you, Mama,' he had retorted, smiling into her amused grey eyes.

After an hour, Hebe, thoroughly bored with resting, summoned both men back to her salon, announcing that she had not the slightest idea what she could do to assist her aunt.

'Send Giles to listen sympathetically,' Alex was suggesting idly when there was the sound of the knocker. 'Who can that be?'

Starling appeared in the doorway. 'Mrs Fulgrave, my lady.' He flattened himself against the door frame as Emily Fulgrave almost ran into the room, 'Oh, Hebe, my dear, Alex… Oh!' Both her niece and the Earl regarded her with consternation from the *chaise* where Alex was sitting beside Hebe who, he had insisted, was to stay lying down for at least another hour. Mrs Fulgrave burst into tears.

It took quite five minutes and a dose of sal volatile before she could command herself again. Giles, his escape cut off by a flurry of hastily summoned maidservants and general feminine bustle, retreated to the far side of the room, hoping that his presence would not be marked. Hysterical matrons, he felt, were even less his style than fast ones.

Finally Hebe managed to ask what was wrong. Her aunt regarded her over her handkerchief and managed to gasp, 'Joanna has run away.'

Eventually the whole story was extracted. Joanna had vanished from her room, but was not missed until it was time for luncheon because she was assumed to be hiding herself away until her unwanted suitor was due that afternoon and Mr Fulgrave was not in a mood to be conciliatory and seek to encourage her to emerge.

When her mama had finally opened her bed-chamber door she was gone, with only a brief note to say she was going 'where she could think.'

After several hours of sending carefully worded messages to her friends in town, all of which drew a blank, her parents were at their wits' end. Mr Fulgrave was prostrate with gout, dear Alex had seemed their only resort.

Alex shot one look at Hebe's white, shocked face and said firmly, 'I am sorry, Aunt Fulgrave, but I simply cannot leave Hebe now.'

'I know, of course, you cannot,' Emily Fulgrave said despairingly. 'I should have thought. It will have to be the Bow Street Runners, but we will have lost a day…'

'I will find her,' Giles said, standing up and causing all of them to start in surprise.

'Oh, Giles, *thank you*,' Hebe said warmly. 'I had quite forgot you were there. Aunt Emily, Giles is staying with us. What could be more fortunate?'

Giles wondered if Mrs Fulgrave would consider that the family scandal coming to the ears of someone else, however close a friend, to be a fortunate matter. 'You may trust my absolute discretion, ma'am, but you must tell me everything you know about what is wrong and where she may have gone,' he began briskly, only to stagger back as the distraught matron cast herself upon his chest and began to sob on his shoulder. 'Ma'am…'

Eventually Mrs Fulgrave was calm, sitting looking at him with desperate faith in his ability to find her daughter. Giles was already bitterly regretting his offer.

Damn it, what else can I do? he thought grimly. Alex and Hebe would fret themselves into flinders otherwise, and the Fulgraves had welcomed him into their family. And the thought of the girl with the pain in her hazel eyes tugged at him, awakening echoes of his own hurt.

Chapter Five

On the thirtieth of June, two days after Mrs Fulgrave had arrived distraught at the Tasboroughs' house, her errant daughter sat up in bed in the best chamber in the White Hart inn at Stilton and decided that, just possibly, she was not going to die after all.

It had been the meat pie she had so incautiously eaten at Biggleswade that had been her downfall. She had known almost at once that it had been a mistake, but she had been so hungry that when the stage had stopped she had eagerly paid for the pie and a glass of small ale.

Up until then the entire undertaking had seemed miraculously easy. She had packed a carefully selected valise of essentials and had donned the most demure walking dress and pelisse in her wardrobe. Her hair was arranged severely back into a tight knot, she had removed all her jewellery and her finished appearance, as she had intended, was that of a superior governess. And governesses were invisible; young women who could travel unregarded on the public stage without the slightest comment.

Finding the right inn from which to depart had taken a little more initiative, but careful study of the London map in her father's study showed her which area the Lincoln stage was likely to leave from, and a shy governess enquiring at six in the morning for the right departure point for Lincoln was apparently an unremarkable event.

In fact, she had felt remarkably pleased with herself and her tactics. Giles would have been proud of her, she caught herself thinking before that fancy was ruthlessly suppressed. Her only worry was how to get from Peterborough to Wisbech and Georgy, but that would doubtless become apparent once she had reached Peterborough.

Joanna pressed her arm against her side, feeling the reassuring bulge of the purse tied to her belt under her pelisse. She had only just received her quarter's allowance and still had, quite unspent, her birthday present from her generous godmother. Of all her worries, how to pay for her journey was the least of them.

Then she had eaten that wretched pie. Goodness knows what it had been made from, or how long it had been sitting in a warm kitchen before she had eaten it. By St Neots she was feeling queasy, past Eaton Socon she knew that at any moment she was going to be violently sick.

The stage had drawn up at the White Hart and she had staggered off, just finding enough voice to request the coachman to throw down her valise before she dived behind the shelter of a barn and was hideously ill. When she emerged shakily some time later the coach was gone, but thankfully the landlady proved motherly and kind to the white-faced young governess who explained that she was travelling back to her employer in Lincoln and had been taken ill.

'I am sure it is something I have eaten,' Joanna explained weakly, 'but I cannot travel like this. Fortunately Lady Brown does not expect me for another week so she will not worry. Is there any possibility of a room?'

The landlady was impressed by the genteel appearance and cultured accents of the young woman before her, and even more reassured by the sight of her guinea-purse. Such a pity that a young lady like that had to demean herself as little more than a superior upper servant.

'You come along, my dear,' she had urged. 'By good luck the best bedchamber is free and I'll have the girl see to you.'

The girl in question was kept more than a little busy over the next night and day. Joanna was thoroughly sick and at one point the landlady considered sending for the doctor, but by the following morning she was pale but recovering and could manage a little plain bread and a glass of water without it promptly returning.

She sat up and considered her situation. It was a setback, for she felt uneasily that until she turned off for Wisbech she was in danger of detection, but otherwise her plan was still holding together. But the delay had made Joanna think, and for some reason a particularly dry and academic book on strategy she had once tried to read came to her mind. She had cast it aside after a few chapters, unable to read further even to impress Giles. What had struck her as so idiotic about it was that the author propounded all manner of cunning manoeuvres without once considering that the enemy would be doing whatever *they* decided was best, thus overthrowing all the plans of their opponents.

It was just what she had been doing: planning her life with Giles without thinking for a moment that he might be doing something entirely otherwise. All at once it dawned on her that she hadn't been thinking about the real man at all, only the object of her dreams, her innocent, ignorant fantasy. Did the man she loved really exist at all?

Giles Gregory meanwhile was finding a perverse pleasure in the hunt. He had never been an intelligence officer, unlike his friend Alex, but no army officer could rise through the ranks without knowing how to hunt down and track the enemy through hostile or strange county.

And this was a foreign country to him, he realised, shouldering his way into the bustling inn yards of London. To a man used to command, and used to the least of his commands receiving instant obedience, the experience of being out of uniform and on the receiving end of the London working man's tongue was instructive.

'Move yer arse!' he was abruptly ordered when he stood too far into the yard of the Moor's Head as the stage swung in through the low arch, then, as he sidestepped out of the way, he was buffeted by a swaggering postilion with his iron-shod boots and aggressive whip. 'Shift yourself, bloody swell cove!'

He swung round to meet the man eye to eye and the postilion backed off, hands raised defensively, muttering, 'Sorry, guv'nor, no offence meant.'

Giles looked him up and down without speaking until the man was reduced to stuttering silence, then said with a hint of steel in his pleasant voice, 'You will oblige me by telling me the inn for the Lincoln coaches.'

'This one, guv'nor. Let me show you the office, sir!'

Giles allowed himself to be shown the way. He was taking a gamble, but close questioning of a tearful Mrs Fulgrave by her niece and both men had elicited the fact that her sister Grace was the most likely refuge for Joanna. 'Then there is her schoolfriend Lady Brandon in Wisbech,' her mother had said, showing a greater awareness of Joanna's correspondence than her daughter had given her credit for. 'And, of course—' She had broken off, looking guilty.

'Who, Aunt?' Hebe had probed. 'We have to think of anyone she could have gone to.'

'Oh, dear. You must not tell your uncle I mentioned this.' Mrs Fulgrave took a deep breath. 'My sister-in-law Caroline near Norwich.'

'I have never heard of her, Aunt Emily.'

'I know, dear.' Emily had looked round imploringly at her audience. 'You will promise not to tell Mr Fulgrave that I told you? His youngest sister Caroline…' she blushed and went on bravely '…she lived with a married man as his wife. They fell in love, and then it transpired that he had a wife living who had run off with another man. So Caroline and Mr Faversham could never marry. It was impossible, of course, but she went and moved in with him. The family cut her off, even after his wife died, ten years later, and he married her, only to die himself within six months.'

'Oh, poor lady,' Hebe cried. 'How sad!'

'I thought so,' Emily said stoutly. 'And so I told Mr Fulgrave. I have written to her every year, but he would never relent because he says it nearly killed his poor father. But it is foolish of me even to consider Caro—Joanna could not know of her.'

'Are you sure?' Giles pressed. 'Where do you keep her address?'

Mrs Fulgrave had removed her remembrancer from her reticule and held it out, open at the right page. Giles studied the address, then delicately lifted one long black hair from the crease in the page. Silently he held it up, dark against Mrs Fulgrave's own light brown hair. 'I think she knows.' Only Hebe noticed that as he noted the address in his own pocket book he carefully laid the hair in its folds.

However, their supposition that Grace was the most likely choice for Joanna to make appeared to be confirmed at the stage-coach office. Not only did the book keeper assure Giles that this was the right departure point for Lincoln, but he remembered Joanna. 'If you mean the young lady governess, sir? Least, I suppose that was what she was. Remarkable handsome young woman, that I do know. But anxious somehow—that's why I recall her, sir—that and her looks, if you'll pardon me saying so. All dressed so demure-like and those big eyes…'

'Where did she buy a ticket to?' Giles demanded, coming to the conclusion that if he took exception to every man who offended him that day he would not get far.

'Lincoln, she said. At least, first she asked about

Peterborough, then she looked confused and said she wanted Lincoln, sir.'

'And what would be the town to change for Wisbech?'

'Peterborough, sir.'

'And what are the stops between here and Lincoln?' Giles dug his hand in his pocket and began to sort coins. The man brightened at the chinking noise.

'I'll make you a list, shall I, sir? All of the stops or just the junction points, like?'

'All of them,' Giles had replied, tapping a gold coin suggestively on the counter.

Within half an hour his curricle, with the matched greys in the shafts and his groom left behind, faintly complaining, swung out on to the Great North Road heading towards Stevenage. Joanna had a full day's start on him and he could not risk simply assuming she was going to Peterborough; he was going to have to check at every stopping place on the list. But then, there were French colonels—some of them still alive to remember it—who had had similar starts on Giles Gregory and who had still found themselves tracked down, outmanoeuvred and defeated. One chit of a girl was not going to elude him now.

* * *

Joanna parted with some reluctance from the comforts of the White Hart the next morning. She was anxious to be on her way and to reach Georgy, but the inn and its motherly landlady, Mrs Handley, had seemed safe; although she would never have admitted it, Joanna was feeling lonely and not a little frightened.

Still, she was taken up by the stage without any problem and Mrs Handley had come out herself to see her off and to remind her which inn in Peterborough to get off at in order to pick up the Lynn stage, which would drop her in Wisbech.

She eyed her new travelling companions from under the brim of her modest bonnet and was re-assured by the sight of a stout farmer's wife with a basket, a thin young man who promptly fell asleep and a middle-aged gentleman in clerical collar and bands who politely raised his hat to her as she got on.

'I trust I do not intrude,' he ventured after a few moments, 'but I heard the good landlady directing you to the Crown and Anchor and I wonder if I might be of assistance? My name is Thoroughgood, Reverend Thaddeus Thoroughgood, and I am changing at that point myself as I do very frequently. I would be most happy to point out the stage office and so forth when we arrive.'

Joanna thanked him politely, somewhat nervous that he might want to continue talking to her, for conversation with a strange man, even a most respectable-looking clergyman, on a public stage was not what she had been brought up to regard as ladylike behaviour. However, the good reverend did not say any more and she thanked him and leaned back, feeling happier now she knew she had a guide should she need one.

They stopped once on the short distance to Peterborough. What with the exit of the stout farmer's wife whose basket somehow got jammed in the doorway, the Reverend Thoroughgood getting up to assist her, slipping on the step and falling heavily against Joanna, and the thin young man leaping up to help everyone, it proved a somewhat chaotic halt. However, they were soon at the Crown and Anchor and the Reverend Thoroughgood helped her down with her valise.

'Now, I shall go and collect my gig,' he said chattily, 'and be off home to Sister. You just need to go through that door there and you'll find our good hostess and a nice parlour and she'll tell you when the Lynn coach comes in. Now, you do have enough money, do you not, my dear young lady?'

'Oh, yes, thank you,' Joanna replied, confidently. Then, 'My purse! It has gone!'

'Great heavens!' the clergyman exclaimed. 'That young man must have been a cutpurse! Mrs Wilkins! Mrs Wilkins!'

The landlady came hurrying out, wiping her hands on her apron. She smiled at the sight of Hebe's companion. 'There you are again, Reverend. Your gig is all ready for you. But, sir—' she broke off at the sight of their agitation '—what's about?'

'My money has been stolen,' Joanna lamented. 'This gentleman thinks it was a cutpurse on the stage.'

'Well now, miss,' the landlady said sympathetically, 'that's a dreadful thing. Why, there is no stopping the impudent rascals. That's the third time we've seen that happen, is it not, Reverend?' She patted Joanna's arm. 'We had better be telling the magistrate, miss.'

'But that won't get my purse back,' Joanna stammered. 'What am I going to do? I have to get to Wisbech.'

There was a silence, then the clergyman said,

'Normally I would not suggest it, of course, but as I have an open gig, and it is still broad daylight, would you consider riding with me to my home where my sister awaits me? You can spend the night most securely under her protection and then in the morning we can consider what is best. To write to your friends in Wisbech, perhaps? Or I may have a neighbour who is driving that way.'

'There now, that is a good idea,' the landlady said approvingly.

Joanna bit her lip. It did seem the best of the alternatives, for the clergyman appeared well known and trusted at the inn and he obviously kept his gig there frequently. A clergyman's sister sounded a most respectable chaperon…

And there was the benefit of it taking her off the main road in case of pursuit. She made up her mind. 'Thank you, sir,' she said decisively. 'If Miss Thoroughgood would not find it an imposition, I would be most grateful.'

The gig was well kept and pulled by a neat black pony and Joanna felt happier as they progressed at a brisk trot through the lanes. The loss of her money was serious, but at least she was not too many miles from Georgy, who was not only the possessor of a vastly generous allowance but was indulged by her husband as to the spending of it. As soon as she knew of Joanna's predicament, she was sure to send both funds and her carriage at once.

The Reverend Thoroughgood did not seem anxious to ask personal questions or to make encroaching observations, so Joanna was emboldened to introduce herself. 'I should tell you a little of my circumstances, sir, for I am sure Miss Thoroughgood will not wish to take a total stranger into her home. My name is J…Jane Wilson and I am a governess on my way to my new employer in Wisbech, Lady Brandon.'

It felt shocking to be lying to a man of the cloth, but he would hardly assist her if he knew the truth.

'We must see you on your way as soon as possible, Miss Wilson,' the reverend said, turning down another lane. Joanna was becoming a little confused. The lanes must be more than usually meandering hereabouts, she decided, for it seemed they must be driving in a circle. 'No doubt but that Lady Brandon will be anxious for you to begin to teach her children, and equally your friends and family will be concerned to hear of your safe arrival.'

Joanna bit her lip. It would look odd indeed if

the only letter she sent during her enforced stay with the Thoroughgoods was to Lady Brandon. 'I do not have any family,' she said, trying to sound brave but lonely. 'And no close friends. A governess's life is a solitary one, I am afraid.'

'I am sorry to hear that,' the Reverend Thoroughgood said solemnly. 'You must turn for consolation to the thought of the good you are doing and the Christian learning you are bringing to young and tender minds.'

'Oh, yes, quite.' Joanna felt that any further discussion of this would be dangerous. She must recall all she could of her own governesses before venturing into conversation on their lives and duties. 'Are we near your parish yet, sir?'

'I do not have a parish: I have always been a scholar rather than a pastor, although I have many friends in London to whom I minister and attempt to bring spiritual light and succour by correspondence and the writing of tracts.'

'Indeed.' Joanna racked her brains; this was far more difficult than making conversation with a duchess. 'That must be very…satisfying.'

'Indeed it is, my dear Miss Wilson. I feel I myself gain much profit by my efforts in the capital. Now, here we are.'

The gig turned into the drive of a modest yellow brick house set within a somewhat overgrown and dull garden of lawn and laurels. It looked not so much dilapidated as unloved and uncared for and Joanna shivered despite the warm afternoon. A clergyman in modest circumstances could not afford to spend much on external appearances, she chided herself. It was most ungrateful to be critical after he had offered to help her in her difficulties.

No groom came round at the sound of the gig and the Reverend Thoroughgood simply dropped the reins as he helped Joanna down. The pony stood patiently, apparently not inclined to wander off, and the front door opened.

'Lucille, my dear!' The Reverend Thoroughgood took Joanna's arm with one hand and her valise with the other and urged her towards the door. 'I have a young lady in distress who has been cast adrift upon the highway by the actions of some pickpocket. She is on her way to her new employer and has no friends or family to turn to.'

The woman who stood on the step, one long white hand raised to hold open the door, surprised Joanna. She was tall, dressed with sombre elegance in a dark gown of excellent cut and, although at least forty-five, retained striking good looks. In Joanna's experience ladies of that age were matrons and dressed and appeared exactly that. This lady had a faintly dangerous and independent air about her.

She looked Joanna up and down, a faint smile on her well-cut lips, then raised an eyebrow at her brother, who hastened to complete the introductions. 'Lucille, my dear, this is Miss Wilson. Miss Wilson, my sister, Miss Thoroughgood.'

Joanna bobbed a curtsy. 'I must apologise, ma'am, for this intrusion. The Reverend Thoroughgood has been most kind to me in my predicament and has offered to allow me to stay for a few days until my letter reaches my new employer and she is able to send a carriage for me.'

'Of course. We are delighted you are here, Miss Wilson. Would you like to come upstairs to your room?' Her voice was cool, not unpleasant, but Joanna sensed a strange current of amusement underlying her words. It made her uneasy, which was ridiculous. She was tired, that was all. Tired, upset by the theft and still not entirely recovered from her stomach upset.

'Thank you, ma'am.' She followed her hostess into a dark hall, up the stairs and into a room. Miss Thoroughgood stood aside as she entered and Joanna walked forward a few steps before turning to see both brother and sister standing in the doorway watching her. 'I…' Her voice died away as she took in their cool, assessing expressions and realised that the room she was in was virtually bare except for a bed and a washstand. The narrow window was barred with iron.

Chapter Six

'I must congratulate you, Thaddeus,' Miss Thoroughgood said, eyeing Joanna up and down in much the same way as she might have assessed the points of a horse. 'This one will do excellently. A real young lady.'

'And a *virtuous* young lady,' he replied, tugging off his clerical collar and bands with a grunt of relief. 'You *are* a virtuous young lady, are you not, Miss Wilson?'

Her flaming cheeks were all the answer he wanted and a smirk of satisfaction crossed his nondescript features, which up until that moment Joanna had found reassuringly bland.

The sudden change in tone was completely disorientating. 'I think there must be some mistake,' she said coldly, taking a step towards them. 'I will leave now.'

'Oh no, dear,' Miss Thoroughgood replied. 'You will not leave this room until we are ready to send you to London.' She turned to her brother. 'When is Thomas collecting the next consignment?'

'He has a carriage making the rounds now, he should be with us by the day after tomorrow.'

'London? What are you talking about? Let me go at once.' Joanna tried to keep her voice steady and confident, but it shook despite her efforts. The brother and sister seemed to grow before her eyes until all she was aware of was their assessing looks, their amused smiles, the way their eyes slid over her body.

The woman addressed her frigidly. 'You go where we send you. You belong to us now. In a day or two you will be in the hands of your new master, on the way to your new…home.'

'Belong? What are you talking about? I have an employer…'

'You are about to get an owner. Milo Thomas, the biggest whoremaster in the capital, is going to pay us very well indeed for such an untouched treasure as you, my dear.'

'Whore…*no!*' Joanna backed away, stopping abruptly as the back of her legs hit the bed. 'You are wrong about me! I am a respectable girl, not…'

'Not yet.' Thaddeus sounded amused at her lack of comprehension. 'Not yet, but you will be. You will learn all you need in one of Milo's closed houses, and you will earn him a fortune. Someone is going to pay very good money to deflower such innocence and beauty, and even more are going to pay handsomely to watch.'

'No!' Joanna pressed her hands to her mouth. She was going to be sick, she was going to faint and then wake up and find this was a nightmare. His words made no real sense to her, except to convey a disgusting, terrifying threat. How could they imagine… She struggled for courage and to think. 'I told you I was a governess, that I was alone in the world. That was not true. I am running away from home and I have a rich and influential family. They will be looking for me— they will pay you to get me back.'

She broke off, panting, and watched the expressions on the two predatory faces opposite her. There was calculation going on and for a moment she dared hope, then Lucille said, 'No. She would, of course, say that to buy time. But even if it were true, if we released her, she has seen us. As it is, a few months in Milo's care and her family, if they exist, will not want her back to shame them.'

She took the valise from her brother's hand and opened it, sorting roughly through its contents. She removed a nail file and a pair of scissors, then tossed it into the room. 'There. Now, rest and do not try to make a noise. There is no one to hear you and you will not want to annoy Thaddeus. He would not leave a mark on you, naturally, but you would be sorry none the less.'

The door closed and Joanna heard the sharp click of a lock, then the further sound of two bolts being drawn. Shaking in every limb she sank down on the bed and tried to think, tried to plan, but all that was in her head were those obscene words. Someone was going to pay to…to… No! She buried her face in her hands and still the Thoroughgoods' words invaded her mind, a rape in themselves. Pay to watch…pay handsomely to watch…

It was impossible. Of course, men went to brothels, she knew that. But surely they went because they wanted women who knew what they were about, who would know how to give them pleasure? How could they want to watch a terrified girl being raped, let alone carry out the act? The sheer perversity and wickedness of such a thing steadied her as she applied her reason to it. There were people who got pleasure from being cruel to animals, there were bullies, people who maltreated their servants; perhaps this was an extreme example of that. But that there should be so many men that a brothel keeper could grow rich from them was appalling. Had she met such men? Could they go about in society hiding such evil behind a mask of respectability?

The thought brought her back to her own fate and, for all her courage, she suddenly gave way to racking sobs, curled up on the musty counterpane where, she supposed through her misery, other girls had sobbed in despair before her. Other girls. Joanna sat up, scrubbing the back of her hand across her wet eyes. Other girls. If she did nothing, not only was she damned to this hell, but all the others who followed her would be. Under no circumstances was she going to be worthy of Giles if she gave up now.

Joanna blew her nose, got to her feet and examined the room. Her legs felt like string, every now and again a sob escaped her, but she forced herself to search. There was nothing that could be used as a weapon. The bed was screwed to the floor, the sheets were thin with age and would tear easily. The washstand was bare of ewer or basin and under the bed the chamber pot was of such thin china that it would hardly bruise a head if she struck someone with it.

The door, as she expected, did not even move when she pressed against it and there was no handle on her side. The window was barred, not with wood, but with iron set into the frame, and the opening sash had been screwed up.

Joanna stared out down the front drive to the glimpse of road at the gate. Could she attract attention if someone passed? No, she would have no warning of their passing, the hedge was so high.

So, she could not escape from here. Then it would have to be the carriage when it came. From what the Thoroughgoods had said, there might be other girls in it, girls in the same predicament. That seemed too easy—a carriage full of frantic, healthy young women would be difficult to control. In the Thoroughgoods' shoes, if it were possible to imagine inhabiting them, she would drug the prisoners. Which meant she must not eat or drink anything, dispose of what she was given, and then feign the right kind of reaction to an unknown drug.

Difficult…Joanna paced away from the window. The practical problem of escape was mercifully blocking out the true horror of her situation, but it lurked in the back of her mind, surfacing every now and again to send shocks of paralysing terror through her before she could wrestle control back again.

Giles…what would Giles do if he were captured? The thought steadied her again, gave her courage, something to fight for. If she never saw him again, if these evil people defeated her, she would at least know she had done all she could and had not been a feeble victim.

There was the sound of carriage wheels on the drive outside and she ran to the window. Surely this was not the threatened Milo Thomas so soon? But all she could see was a curricle, the reins looped around the whip, a pair of handsome matched greys in the shafts standing steaming, their heads down.

Probably a friend of the Thoroughgoods. But what if it were not? What if this were some innocent neighbour or passer-by? Joanna looked around the room wildly. Faintly from below came the thud of the knocker sounding. How could she open the window? The door below must have opened, for she could just hear the rumble of masculine voices. Desperately she snatched a sheet from the bed, wound it around her fist and punched a hole through the glass.

'Help! Oh, help!' she screamed, hitting the glass again until it showered down on to the front step below. 'Help!' There was a scuffle from below, then silence.

Joanna snatched up a long sliver of glass from the floor and ran to the door, standing at the hinge edge, desperately trying to quieten her gasping breath. There was a noise on the landing and the sound of bolts being dragged back. The visitor? Or Thaddeus Thoroughgood? If it was Thaddeus she was going to stab him, she had no doubt about it, not even the slightest qualm. The back would be the place…

The door swung open, she took a step forward and a voice she could not believe she was hearing said, 'Joanna?'

'*Giles?*' She must be hallucinating, delirious, the whole thing was a dream. Then he came into sight around the door and she was stumbling forwards and into his arms, the lethal glass dagger falling unregarded to the floor. She was saved: and saved, miraculously by the man she loved. 'Giles, oh, Giles…how did you find me? These people…oh!' Over his shoulder she saw Lucille, a poker clenched in her fist, her arm upraised to strike. 'Behind you!'

Naturally Joanna had never seen a fight, let alone men boxing, but even she could appreciate the economy and power of the single blow that Giles delivered as he swung round. It took Lucille perfectly on the point of the chin and she went down with a thud, quite still.

'Damn it!' Giles knelt beside the recumbent form. 'I've never hit a woman before.'

'I hope you have broken her neck,' Joanna said vehemently, startling him. He had expected tears, fainting, but not such fierceness. She must have been terrified: he recollected the feeling of her quivering body as she hugged him so fiercely. 'Where is her brother?'

'Unconscious on the hall floor. Joanna, never mind them, are you—'

'Yes, I am fine, thanks to you,' she said, regarding Lucille with a wary eye. She did not appear to understand what he was really asking, and he did not persist. Time enough for that. 'Giles, we must not risk these two escaping before we can get the magistrate. I cannot begin to tell you how evil they are.'

Giles had formed a very good suspicion of exactly what he was dealing with as soon as he heard the landlady's tale of the kind clergyman and the string of unfortunate young ladies who all had their pockets picked on the stage. The last few miles, springing the already tired horses, had been a battle between his imagination and years of disciplined calm under extreme pressure. Now he simply nodded, accepting what she said without questioning her. 'Is there a room where we can lock them up?'

Joanna put her head around the adjacent door. 'This one, the window is not broken. Oh—' She broke off, turning to him, her eyes wide with horror. 'Oh, look.' The room had manacles bolted to the wall at the bed head.

She had gone so white that Giles thought she was about to faint. He put an arm around her and she looked up into his eyes, her own dark with, he realised with a jolt, burning anger. 'Put them in here,' she said fiercely. 'Shackle *them* to the bed.'

Before he could respond she was running downstairs, the poker in her hand. 'Joanna, stop!' For a horrible moment he thought she was going to strike the unconscious man who sprawled on the dingy tiled floor, but she was only standing over him, watchful for any sign of returning consciousness.

Giles crouched, hauled Thaddeus over his shoulder and stood up in one clean movement, only a slight grunt of expelled breath revealing the effort it took. Joanna ran upstairs after him, and, when he turned from dropping Thoroughgood on to the bed, she was already dragging his sister into the room by both arms.

He picked up the unconscious woman and laid her on the bed beside her brother, then snapped a shackle around one wrist of each. 'Now, where are the keys, I wonder?'

'Here.' Joanna, who had been carefully checking the room for anything that might give the Thoroughgoods assistance, picked up the key from the bare washstand. She bent over Lucille, pulling the hair pins from her head and the reticule from her waist. 'They might pick the lock,' she said tersely. 'What has he got?'

Giles raised his eyebrows at this ruthless prac- ticality, but if it was helping Joanna he was not going to try and distract her. He removed Thaddeus's tiepin and patted his pockets, coming up with a roll of banknotes, a leather wallet and a pretty guinea purse.

'That is mine!' Joanna reached across and took it, clutching it tight in her fist. 'He stole in on the stage.'

'I know,' Giles said, keeping his voice low and

calm, sensing that it would take very little to tip her over the edge. 'Come downstairs now, they are quite secure.'

'Lock and bolt the door.'

'Yes, of course.' He reached up and pulled across the topmost bolt, allowing her to turn the key and shoot the lower bolt. Let her be certain her nightmare was safely shut away.

'Now, come downstairs and I will see if there is anything for you to eat or drink in the kitchen.' Joanna let him guide her down the stairs, her arm quivering under his hand. All at once she stiffened.

'Miss Thoroughgood! Miss Thoroughgood, ma'am!' A thin voice was calling from the back of the house, coming closer, accompanied by the sound of shuffling footsteps.

Giles pushed Joanna firmly behind him and called, 'Who is there?'

'Just me, Mrs Penny, Mr Thoroughgood… Oh! Who are you, sir?'

It was a woman, perhaps in her fifties, perhaps older, skinny in a shabby hand-me-down dress covered by a large sacking apron, her straggling grey hair pulled back into a bun. She stood wringing her hands in front of her, obviously completely unable to cope with the unexpected sight of two strangers in the hallway. Giles noticed with a pang how red and sore her hands looked.

'Do you work for Miss Thoroughgood?'

'Yes, sir. I comes in three times a week and does the rough cleaning.'

'Does she have any other servants?'

'No sir, just me.' She did not seem able to ask what they were doing there, just stood and stared at them.

'Well, Mrs Penny, I am sorry to tell you that Mr and Miss Thoroughgood are a pair of rogues of the worst kind and are going to be handed over to the Justices and will come to a very bad end.'

'Gawd, sir!' Her eyes widened. Giles could not believe for a moment that she had any idea what had been going on in the house.

'I am Colonel Gregory, and this young lady is my…my sister. Now, Mrs Penny, where is the sitting room?'

'In the front, sir…Colonel, sir.' She threw open a door on to the most comfortable and well-kept room they had seen so far. Giles steered Joanna firmly towards the sofa. She moved when he pushed her, but made no effort to sit.

'Can you make the young lady a cup of tea, Mrs Penny?' The woman nodded, but he saw the anxiety in her eyes and how her hands were twisting in the apron again. 'Now, you are not to worry. No one will think you have had anything to do with this. What are you paid?'

'Sixpence a week, sir.'

'And when were you last paid?'

Her brow wrinkled with the effort to remember. 'Three weeks ago, sir.'

Giles fished in his pocket. 'Here,' he handed over a coin which made her gasp. 'That will pay your back wages and is some extra for your trouble today. Now, the tea?'

'That was kind,' Joanna observed faintly as he pushed her gently onto the sofa.

Giles sat down beside her, but did not try to touch her. He was puzzled that she showed no surprise at seeing him: perhaps the shock was just so all-encompassing that she would not have questioned any familiar face.

'Joanna, did he touch you?' he asked, and this time he saw she understood him.

'Oh, no. There was no danger of that.' Her voice was calm and, although faint, quite clear. 'He wanted a virgin, you understand. He made it very plain what for, and that was where my value lay.'

Giles had suspected that as soon as he realised that there was a woman in the scheme.

Thoroughgood was not a solitary pervert, kidnapping girls for his own gratification. No, he was a trader in a very specialised commodity. But he had hoped that Joanna had not realised and that nothing had been said to shatter that innocence. He wanted to take her in his arms; even without touching her he could see the fine tremor running through her entire body. Her skin was so pale it seemed translucent and her eyes appeared unfocussed. But how would she react to being touched by a man now?

She did not respond when Mrs Penny came in with the tea. Giles nodded thanks to the woman and told her to get on with the tasks she normally carried out but not to venture upstairs, whatever she heard.

He pressed a cup into Joanna's hand, but she could not hold it steady so he put it down again to let it cool. After a moment she turned and looked at him, although he could not tell whether she really understood who she was talking to.

'He said that they would get a very good price from the man who…from the man—' She broke off, biting her lip. 'And money from those who would pay to watch. They said a man called Milo Thomas would come and collect me in a coach. I think there will be other girls in it.'

'How can that be?' Joanna asked him, her face reflecting her desperate need to understand. 'I know men go to brothels, have mistresses. Of course I do. And I am not so foolish as to believe that women would not turn to such a way of life if they had better alternatives. But surely men want someone who knows how to make love? Is that not more pleasant? Yet there must be many men like those he was talking about, otherwise how could the brothel keepers and people like the Thoroughgoods make money from them? How could it be worth the risks?'

Giles wished vehemently that he was not the one having to answer her questions. In fact, he would rather have found himself surrounded by French cavalry at that moment. If he got this wrong…

'The vast majority of men are perfectly decent and normal,' he said, keeping his voice as steady and quiet as he could. 'Just as you imagine, they want to enjoy themselves, and they want the woman they are with to enjoy herself as well, whether it is within marriage, or outside it. Normal men,' he added, with a hint of a smile, 'would feel it a slur on their manhood if the lady did *not* find pleasure in their attentions.

'But there are some who like cruelty, like to

inflict pain. I think it must be about feeling powerful, that men who do not feel assured of themselves like to dominate someone weaker. Some stick at bullying their families and servants, others maltreat their horses. Some, just a few, go further. It is not many, Joanna, you must not assume that half the men you meet and know socially are like this, hiding a wolf's teeth under a human smile. But the ones who enjoy such things can usually pay for it, and pay very well to get exactly what they want.'

She looked at him, and he could see her eyes were beginning to focus a little and knew she had listened and understood. As he watched, her rigid calm began to falter and the tears started to well up in her eyes, which had turned a dark, dull brown.

'Joanna, come here.' Without stopping to think whether she might fight him, he leant forward, took her in his arms and lifted her on to his knee, holding her tight against his chest. 'Most men are decent men who respect women. Men like your father, like Alex, like William will be when he grows up.'

He could feel the front of his shirt becoming wet. She was crying almost silently. Then she nodded and he heard her voice, muffled. 'Like you.'

'Yes. Like me. I would never hurt you, Joanna.' For some reason that seemed to make things worse: in the tightness of his embrace he could feel her sobbing fiercely. Not knowing what to say, or whether it was better just to let her weep, he simply held her, his face buried in the silk of her hair, his body shaken with the force of her sobs. Never, in his entire thirty years, had he felt so violently protective towards a living creature, nor had he ever known himself to be in such a killing rage. He could not trust himself to open that door upstairs without a restraining presence or there would be murder done.

Finally the sobs died down and he tentatively let his arms fall away from her. Joanna sat up a little, but otherwise made no attempt to move from his knee.

'Would you like some tea?' She nodded and reached out for the cup, sitting there sipping it like a trusting child in his lap.

She put it down at last and turned to face him, her eyes still drowned in tears. 'He did not touch me, but it still feels like...' she struggled with the word '...like rape.'

'Because he forced those words into your mind, he forced that image into your imagination?'

'Yes, exactly that. You understand so well. Now I cannot make them go away.'

Giles thought carefully before he spoke, then simply trusted to his instincts. 'They were only words. They were only images, they were not reality, because you would not let them be. You were fighting back, you were not a victim. Those things would not have happened because you were never going to give up.'

'You saved me,' she pointed out.

'Only because you helped me. If I had not come today, you would have been scheming, plotting, resisting.' He smiled at her. 'Where did you find the courage, Joanna?'

'Thinking of the other girls,' she said simply. 'And thinking of what…of what someone who is very important to me would have expected of me.'

For some reason Giles felt that he had been punched in the solar plexus. Of course—this mysterious man who had so upset her at the Duchess's ball that this entire train of events had been set in motion. He could hardly cavil at anything that had given Joanna the strength to resist, but why was she wasting her emotions on this damned man? She was worth more, this pattern-book débutante who had kicked over the traces.

'Remember that you had the courage to fight,' he said, when he had trampled on his anger. 'And talk about it, don't bottle it up.'

'Who can I talk about it with?' she asked.

'Me. Hebe. Alex.'

'*Alex?* Goodness, no!' Joanna sounded almost normal again. 'I am scared of Alex.'

'Why on earth? He usually has to fight the ladies off—or at least he had to until he had Hebe to do it for him.'

'He looks so…sardonic,' Joanna said. 'Hebe told me that her maid on Malta said he looked like "a beautiful fierce saint". He was furious, apparently.'

Giles grinned, saving that one up to torment Alex with on some future occasion. It was enough that talking of their friends had restored Joanna a little. 'Will you be all right if I go and talk to Mrs Penny? I want to find out where the nearest magistrate is.' She nodded, so he placed her carefully back on the sofa, found a clean handkerchief in the depths of his pocket for her and went in search of the charwoman who was scrubbing the kitchen floor.

'Magistrate, sir? The nearest one is the Squire.'

Patiently Giles extracted the information that Squire Gedding was a good man, firm but fair, and his lady was as nice as you could find anywhere.

'When my Jimmy had a bit of trouble with a pheasant—out of work he was, on account of him having hurt his arm—Squire had him in front of his desk and was right fierce. Told him he was a bloody fool and ought to have come to see him, not go trampling about in his coverts scaring the birds. And he gave him a job in his stables, and Mrs Gedding, she went right 'round with food for the little ones, and medicine for Susan, that's my daughter-in-law…'

Giles let her ramble on, feeling a considerable relief washing over him. A country squire with a firm hand but some imagination and a kindly wife were exactly what he had need of just now. 'How far away does Squire Gedding live?' he asked, cutting into further reminiscences of the Geddings' goodness.

'Less than two miles, sir. In the middle of the village.'

'That close?' Giles said with considerable relief. The sooner he got Joanna into the hands of a respectable lady, and the Thoroughgoods into the grip of the forces of law and order, the happier he would be. There were muffled shouts from upstairs and Mrs Penny started nervously. 'Do not worry, Mrs Penny, they cannot get out. Will you come with us in my carriage and direct us to the village? I will drop you off at your home.' She nodded, obviously anxious. 'If you go and make sure the fire in the kitchen is banked down,' Giles continued firmly, 'then I will lock up and we will be on our way.'

The three of them were soon outside. The greys stood patiently, too tired to show any inclination to wander. Giles helped both women up and then squashed into the seat beside them, thankful that Joanna was slim and Mrs Penny positively skinny.

The journey to the village did not take long despite the tired horses and the fact that dusk was falling rapidly. The charwoman indicated a cottage by the side of the road and was helped down, much to the amazement of the younger woman who came to the door, one child in her arms, another clinging to her skirts. 'There now, Mrs Penny. Thank you for your help. Squire will probably want to talk to you about this, but, in the meantime, be sure not to gossip about it.'

Giles glanced anxiously at Joanna, who was beginning to sway now that Mrs Penny's skinny form was no longer supporting her. Fortunately the Squire's house was as easy to find as Mrs

Penny had said, and as he drove on to the gravelled apron at the front a groom came round from the side of the house. 'Good evening, sir, may I take your horses?'

'Thank you. Is the Squire at home?' Giles put a steadying arm around Joanna, whose eyes were fluttering closed.

'Yes, sir, and Mrs Gedding, sir. Will you be staying, sir? I can stable the team and give them a good rub down and a feed.'

Giles was too concerned to get Joanna inside to pay much attention to the niceties such as introducing himself to the Squire first. 'Thank you. Just hold their heads while I help the lady.'

Between them they lifted Joanna down safely. Giles was not sure whether she had fainted or was simply asleep, but her head fell against his shoulder as he carried her and her face was buried in his coat front. A wave of fierce protectiveness swept over him, startling in its intensity: somehow he was going to make this all right for her.

A sensible-looking maid opened the door to him, took one look at his burden and said simply, 'You'll be wanting Mrs Gedding, sir.'

He followed her across the hall and through the door she held open and saw a big, grizzled man sitting on one side of the hearth, a plump, cheerful lady opposite him, obviously in full flow of speech. She broke off at the sight of the apparition on her threshold, then jumped to her feet and hurried over.

'Ma'am, I apologise for the intrusion,' Giles began. 'My name is Colonel Gregory and—'

'You need help,' she finished for him. 'Bring the poor lamb in, everything will be all right.'

And Giles, who could not remember feeling so relieved since he had seen a relief column of cavalry cutting their way through to his bridgehead at Vittoria, decided it probably would be.

Chapter Seven

Joanna stirred, yawned without opening her eyes and snuggled down into the bed again. She felt completely drained, she realised, sleepily beginning to wake up, but that was no wonder after such a dreadful night made hideous with nightmares. How had she imagined such appalling creatures? That clergyman, his sinister sister, their unspeakable plans for her...but her imagination had at least conjured up Giles to rescue her.

Then a cold, queasy hand gripped her stomach and she woke fully, remembering the day before, realising that it was all true, that it was no nightmare. 'Giles!' Joanna scrambled up against the pillows, searching the room with wide, frightened eyes, but it was not the shabby, dark room with its barred window. This was an airy, pretty chamber with delicate furniture, white muslin curtains stirring gently at an open window and a bowl of tumbling roses on the sill.

The door opened and a smiling lady looked in. 'Are you all right, my dear? I am Mrs Gedding and this is my home. You are quite safe here.' She came further into the room and Joanna saw she was a motherly-looking person with an air of commonsense kindness about her. She relaxed back against the pillows, her panic ebbing. 'My husband is the squire and a magistrate, and he and your young man are off dealing with those dreadful people,' she added reassuringly.

'My young man? Oh, you mean Giles? Oh, no, he is not…I mean…' Joanna was afraid she was blushing and when she saw the twinkle in Mrs Gedding's eyes she was sure of it. 'He is a friend of the family,' she added hastily, then realised with a shock that she had no idea how it was that Giles had saved her. How on earth had he come to be there? It had seemed so right, so perfect that it was the man she loved who had rescued her from that nightmare that it had never occurred to her to question it.

She recalled, as though from a long time ago, her fierce anger with her captors and Giles's calm handling of her fears. 'Are they, the Thoroughgoods, I mean…?'

'Off to Peterborough gaol last night,' her hostess said firmly. 'Two armed constables with them in a locked carriage. They'll be out of harm's way now, and there they'll stay until Quarter Sessions. The Colonel and my husband have gone back to the house today to search it for more evidence and to see if they can set an ambush for that Milo Thomas you told the Colonel about.'

She smoothed the bedcovers and watched Joanna for a moment, her head on one side like an inquisitive robin. 'You'll do better knowing all there is to know, I can tell. Some people don't want to know, other people need to. You've got too much imagination to be sheltered with half-truths. The Colonel told us how brave you were. Now, would you like a bath and some breakfast? Or would you like to talk to me about anything?'

Joanna smiled back. In the absence of Giles's arms around her, she could not have felt more secure than she did with this frank, friendly lady. She hugged the comment about Giles's opinion to herself and considered the question. 'Not at the moment, thank you,' she said. 'I asked Giles about why, and that sort of thing. That was what I could not understand. Why? And what made men like that? He explained it all.'

'Did he, indeed!' Mrs Gedding's eyebrows shot up. 'Well, he is an extraordinary young man if he could do that without turning a hair.'

'I think I could talk to Giles about anything,' Joanna said thoughtfully, then remembered exactly what they had been discussing and smiled faintly. 'He is *very* kind—and brave,' she added. 'I expect he had rather have faced a cavalry charge!'

Mrs Gedding smiled back. 'Bath and breakfast? I have no idea what has happened to your luggage; probably it is still at the Thoroughgoods' house. Even the most thoughtful and courageous man may be relied upon to forget such essentials as clean undergarments and tooth powder in a crisis. Never mind, my younger daughter's things are here—she is staying with her married sister, and she will not mind at all if you borrow whatever you need.'

A bath and clean, pretty clothes restored Joanna's spirits and she sat down to breakfast ravenously hungry. 'I do beg your pardon, ma'am,' she apologised when she realised she had finished the entire plate of toast, 'but I have eaten hardly anything since I left home but a meat pie at Biggleswade, and that made me ill.'

'Ah, yes, your home.' Mrs Gedding refilled her tea cup. 'The Colonel has written to your parents, and I have added a note. I have left the package open, so if you would like to add something of your own we will get it sealed up and off to Peterborough to catch the post as soon as may be.'

'Oh. Yes. Thank you.' Joanna bit her lip. She had meant to be with Georgy at least two days ago, with a reassuring message on its way to London as soon as she arrived—without any direction for finding her, of course. 'I should never have done it,' she blurted out, suddenly acutely conscious of the anxiety she must have caused. 'I was so miserable and confused. I cannot imagine what you must think of me.'

'That you were very unhappy, Joanna dear, and not thinking very clearly,' Mrs Gedding said prosaically. 'We all do stupid and thoughtless things at least once in our lives. Now, in his letter the Colonel has explained a little of what has happened—not the worst of it, naturally—and has told your parents that he must stay a day or so until the evidence is all collected together and you have rested. I have promised your mama that I will look after you and that we will find you a suitable chaperon before you travel back to London. All that remains for you to do is to rest and get stronger. But write your note first.'

'Yes, ma'am,' Joanna said meekly. The letter was hard to compose. In the end she managed a few lines to say how sorry she was, and that she was quite safe and that Mrs Gedding was very kind. But it was more than she was capable of to apologise for running away before Lord Clifton called to make his offer. The ink was blotted here and there with large teardrops, but she did not want to ask for more good notepaper and she hoped Mama would recognise tears of real regret.

Her hostess was bustling about with lists when she brought her the note. When it was sealed with the others and the groom dispatched with it, she asked politely if there was anything she could do to help.

'It won't do you any good to sit and brood, will it, my dear? No, I did not think it would. But you must not exert yourself too much yet.' Mrs Gedding thought for a while then said, 'I know, *pot-pourri*. Come along.'

Joanna found herself shown out into the back

garden, a basket over her arm and a pair of scissors in her hand. 'Oh, how beautiful!'

The garden was a mass of roses, of old-fashioned flowers, of weeping trees and winding paths scythed through the grass. The scent was magical and almost took her breath away.

'I love it,' said Mrs Gedding simply. 'It has taken me twenty years to make it look as though it just happened by accident. Not many people appreciate it.'

'It is Sleeping Beauty's garden,' Joanna declared. 'Is there a turret hidden in the midst of it?'

'No, but that is an excellent idea. I must ask Mr Gedding to have one built as a summer house. Now, my dear, the sun has dried the dew off the roses, so if you will be so good as to start picking heads from the ones that are just open, they will be perfect for drying.'

Joanna spent an idyllic morning exploring the garden. The maid brought out a chair and a rug and some larger baskets and she wandered up and down the paths, snipping rose heads into her basket, smelling the other scented bushes, thinking about the perfect place to position Sleeping Beauty's turret. Occasionally she would tip her basket into the bigger one by the chair and sit and rest for a little.

Mrs Gedding came out with some lemonade and they talked of their families and the contrast between village and town life, then her hostess went back inside and Joanna sat, surrounded by her baskets brimming with roses, and finally let herself think about the previous day.

She probed her memory like someone exploring a sore tooth, very cautiously, wincing as she realised just how careless and gullible she had been and what dreadful danger she had escaped. Giles's words of praise were balm to her self-esteem, but her conscience continued to prick her when she thought of her parents' anxiety.

And how, of all the miracles, had it been Giles who had found her? On the thought he appeared from the back door, carrying a chair and a folding table, the maid with a loaded tray behind him.

'Hello.' Joanna's heart gave a sudden, hard thud and she found that all she could do was to smile back at him. 'Mrs Gedding thought we might like to picnic out here. The Squire has come back to arrange for a clerk to assist us this afternoon: there is so much paper we are unearthing that we are going to have to get it listed and ordered before we can start to make sense of it all, let alone mount a court case.' He set down the chair and unfolded the table. 'May I sit down?'

'Oh, yes, of course, I am sorry, my wits are gone a-wandering.' He looked exactly as she remembered him from London. This morning she had been half-afraid that it was all a delusion and it wasn't the real Giles. Now, sitting beside him, watching the dappled shade from the tree cast patterns over his dark blond hair and returning the smile that crinkled the corners of his grey eyes, she knew he was real and a ridiculous, hopeless wave of love swept over her.

'Gi…Colonel Gregory…'

'Giles will do very well, Joanna.' He leaned forward and poured two glasses of lemonade. 'How are you today?'

'Much better than I deserve,' she replied ruefully. 'I cannot thank you enough. I was praying for a miracle, and there you were! But I do not understand how you came to find me.'

'Well, your father is laid up with gout and your mama hurried round to the Tasboroughs' town house in a fine state of alarm, as you might expect, hoping that Alex would be there. But, of course, she had not stopped to think about Hebe's condition. Fortunately I was staying and I knew Alex would not want to leave his wife, so I offered to hunt you down. You gave me a fair run for my money.' He lifted a plate and offered it to her. 'Ham? A slice of bread and butter? Or I think that is a slice of raised pie…'

'Ham and bread, please.' Joanna cut up her food, thinking over what Giles had said. 'Hebe is well?'

'Oh, perfectly, but she doesn't rest as much as she should, and I put the idea into Alex's head that she is expecting twins, so you can imagine the state he is in. I should imagine he and your mama between them are exercising Hebe's powers to calm and reassure to the utmost.'

Joanna digested this information, decided she could not possibly ask why Giles thought Hebe was expecting twins and said, 'How lucky you were still in London. I thought I heard someone say you had gone to see your father. Is the General well?'

Giles shrugged and Joanna saw the anxiety in his eyes, although he kept his voice light when he said, 'Not entirely. He does too much, will not admit he is not in the best of health and drives my mother distracted.'

'But you came back to town despite that?'

Joanna bit her lip, wondering if she had over-stepped the mark and was being intrusively curious, but Giles did not appear to find her question impertinent.

'We had a blazing row and he disinherited me,' he said with a smile that did not reach his eyes.

'Oh, Giles! How dreadful!' Joanna's bread and butter dropped to the plate unheeded as she stared at him. 'But why on earth?'

'I told him I intend to sell out. Oh, and there is the question of my marriage, of course.'

'Giles, you should not jest about it,' Joanna said, shaken to the core. 'Of course you are not going to sell out. Why, you are going to be a general—'

'Not you, too!' He got up and took two angry strides across the grass, then turned back with a shake of the head. 'I am sorry, Joanna, I did not mean to shout at you. My father is a sick man who is not getting any younger. He needs my help and support with the estate, even if he won't admit it. And we are at peace now: I do not want to spend the rest of my career as a peacetime soldier, always on parade, or worse, putting down industrial unrest in the north of England. I did not join the army to ride down starving mill workers or hungry farm labourers.'

Joanna put a hand on his arm as he sat down again, his lips tight, his eyes shadowed. 'I am sorry. That was very stupid and thoughtless of me. Of course, you must do what is best for your family. But has he truly disinherited you?'

Giles smiled, this time with real humour. 'He doesn't mean it. He will be regretting it now, although I doubt if he is regretting the strip he tore off me and the lecture I got on doing my duty and settling down with a conformable, suitable wife!'

Joanna took a drink of lemonade as the best way of hiding her reaction. So, the old general did not consider Lady Suzanne a suitable wife. Why ever not? She seemed eminently eligible to Joanna, but perhaps he thought her too flighty to make his son a good match. A faint glimmer of hope stirred in her breast. Would Giles heed his father? Would the General's opinions make him reconsider?

But, no, surely if he loved Suzanne he would not give her up, and much as it hurt, Joanna would not want him, too. She could only think less of him if he was the sort of man who could turn from true love under pressure.

'You are looking very serious,' he said after a moment. 'How do you feel?'

'Much better, truly,' Joanna reassured him. 'I was just worried about you and your father. Now you are even further away, and it is all my fault. What if he wants to contact you and make peace?'

Giles laughed. 'My mama, who packed me off back to town to indulge in a course of carefully calculated dissipation, assured me it would be at least two weeks before he would admit to any regrets in the matter and another two after that to digest the rumours of my behaviour, which my assorted well-meaning aunts would send back.'

'Dissipation? But what…?'

'The plan, according to Mama, is that he will summon me back in order to engage me in some salutary hard work and will then get accustomed to having the prodigal around and will be reconciled to my assisting with the estate.'

'Goodness,' Joanna said rather blankly. 'Do you think it will work?'

'Mama has been winding my father around her little finger for thirty-five years and I have never known her wrong yet.'

'Yes, but you are hardly engaging in dissipation, are you? What sort of dissipation, anyway?'

'Cards, horses, um…'

'Um?'

'I do seem to be having the most improper conversations with you, Miss Fulgrave! Wicked widows and fast matrons is what my outrageous mama had in mind, I think.'

'More than one mistress at once?' Joanna asked, trying to imagine her own mother recommending such a course of action to William in fifteen years' time and failing utterly. 'Isn't that terribly expensive and complicated?'

'As I have never had more than one at a time I have no idea. Expensive, certainly. But complicated?'

'I shouldn't imagine they would take very kindly to sharing you,' Joanna said, frowning over the practicalities. 'You would have to keep them apart and remember what you had said to each… Have you had many?'

Giles sank his head in his hands with a groan. 'Oh lord, what have I let myself say! Your mama would have fits if she knew. Yes, I have had mistresses, in Portugal and in Spain, and only one at a time, and we parted very amicably in every case, before you ask! And, no, I am not going to tell you about any of them.'

'I am sorry,' Joanna said penitently. 'I did not mean to put you to the blush, but I feel that I can ask you about things that no one else will explain. I mean, it is obvious that lots of men in society have mistresses, and even I can guess that some ladies are, well…not entirely faithful to their husbands. But no one ever says anything about it and it seems a bit late to find out after one is married.'

'I cannot imagine,' Giles said, putting one hand over hers and squeezing it reassuringly, 'that any husband of yours would contemplate setting up a mistress for one second. Especially this mysterious suitor you are so imprudently fleeing from. He seems most devoted!'

Joanna ignored the reference to Lord Clifton, for she was fighting the urge to curl her fingers into his and return the pressure. Somehow it hadn't hurt to know there had been other women in his life: she had expected it, the man was not a monk. But being so close to him, his kindness, almost overset her.

'I don't expect to marry,' she said, attempting to laugh it off and freeing her hand to reach for an apple, 'so it really doesn't arise. I meant, it was a bit late for young ladies in general to find out about that sort of thing.'

'Not marry? Why ever not?' Giles took the apple from her hand, picked up a knife and began to peel it, the ribbon of red skin curling over his hand.

Joanna shrugged, trying not to look at his long fingers dexterously wielding the knife. What would it be like to be caressed by them? She shivered. 'My *mysterious suitor*, as you term him, is not someone whose regard I return—in fact, I dislike him excessively. My affections are engaged elsewhere, but the man I love, loves someone else.'

'Is that what upset you at the Duchess's ball?' He handed her back the apple. 'You found out about it?'

'Mmm.' Goodness, how had she let herself talk about this?

'But just because one man has let you down, it doesn't mean you should give up on the entire sex,' Giles said, watching her with a frown between his straight brows. 'There are many other men— the one who is attempting to make you an offer, for example. Are you sure you know him well enough to have formed such a negative impression?'

'Quite sure! I dislike the way he looks at me— and he tried to blackmail me after I had got into a scrape.' She caught his quizzical expression and nodded, 'Yes, that night at Vauxhall. And, yes, it is Rufus Carstairs, I suppose you have already guessed. But as for marrying someone I do not love—how can you say that?' Joanna was hurt and surprised that he could fail to understand. 'If the lady you love spurned you, could you just shrug and walk away and think "I'll find someone else"? Of course you could not, not if it were true love! I will never feel like this about anyone else, and I will not marry anyone I don't love.

'Imagine being tied to someone you did not hold in the deepest affection! I know some unfortunate women find themselves having to accept distasteful suitors, or men have to make duty marriages to restore their family fortunes, and I truly pity all of them. I would rather remain a spinster than marry anyone other than…him. And,' she added vehemently, 'I *cannot* like or trust Lord Clifton.'

Giles appeared taken aback by her vehemence, but, although he had raised his eyebrows on hearing who her suitor was, he said nothing, so she asked, 'Will you obey your father in the question of *your* marriage?'

'No!' he retorted hotly. 'I will not!'

'You see? In matters of the heart, feelings run very deep.'

He regarded her thoughtfully over the rim of his glass. 'You are sure that this unfortunate experience has not made the entire business of marriage distasteful to you?'

'Oh, no,' Joanna looked directly into his concerned grey eyes and smiled ruefully. 'Oh, no, not if it were marriage to the man I love.'

Chapter Eight

That evening brought a report that Milo Thomas had been intercepted near Lincoln and three distressed young women rescued. Joanna wondered anxiously about the reception they would receive when they returned to their homes and whether they would have the reassurance and support she was enjoying from Giles and from the Geddings.

'And what about the ones who are already in those dreadful places?' she asked vehemently as they sat down to dinner. 'What is going to happen to them?'

'I will be laying evidence with the Bow Street magistrates,' the Squire said reassuringly. 'They will check all of the addresses in Thoroughgood's notebooks and ensure that every young woman there is free to leave. If any have been kidnapped and, er…forced, then the justices will take the appropriate action.'

'Yes, but what becomes of the women?' Joanna persisted. 'What on earth happens to them?' There was an uncomfortable silence around the table. 'When I get back to London I am going to *do* something about this.'

'My dear,' Mrs Gedding said gently, 'there is nothing that an unmarried girl of good family *can* do about it.'

Joanna knew that was likely to be only too true. 'Oh, I wish I were a rich widow!' she declared vehemently. Giles sat back in his chair with a gasp of laughter and she caught his eye, defiantly. 'Well, I do! Not that I would wish anyone dead, of course not, but it seems to me that the only women who have any freedom of action at all are rich widows.'

The Squire looked faintly scandalised and, although Mrs Gedding sent her an amused look of understanding, Joanna thought it best to take herself off to bed as soon as possible at the end of the meal.

When she woke the next morning, it was to the feeling that she had been ill, in a fever, and that now she was back to normal. The spectres of the Thoroughgoods and her terrifying experience had become less nightmarish, although her determination to do something about the plight of the girls forced into brothels was no less ardent. Perhaps Hebe, when she had recovered from the birth, would be able to help.

But with the sense of recovery came the anxiety about how her parents would react and the more pressing realisation that not only was she in the same house as Giles but that she had been having conversations of quite shocking frankness with him. As she dragged the brush ruthlessly through her hair, she thought it was only by some miracle that he had not guessed the identity of the man she loved, the man whose presence she was fleeing from.

She was so preoccupied with these thoughts that she walked straight into Giles in the hall outside the little parlour that did service as a breakfast room. Joanna knew she was blushing frantically, but could think of nothing to say, other than to stammer, 'Good morning.'

Giles opened the door for her and ushered her through. The room was deserted. 'Good morning, Joanna. May I pour you some coffee?'

Joanna sat down abruptly, making a business of shaking out her napkin so as not to meet his eyes. 'I…yes, thank you.'

Giles put the cup in front of her and took a seat opposite. 'Might I trouble you for the bread?

Thank you. You are feeling more yourself this morning, I think.'

'What?' Joanna looked up, startled, and saw he was regarding her with an expression halfway between amusement and sympathy. 'I am feeling better, yes, but how do you deduce that?' Her heart was beating irregularly: did he really under-stand her so very well?

She waited, biting her lower lip, while he buttered his bread, a slight frown between his brows. 'How do I know? Well, yesterday we were having ex-tremely frank conversations without you turning a hair. In fact, you were quite unnaturally calm, which convinced me you were still suffering from shock. This morning you react as any gently bred young lady would at the realisation that the man she has just bumped into was the very one with whom she was discussing mistresses, houses of ill repute and the perils of the married state only the day before.' He smiled as she bowed her head in confusion. 'You blush very prettily.'

'Oh!' Joanna gasped indignantly. 'You are just saying that to make me blush more! Really, Gi…Colonel Gregory…'

'That is better,' he said approvingly. 'I would have hated to see you revert entirely to—what was it your mama called you? Oh, yes, the "perfect débutante".'

'I was never that,' Joanna said sadly, 'although I did try so hard. Colonel, was Mama *very* angry?'

Giles stood up to carve a slice of meat from the joint on the sideboard. 'Cold beef? No? I do wish you would stop calling me *Colonel*. What is wrong with Giles? After all, I am a family friend, almost a friend of your childhood.'

'It seems hardly proper.'

Giles's expression was so comical that Joanna burst out laughing. 'Oh, Giles, do stop looking at me like that! I realise that after everything that has occurred it must seem finicky of me to cavil at first names, but believe me, I truly am trying to behave myself as I should. But do tell me about Mama.'

Giles flipped open the lid of the mustard pot and looked round for the spoon. 'She was not angry at all when I saw her, but you must remember she was very much shocked and upset and anxious to have you found. I cannot vouch for her mood when she knows you are safe. And, of course, she was most anxious to keep the news from your highly eligible suitor.'

'Hmm,' Joanna murmured, depressed. 'I know exactly what you mean. When one is frightened for someone the fear is all there is. The moment they are safe you can be angry at how foolish they have been. I remember how I felt when William was stuck in the big oak in Green Park. Once the keepers had got him down safely I could have boxed his ears, yet only a minute before I was frantic with worry that he would fall out and break his neck.'

'Well, I think it is unlikely that you will escape without a lecture,' Giles said kindly, 'but I am sure your parents will soon forgive and forget. And no one else in society but the Tasboroughs knows of this adventure, so you will be able to emerge next Season as though nothing had occurred. Although,' he added frankly, 'do you not think it would be a good idea not to strive to be quite such a pattern card of perfection? It must be very wearing for you, never allowing yourself to kick over the traces.'

'Young ladies are not permitted to kick over the traces, as you put it,' Joanna retorted. 'Look at the fuss it causes.'

'I meant indulging in the odd bit of mischief and high spirits, not running away and being kidnapped,' Giles countered. 'Suzanne is always up to something or another and it does her reputation no harm.'

'I am sure if I were as beautiful, well connected and rich as Lady Suzanne,' Joanna snapped, 'I could get away with almost anything. We lesser mortals have to be more careful.'

'But not to the point of becoming a by-word for your virtues! It is a testimony to your character that your reputation does not result in jealousy amongst the other débutantes and that you have so many friends.'

'I am sure those who do not think so well of me will be most amused to see me take part in a third Season, still unspoken for,' Joanna said bitterly. 'I never intended to behave in any way to make other débutantes seem less…correct. I was only trying—' She broke off. It was so easy to talk to Giles that she was in danger of saying far too much and betraying herself to him.

'Trying?' he prompted.

'Trying to make sure I would be a perfect wife for…him.' *For you, only for you*, her inner voice repeated.

'Ah. The mystery man. Are you so sure he wants perfection?' Giles appeared annoyed rather than curious.

'He deserves it!' she said hotly. 'He needs a wife with perfect social skills: it is very important in his position.' Only now, of course, Giles had voluntarily ended his glittering career. Now he had no need of a Society hostess who also understood the army, only a well-bred, suitable wife and in Lady Suzanne he most certainly had that, whatever his father thought.

'Who on earth is he, this paragon who must have such an impeccable wife? A duke? A leading politician? A diplomatist?'

'I am not going to tell you. It is hopeless now, anyway.' Joanna took a mouthful of her cooling coffee and refused to look at Giles.

'Then stop trying to be perfect. Relax and enjoy next Season for a change.'

'To what end, pray? To put off being on the shelf for a few more months?'

She realised that they were glaring at each other across the table. It hurt so much that Giles seemed to care about what was troubling her; his indifference would have been easier to bear. And he must care to become so involved and angry about it.

Then his face lightened and he smiled at her. 'Come now, it is far too nice a day to be inside squabbling. Squire Gedding has no need of me this morning and I have a treat for you. You do ride, I assume?'

'Why, yes, I love to ride. But ride what?'

'Did I tell you that part of my scheme now is to breed horses on the estate? No? Well, that is what I intend to do; it will mean that I am not spending all my time breathing down the General's neck, and I think it might be a satisfying undertaking. I was talking to the Squire about it and he tells me a neighbour of his has a fine mare he wants to sell. He is bringing it over this morning for me to look at; I thought you might like to ride it so I can see its paces.'

'Oh, yes, please!' Joanna jumped up, then recollected her small stock of clothes. 'But I have no habit. And what about a saddle?'

'Mrs Gedding tells me her daughter's old habit is here, and the saddle she herself used when she still kept a riding horse is in the stables. Listen— I imagine that is the neighbour now.'

The breakfast parlour windows opened out on to the side of the house where the carriage drive led to the stables and, sure enough, Giles's sharp ears had picked up the sound of hooves. A man on a black hunter came into sight leading a pretty grey mare on a long rein towards the yard.

Mrs Gedding appeared in the doorway. 'Good morning, my dear. Have you had enough breakfast?

I expect the Colonel has told you all about James Pike's grey mare. If you would like to ride her, the girl has put out Jennie's old habit on your bed.'

With a smile Joanna thanked her hostess and ran upstairs to change, her heart pounding. The encounter with Giles over the breakfast table had left her feeling flustered and almost frightened. But she had no opportunity to reflect alone, for the maid was waiting and Joanna had to submit to being unbuttoned and undressed, standing patiently while the habit was tossed over her head. The girl discovered with a cluck of displeasure that a section of hem had dropped and one button was loose. Joanna nodded absently as the maid asked if Miss would mind waiting while she fetched the sewing things and did a hasty repair.

She sat on the edge of the bed while the maid rapidly whipped stitches along the hem and shrugged out of the jacket for the button to be replaced, without really being aware of what was going on. Giles, and her feelings for him, seemed to fill her mind to the exclusion of all else. She found she liked him so much it was a shock. She had known almost from the moment she met him that she loved him, but now she knew that she had fallen in love with the *idea* of the man, not the man himself. Perhaps if she had never seen him again after that evening at the Duchess's ball she would have gradually fallen out of love with her memory of him. But now fate, and her own foolishness, had thrown them together so closely that there was no escaping the impact of his personality on her.

And not just his personality. Joanna had never felt so aware of a man before—even the thrilling sensation of being held in his arms as they waltzed paled beside the effect of being so close to him daily. She was getting to know the tiniest details: the impatient way he pushed his hair off his forehead, the black flecks in his grey eyes that turned them dark when he was angry, the way he would tug at one earlobe when he was thinking, the way he would throw his head back and laugh, the scent of Russian Leather cologne…

She had fallen in love with an heroic ideal of a man, now she was in love with the real thing. And not just in love: she *wanted* him, she realised with a sudden shock, which sent the colour flooding into her cheeks. Wanted his kisses, wanted to be held in his arms.

'Oh, I'm sorry, Miss, I've kept you waiting in

this warm room,' the maid said apologetically. 'You're quite flushed, Miss.'

Joanna cast a harried glance at the mirror and tugged down the veil on her hat. 'It will soon pass, thank you.' She took the gloves the girl handed her and ran downstairs to where Giles was patiently waiting in the hallway, talking to Mrs Geddings. 'I am sorry to have kept you,' she apologised. 'The hem needed a few stitches.'

The mare had been saddled up and was standing quietly in the little paddock that opened off the stable yard, a groom at her head. A short man in a buff coat was talking to the head groom, but broke off when he saw Mrs Gedding and her guests. Introductions were made and Giles and he ducked under the rails to look at the mare.

Joanna watched as Giles ran his hands down her legs, checked her teeth, lifted a hoof, which the animal allowed without fuss, and asked the groom to remove the saddle. He ran his hands down her back, making her withers twitch, but otherwise provoking no reaction. Then he vaulted neatly on to her back and gathered up the reins.

He was far too big a man for the mare, but she walked on obediently, stopping when commanded, and standing like a rock even when Giles dropped the reins on to her neck and clapped his hands loudly. One dark grey ear swivelled back, but that was all.

He swung down and led her back to Joanna, who was leaning on the fence. 'She seems steady enough, if you would care to try her. The question is, will she prove too steady? I'm not looking for an armchair ride. I want to breed a line with spirit.'

Joanna smiled as the mare pushed her soft muzzle into her hands, looking for caresses and tidbits. 'Oh, no, you must earn your apples! What is her name, Mr Pike?'

'Moonstone, ma'am,' he replied, looking embarrassed. 'That's what my youngest daughter called her when she was foaled. Seems a bit fancy-like.'

'It suits her. No, stop it, there is nothing for you in my pockets!' She gathered up the reins and glanced round. 'Please will you give me a leg up, Mr Pike?'

He cupped his hand for her booted foot and tossed her up into the saddle. Joanna concentrated on adjusting her skirts and the reins, not looking at Giles. She wanted, very badly, to impress him with her riding and it was making her nervous.

Moonstone responded promptly to the pressure of her heel and Joanna circled the paddock once at a walk, then at the trot and finally shortened the reins and urged the mare into a canter. She responded willingly and Joanna soon forgot she had an audience. The paddock was dull riding though, but at one end the fence bordered a larger meadow and as she cantered past Joanna could see no sign of a ditch or other obstacle. When they reached the far side she wheeled the horse and set her direct across the field towards the fence.

The mare's ears pricked forward and she lengthened her stride, anticipating the jump. There was a shout behind them, which Joanna ignored, and then the mare was bunching the muscles of her hindquarters and leaping smoothly over the rails, Joanna balanced lightly on her back. They landed safely and Joanna let her have her head.

The exhilaration of galloping was wonderful. At the end of the meadow she turned the mare, took her back at the same pace, only collecting her up before the jump, and returned to the waiting onlookers with face flushed and veil all awry.

'She is a beautiful ride, Mr Pike!' Joanna pushed back her veil and saw that although Mrs

Gedding was looking pleased at her performance, Giles's expression was positively thunderous. He stalked into the paddock to her side and she leaned down and whispered, 'I am so sorry! Was I sounding too enthusiastic? I should not have done so before you had agreed a price—but she is a lovely ride, such even paces and so willing.'

'It is not that at all,' he ground out. 'Are you completely careless of your safety? There might have been a ditch, a fallen tree, goodness knows what on the other side of that fence and to jump a good five foot before even trying her at a smaller obstacle—what folly!'

'Of course I looked first,' Joanna said pacifically. It was wonderful to realise that he was so anxious for her. 'And I think I ride well enough to manage such a jump, do you not agree?'

Giles looked up at her, the anger fading out of his face. 'You ride extremely well,' he conceded. 'But I was having visions of explaining to your mama just how you had come to break your neck while in my care.'

Mr Pike walked out to take Moonstone's head while Joanna let Giles lift her down. His hands fastened firmly on her waist, but the moment her feet touched the ground he let go and she was left chiding herself for being so immodest as to want his hold to linger.

The two men strolled away, the mare following behind. Joanna went to join Mrs Gedding, who was fulsome in her praises. 'What a good seat you have, my dear! I was never in the slightest fear for you, although you should have heard the Colonel's language when you took that jump!' She chuckled. 'On second thoughts, perhaps it was best that you did not. I believe he had no notion he was swearing until I laughed.' She regarded Joanna, who was carefully gathering up her skirts to keep them out of the long grass. 'Would you care to keep that habit, my dear? It is an excellent fit and my Jennie will never get into it again, not after two babies. I am sure you have far finer at home, but perhaps the Colonel will let you ride while you are here.'

'Why, thank you, ma'am, that is most kind, I would be very grateful if you are sure your daughter would not mind. Oh, look, they appear to have reached agreement.' The men were shaking hands and Mr Pike ducked back under the fence to remount his hack.

'Good day, Mrs Gedding, ma'am! My compliments to the Squire.'

'Good day to you, Mr Pike! You and Mrs Pike must dine with us soon.'

Giles rejoined them, looking pleased. 'A good morning's work, I believe. Would you like to take her out on to the roads for a while, Joanna? I'll have the gelding the Squire has loaned me saddled up and we can explore a little.'

'If you do not need me, ma'am?' Joanna tried not to look too enthusiastic, but could not help her wide smile when Mrs Gedding shook her head.

'No, dear, thank you. Off you go and get some fresh air, it will do you good.'

Joanna had never seen Giles on horseback and could not help watching from under her lashes as he rode out of the yard on the raking bay the Squire had found for him. For a big man he rode lightly, his hands relaxed on the reins, but Joanna could tell that the gelding knew exactly who was in command and that at the slightest sign of trouble those long, well-muscled legs would close and quell it.

The enclosures of recent years had left long, wide grass verges bordering the quiet roads and the two riders found plenty of opportunities to canter and many ditches to hop over. Giles made no comment about her riding, but Joanna was aware that he was watching her. A pheasant erupted from under Moonstone's nose sending her skittering across the road, but he made no effort to catch her rein, merely steadying the gelding until she had soothed the mare and brought her back alongside him.

'What will you do when you get home?' he asked after they had reined in from a long canter and were walking the horses up a slight incline.

'I doubt I will have much say in it,' Joanna responded ruefully. 'Go to Bath as Mama says, I suppose. I would prefer that we all went to Brighton, which was what was planned, but if Papa's gout is bad, I have no idea what will be decided. In any case, that might be regarded as too much of a treat after my behaviour.'

'Could you go to Hebe?'

'Of course, under normal circumstances. But the baby is due, and Alex will be cross with me for worrying Hebe and making all this to-do, and I expect I would find myself looking after little Hugh the whole time. And,' she added gloomily, 'no doubt there would be all sorts of gossip about why I'm not in Brighton with the family.'

'Chicken pox?' Giles suggested half-seriously and received a reproachful look.

'Where will you go?' Joanna thought it was a reasonable question in response to his and one unlikely to make him suspicious of her motives for asking.

'Well, unless there is a message saying that the prodigal is forgiven and I'm to hasten home, then my campaign of dissipation will best be advanced in Brighton, I imagine.' He reined in and pulled his pocket watch out. 'I thought so, we had better turn and make our way back or we will be late for luncheon and I promised the Squire some more help at the Thoroughgoods' house this afternoon.'

'There must be a lot of paperwork,' Joanna commented.

'Yes. We believed we had it all, but I thought it worth checking the panels in the study and, sure enough, we found a concealed cupboard with another stack of ledgers and letters.'

Joanna rode in silence for a while, firmly biting back the question on the tip of her tongue. Finally it got the better of her. 'Will Lady Suzanne not be in Brighton? I should imagine that might restrict your efforts to create a mild scandal. Your father will hardly believe you have plunged into a life of dissipation if he hears that you are squiring her about in Brighton.'

'Indeed it would, and I have absolutely no desire to end up with another argument with Papa over Suzy and my intentions in that quarter! No, fortunately Lord Olney disapproves of Brighton. He will probably be taking the whole family up to stay with his mother in Harrogate.'

'And what,' Joanna said tartly, 'will Lady Suzanne say when she hears about your activities in Brighton?'

'Darling Suzy will no doubt tease me unmercifully.' He grinned. 'That young woman understands me very well indeed. Come on, let's canter or we will be late.'

Darling Suzy! Joanna dug her heel into Moonstone's flank and gave the mare her head. Giles was so relaxed about Lady Suzanne, so confident about her reactions. His voice when he spoke about her was warm, affectionate, caressing. What she would not give to have him speak to her in that way. She closed her eyes for a moment against the tears that stung her lids and followed the big bay hunter.

Chapter Nine

After luncheon Joanna spent the rest of the day with the rose petals she had collected for the *potpourri,* separating them and spreading them on muslin to dry in the stillroom.

It was a pleasant occupation in the cool, scented room, but one which gave her far too much time to think. Would her parents allow her to go to Brighton? And if they did and Giles was there, was that better or worse than being separated from him entirely? And what about Lord Clifton? Was he going to persist in his suit?

Her thoughts went round and round like a dog in a turnspit. She had run away, wanting time to think. But now, when she had it, it seemed she was no further forward in planning her life.

Dinner time passed with no sign of the men,

only a note from the Squire saying that they had decided to work on and finish all there was to do that day. They had sent out to the nearest inn for food, he assured his wife, and he thought he would probably go direct to Peterborough that evening to ensure that all the evidence was safely delivered, so she was not to expect him home that night.

By ten Giles had still not returned and Joanna found she was restless and quite certain that if she went to bed she would not sleep. The ladies had retired to the sitting room with its big window on to the garden and the scents of the sun-warmed flowers still drifted in through the open casement, mingling with the song of the nightingale in the long hedge.

'May I sit up, ma'am?' Joanna asked as Mrs Gedding put down her sewing at last, got to her feet and announced that she was for her bed. 'I am not tired and I am sure the Colonel will lock up if you want to send the servants to bed.'

'Very well, my dear. Everything will be secure except for this window and the front door, if you will be so good as to ask him to attend to those and to make sure all the candles are out. The decanters are there, on the sideboard—I am sure the Colonel will welcome a drink when he returns.'

She hesitated, drawing her shawl around her shoulders. 'Or should we close the window now? It is just becoming a little cool.'

'May I leave it? I am quite warm and the evening is so lovely. Or…' Joanna glanced at the grate with its fire basket full of pine cones '…might I light the fire? It will just keep the chill off.'

'Of course. The tapers are on the mantel shelf. Just make sure the embers are raked right out before you go to bed, dear. Goodnight.'

Joanna found some old papers in the log basket and after one false start managed to light a small fire. She heaped on pine cones, enjoying the crackle and the bright blue light they produced. The fire was not so much a source of warmth as of company and she sat on the floor, leaning against the arm of one of the wing chairs, close enough to the hearth to toss on cones as they burned up.

The longcase clock in the hall chimed eleven and then the quarter before she heard hoofbeats on the carriage drive. She got up and put the front door ajar, leaving the sitting-room door open as well, and set the tray of decanters and a glass on the side table next to the wing chair. The candle on the mantelshelf was guttering so she trimmed it and lit another. With the firelight they cast a soft glow in the room and a few moths blundered in from the garden.

When she heard his step she called, 'Giles! Will you lock the front door, please? Everyone has gone to bed.'

There was the sound of the lock and of bolts being shot, then Giles appeared in the doorway. 'Joanna! Still up?' Even in the dim light she could see how tired he looked.

'Come in and let me take your coat,' she urged. 'See, the decanters are here. Sit down and have a drink—you look too tired just to go to sleep.'

Obediently he shrugged out of his riding coat, stretching with a sigh as he did so. Joanna took it and hung it carefully over the back of a chair, smoothing out the creases with a hand that lingered on the cloth, warm from his body.

When she turned back to him he was standing, a tall figure in his shirtsleeves, by the window where the moonlight was just beginning to spill on to the boards. 'God! Those nightingales! Heartbreakingly beautiful, isn't it? They would sing on the battle-fields, you know. Some of the soldiers were super-stitious about them, said they were Death's bird.'

Joanna shivered at the thought. 'Come and sit down. Have you and the Squire finished now?'

He sank into the wing chair and lifted the brandy decanter, stretching long booted legs out in front of him. 'Yes, all complete, thank goodness. I fancy we have cooked the Thoroughgoods' goose for them.' He splashed some spirits into the glass and raised it to his lips. 'Ah! That is good. What are you doing up at this hour with everyone else in bed?'

Joanna came and sat down again in her place by the hearth, leaned against the arm of his chair and tossed a handful of pine cones into the blaze. 'I wasn't tired and the scents and the sounds from the garden are so lovely I stayed up.'

Giles did not seem to want to talk, and Joanna was too content just sitting with him in the firelight to disturb the mood. Gradually she relaxed until her head rested against the chair and after a few minutes she was conscious of a light touch on her hair which she had twisted into a crown on the top of her head. Giles seemed to be stroking it gently as he might a cat that had settled in his lap and she realised that he was probably quite unaware he was doing it.

Unlike the cat, which would have stretched and

curled tighter to his caressing hand, Joanna kept as still as she could, willing him to continue.

'That smell of burning pine cones,' he said, almost to himself, his voice deep and quiet. 'It reminds me of campfires when we were in the foothills of the Pyrenees.'

'Tell me about it,' she said softly, as though speaking to a sleepwalker.

'Memory is a strange thing: the bad times, the nights when it was raining or snowing, or when the enemy was close and no one could relax or sleep, the nights when we were all hungry and cold or wet and the wolves were howling and the wounded moaning—all those nights seem to blur into one nightmare. But the good times, the nights when it was dry and warm and there was no alert, I can remember almost every one quite clearly. It was best in the foothills; we had clean water and there was plenty of wood to burn and trees to shelter amongst.

'The men set the tents out in lines, each with its fire in front. It was like a village, people wandering up and down, the women gossiping, sitting in front of the tents in the firelight mending or cooking, the smell of the burning wood and the pine cones, someone singing, a sleepy child crying.'

Joanna could tell from his voice that Giles was smiling at the memory. The caressing fingers in her hair had found the pins and one after another they fell out on to the floor or into her lap until the mass of black hair fell softly around her shoulders.

'They were happy times?' she asked.

'Yes. They had a simplicity, an honesty. It was like a big family: one with its rogues and its problem children for sure, but still a family tied together with intense loyalties and one purpose.'

'And what would you be doing on those evenings?' He was running his fingers through her loosened hair now, lifting it and letting it fall. It was hypnotically sensuous and reassuring. Joanna could feel her eyelids drooping, although she had no desire to sleep.

'If I were not on duty I might walk along the lines, visit men who had been wounded, talk to anyone who wanted a word. Sometimes I'd eat with a group of them, sometimes sit and listen if they were making music. Other times I would sit outside my own tent, talk to my servant, write my journal or letters. Be thankful for the peace and the stillness. As I am now. You are very tranquil company, Joanna.'

She smiled, her eyes on the dancing blue

flames. It had been one of her dreams of when they were married, to be a restful presence for him at the end of a long, hard day. It would never happen again, but now she could savour it.

One of the pine cones exploded with a sharp crack and landed on the hearthrug in a shower of sparks. Joanna bent forward, but Giles was before her, going down on one knee and reaching out to scoop the burning fragment back with a deft flick of his long fingers. He pinched out the remaining sparks and half-turned, finding himself face to face with Joanna as she knelt beside his chair.

Her hair flowed over her shoulders and down the curves of her breast and as she regained her balance the last of the pins fell to the ground.

Giles put out a hand and lifted a heavy lock of hair. 'Did I do that?'

'Yes, of course you did. You were sitting there, stroking it as if it were a cat, and all the pins fell out.' Joanna tried to keep her tone lightly amused, but her breath was tight in her chest. He was so close that she could see the firelight catching the golden stubble on his chin. He smelt of leather, a faint scent of brandy and the indefinable masculine smell that was simply *Giles*.

'You have beautiful hair,' he said simply, then leaned forward and kissed her on the lips.

His mouth was warm and gentle and for a moment Joanna froze, not with alarm but in pure shock. Then she put out a hand to his shoulder to steady herself and tentatively leaned into the kiss. Giles's hand cupped the back of her head, pulling her to him, and the pressure of his lips increased, parting her own slightly. He tasted of brandy and his body, so close to hers, was hot.

No man had ever kissed her like this and she was conscious of her ignorance and inexperience. What should she do now? What would he do? The answer made her gasp as his tongue insinuated itself between her parted lips, touched the tip of her own tongue with a fleeting, startling intimacy and then she was hard against his chest, one of his hands in her hair as the other caressed her neck, sliding sensuously down to her shoulder where the sensitive skin was exposed by the lace of her fichu.

His mouth now was firm, demanding things that her body seemed to half-understand but did not know how to respond to. She seemed to have stopped breathing and to be both freezing and burning at the same time. Her entire world was focused on the sensation of his mouth on hers, the invasion of his tongue and she was unaware that her fingers were clenched tight in the thick linen of his shirt.

Then, as suddenly as he had kissed her, he released her. Joanna opened her hands and sat back on her heels with a bump, her lungs filling with a deep, racking breath.

Giles got to his feet in one swift, violent movement and stood beside the chair opposite her, his face stark. 'Damn it! I am sorry, Joanna, I don't know what came over me. No, what am I saying? I know perfectly well what came over me and I should not have let it happen.'

'I…' Her voice seemed to have vanished along with all the strength in her legs. Her skin seemed unnaturally sensitive and a hot, disturbing feeling burned inside her.

'I am sorry I frightened you, Joanna. Of all the stupid things to do when I imagine the last thing you want is a man so much as laying a finger on you. I had forgotten where I was, who I was with. You look so…so hauntingly different in the fire-light with your hair down like that.'

Even in the gloom Joanna could see the tension in Giles's face, the way he was gripping the chair back until his knuckles showed white. It was incredible, impossible, but it seemed that kissing her had affected him as profoundly as it had affected her. And yet, he did not love her. As a glimpse of the power of physical desire, it was disturbing and enlightening.

'Giles—' she swallowed and managed some control over her voice '—you did not frighten me, I promise.'

'You are too innocent, too—'

'No,' she interrupted sharply. 'I may be inexperienced, but I am not innocent of what has just happened. You kissed me, that is all. We were alone, it is late, neither of us was concentrating on the proprieties. It happened, and I am sure I should not say so, but it was very…interesting.'

He made a sound which Joanna thought was a choked laugh. 'You see,' she persevered, 'I have never been kissed before, not properly, and I do not expect to be again, so it was interesting to find out what it was like.' There, that should explain why she had not slapped his face, or shrieked or done any of the other things a well brought-up young lady ought to have done.

'Joanna, you simply cannot go around allowing yourself to be kissed because it is *interesting!*

How many other experiences do you think you might sample out of interest? You are playing with fire…'

'Nonsense!' Joanna got to her feet shakily. She felt as though her legs were going to give way at any moment and she grabbed hold of the chair back.

'Nonsense? Joanna, I do not believe for one moment that you have any idea of the danger you are in when you trustingly let yourself be kissed like that. And *don't* stand there looking at me like that with those big hazel eyes: there is just so much a man can take.'

'You are trying to scare me for my own good,' she retorted. 'I don't believe for one moment I am in any danger from you, Giles. I trust you.'

Giles stood looking at the defiant, piquant face. Her eyes were huge in the firelight and the shadows flickered over her mouth, swollen from the pressure of his mouth. Her hair fell like black silk, rising and falling with her rapid breathing and she said she trusted him!

He took a deep breath and said, 'Joanna, will you please go to bed. *Now.*'

'Very well.' Anyone who did not know her would have missed the slight tremor beneath her composed tone, but Giles caught it. He did not believe now that he had frightened her, but he knew he had not been in any way restrained, that he had simply followed his instincts in a way that left him feeling utterly shaken at his own indiscretion. He was no rake, never had been. He was no monk, either, but he had never trifled with virgins, and he had no intention of starting with this one.

'Go on,' he said again, making his tone light with some effort. 'And leave me to contemplate exactly what your mama would say if she knew about this.'

Joanna, who had been making her way to the door, stopped in her tracks and stared at him, her eyes wide. 'You would not tell her!' He realised with a shock that she was truly alarmed at the prospect, far more alarmed than she had been by the kiss itself.

'I ought to,' he said ruefully, 'but I will not, unless you wish me to confess.'

'No! She would be so angry.'

'At me, with full justification; not with you.' It seemed incredible that Joanna should appear so worried at the prospect of her mother's displeasure. Mrs Fulgrave had always seemed a most amiable and reasonable woman.

'Oh…well, you do not deserve her censure for

such a thing, after you have rescued me and looked after me. You are a friend of the family, I would not want to put any barrier in the way of that continuing,' she finished formally, apparently getting control of her feelings with an effort. 'Goodnight.'

Giles, finding himself alone, stood staring at the fire for a long moment before, with a little shake, pulling himself together and raking out the dying embers. He shut and bolted the window and snuffed out one of the candles. Picking up the other with one hand and his coat with the other, he walked slowly upstairs to his bedchamber, trying to sort out his feelings.

Colonel Giles Gregory was not a man who was given to self-doubt or lengthy introspection. He was self-confident, assured, used to being in command of himself, his emotions and those around him. If he felt himself in error, he had no trouble owning to it and when he confronted a problem he would apply his intellect and experience to it, asking advice when that seemed the best course of action.

He shut the chamber door behind him and tossed his coat on to a chair, tugging off his cravat with an impatient jerk. There was no problem about what to do in this situation: he simply had to make sure he did not allow himself to relax to the point of carelessness when alone with Joanna and to see she got home, suitably chaperoned, at the earliest possible opportunity.

No, he thought, glaring at his reflection in the glass with as much irritation as he would if he was lecturing a subaltern caught in some indiscretion, the problem was that his normally well-regulated emotions were now decidedly disordered.

Giles sat down and began to tug off his boots. 'Pull yourself together and apply your brain,' he muttered, leaning back in his shirtsleeves, his stockinged feet propped on the fender.

He was feeling aroused—damnably aroused. It hardly required any intellectual effort to deduce that. Giles trampled firmly on the demands his taut body was sending him, and, beyond resolving to seek out some accommodating feminine company when he returned to town, did his best to ignore it.

Joanna had got under his skin in a totally unexpected way. How long had it been since he'd thought about that time in Spain, relived the sounds and smells and emotions? A long time, he realised. And when he had, there was no one to talk to about it. His father and Alex would understand, they had the same experiences, but it was not something you discussed with another man. And yet…it had been curiously comforting to do so. How had she managed to so disarm him, to take him so far off guard and out of himself?

He had thought her an unhappy girl, hurt by some man she would soon forget, but he had been wrong. Joanna was not a child with an infatuation. She was a young woman who had experienced two Seasons and who had devoted herself to becoming the perfect wife for some insensitive lout who had hurt her by rejecting that dedication, that love. What had she said just now? 'I have never been kissed before, not properly, and I do not expect to be again.'

At least that man had not seduced her and then cast her off. Giles winced, remembering the matter-of-fact way she had announced that she did not expect to experience another kiss. What was she going to do with herself now? Return home and dwindle into an unpaid companion to an elderly relative? Become the spinster support of her mother? What a waste!

Giles wearily got to his feet and began to shed the remainder of his clothes. It was as he pulled his shirt over his head that he realised there was another element to that evening's encounter, which was fretting him like a stone in his shoe. He stood, one hand on the bedpost, trying to analyse it.

Joanna had been so trusting when he had imprudently kissed her, so calm in the face of what should, after her terrifying recent adventure, have been an alarming experience. She trusted him, she had said so. Suzy trusted him, too—her 'darling Giles'. Trusted him enough to kiss him and flirt with him, wheedle and flutter her eyelashes, without a thought in her pretty head that he might step over the line and take advantage of what she was so charmingly offering.

'You're getting middle-aged, my boy,' Giles told himself, casting a disparaging glance down at an admirably flat and well-muscled stomach. 'That's what it is. You're no longer a devil with women, just a nice, reliable, safe friend to flirt with.' With a wry grin at his own self-pity, he blew out the candle.

In a bedchamber at the other end of the landing Joanna was also wrestling with her emotions. The memory of the kiss itself seemed to warm her whole body and to fill her with a dull yearning ache. She knew she had added a physical desire for Giles to what had always, in her inexperience, been a purely spiritual longing. But how could she not have let him kiss her? How could she not have responded? The pressure of his lips on hers was still tangible: would she feel it still when she woke in the morning or would it become like a dream?

But wonderful though that simple kiss had been, she treasured more the way Giles had let her share his memories, his recollections of ordinary life with his troopers. Not the glory or the tragedies, just the scents and smells, the music, the rough camaraderie. That was what she had always hoped for, that as his wife she would be someone to whom he could talk without reservation about whatever mattered to him, the big things and the most trivial.

Like the kiss, his voice describing the firelit camp was a door opening into a world of intimacy and trust. A door that she must shut again. Neither his kisses nor his trust belonged to her: they were another woman's and she must learn to do without either.

Chapter Ten

If Mrs Gedding noticed that her guests were somewhat constrained the next morning she gave no sign of it and carried the burden of conversation at breakfast with her usual cheerful good humour. Had she been privy to the very different preoccupations of Miss Fulgrave and the Colonel she might have been apprehensive, but both managed to give the impression of merely having slept badly.

Giles was trying to concentrate on what his plans should be once he had safely delivered Joanna back to her mama, but was finding the thought of escorting a disturbingly unpredictable young lady preying on his mind. He gave himself a brisk mental shake. What possible problems could one young woman present to an experienced senior officer?

On one occasion he had simultaneously delivered a general's temperamental Spanish mistress, fifty French prisoners, a wagon train of army pay and six field guns through enemy territory and had arrived with every coin, gun and prisoner intact. And he had achieved this without offending the lady, who had made it quite clear that she was offering to make the journey very pleasant indeed for him.

That aspect of the experience made his mouth quirk in a reminiscent smile and Joanna, watching him covertly over the rim of her coffee cup, caught her breath. Was he remembering last night? The sensual smile faded, leaving her back with her circling thoughts.

What was she going to do? It did not help that she had no idea what she wanted. She must give up all hope of Giles, that she understood very clearly. His flat refusal to bow to his father's disapproval of the match with Lady Suzanne was clear enough indication of that.

Surely Mama would not be too angry now she knew she was safe? Surely she would understand that only real unhappiness would have driven her daughter to such extremes? Joanna, hating the thought of being estranged from her parents, felt utterly miserable that they would feel she had let them down and behaved badly.

Show some backbone! she lectured herself silently. *Mama will write soon and be forgiving, surely. And then we can all go to Brighton and no one will know I am in disgrace and I will be able to think about what to do with the rest of my life once I have got rid of Lord Clifton...* Having some sort of plan made her feel better and by the time the maid brought in the morning post the heavy look had vanished from her eyes.

'A letter for you, Joanna.' Mrs Gedding passed it across with a sympathetic smile at the sudden flare of apprehension in her eyes. 'Your mama, I expect. One for you, Colonel…two, no, three for Mr Gedding. Thank you, Anna. From Mrs Thwaite by hand? Ah, good, I hope this is the reply I was expecting. Do, please, both of you read your letters, if you will excuse me perusing this.' She bent her head, crowned with its frivolous cap, over the note and Joanna nervously slit the seal on her letter.

She ran her eyes rapidly over the page unable to focus at first, then phrases and words jumped out at her with the force of blows. *Your poor father…Dr Grace…William quite distraught… wicked, wicked girl...*

Papa! Joanna took a shuddering breath, willed her hand to stop shaking and made herself read the letter from the beginning. After the first few sentences she realised with relief that it was her father's gout that was so severe that the doctor had been called and not, as she had first feared, that her disappearance had brought on a seizure of some kind. William, apparently, was distressed at the absence of his sister and the fact that no one knew why she had gone and as for her mother…

Words, Mrs Fulgrave declared, quite failed her. This fact did not, however, prevent her from writing at length of her opinion that Joanna was the gravest disappointment to her parents, that she had behaved in a way which was incomprehensibly wicked and wilful and that her poor mama had been at a loss to know what to do with her. It was only the intervention of Providence in the shape of Colonel Gregory that had prevented the most appalling consequences and it was to be hoped that she was fully repentant and thankful.

Naturally she could not be inflicted upon her elderly relative in Bath after such behaviour. Dear Hebe had begged that Joanna be allowed to go to her at Tasborough and the Earl had assured Mrs Fulgrave that she would be kept under the strictest watch and that she would be able to make herself useful. The last word was underlined several times with some force.

Blinking back the tears, Joanna looked up and met Giles's eye. He raised one eyebrow. 'Mad as a wet hen?' he enquired.

'Really! Colonel!' Mrs Gedding chided, failing to hide the fact that she was amused.

'Mama is displeased,' Joanna agreed with dignity, swallowing hard. She was in no mood to be teased. Presumably Mama had found Giles's actions commendable throughout—as indeed they had been. 'She says I must go to Tasborough and that she has told our acquaintance, including Lord Clifton, that she cannot refuse her dear niece's request for my company.'

'Ah. She expects that Alex will keep a strict eye on you, I imagine?'

'Yes,' Joanna agreed drearily. 'She also says that she is taking Papa and William to Bath to take the waters. Papa, I mean; William will not be taking the waters. Mama points out that William will be very much bored in Bath and it is all my fault that they are not going to Brighton.'

'How can that be your fault?' Giles enquired. 'Surely you cannot be blamed for your father's gout—she tells me in her letter that that is what continues to trouble him.'

'The doctor informs her that anxiety and strain all aggravate a naturally gouty tendency,' Joanna said, scanning the letter again for the lengthy description of poor Papa's sufferings, all of which were made infinitely worse by thoughts of his undutiful daughter. 'She quotes Shakespeare, something about a thankless child.'

'*King Lear*,' Mrs Gedding supplied helpfully. '"How sharper than a serpent's tooth it is to have a thankless child".' She regarded Joanna's white face. 'She is very upset, I fear, my dear. But never fret, once she has you home safe all will be forgiven, you will see.'

'I do not know when that might be. If I am to go to Tasborough for the summer it could be weeks before I see her.'

'Good thing,' Giles said briskly. 'By the time she does see you again this will all be ancient history. And you will enjoy being with Hebe.'

'And Alex, and little Hugh, and the new baby,' Joanna said bitterly. The last thing she wanted just now was to be in the heart of a happy young family, especially with a new baby about to arrive. She wanted her own babies—Giles's children—not to be a doting nurse for little relatives.

'You really are going to have to get over this antipathy towards Alex, you know,' Giles said casually, spreading preserves on his toast. 'You'll enjoy yourself once you are there.'

For the first time since she had known him Joanna found herself staring at Giles with real anger in her heart. She had confided in him! She had believed he understood how she felt; surely he would know, instinctively, why she was so upset at this banishment? No, apparently he did not. This man she loved was proving to be very much a human being, she realised. He kissed young women he was not in love with, he quarrelled with his father, he did not understand how she felt after all she had told him...

'Don't glare at me,' he said with a grin, which only added fuel to her anger. 'I have to escort you all the way back to Hertfordshire, always assuming we can find you a chaperon.'

'Now there I think I have the perfect solution,' Mrs Gedding announced, flourishing the note she had received. 'Mrs Thwaite, our vicar's wife, has dispensed with the services of her governess now that her youngest daughter has left the schoolroom.

Miss Shaw is returning to London to stay with her sister whilst seeking a new post. She would be quite happy to assume charge of Joanna and is ready to leave at your convenience. Mrs Thwaite says…' Mrs Gedding peered closely at the foot of the note where the vicar's wife had almost run out of paper '…she says Miss Shaw will call today at eleven to discuss the arrangements.'

'What have you told Mrs Thwaite about me, ma'am?' Joanna asked apprehensively.

'Only that owing to family circumstances you find yourself stranded here without the female company you were expecting. I referred to your papa's poor health and the fact that you had a sister in Lincoln, and I flatter myself that without uttering one untrue word I have managed to give the impression that various plans have simply come adrift.'

Mrs Gedding might have thought she had pulled the wool over her neighbour's eyes, but as soon as Joanna was introduced to Miss Shaw she was convinced that the governess was not deceived for a moment.

Miss Shaw was an acidulated woman in her mid-thirties, and if Joanna had wished to find a spinster unhappy with her lot and soured by her experiences, she could not have hoped for a more depressing example. The governess appeared to find some satisfaction in appearing as downtrodden as possible in her severe grey wool gown, her hair dragged back from her thin face and not so much as a piece of mourning jewellery to ornament her bodice.

She kept her hands clasped together throughout the interview, casting sidelong glances at Giles and answering Mrs Gedding in a respectful undertone. But the looks she sent in Joanna's direction were sharp and judgemental and it was quite apparent that she guessed her temporary new charge was in disgrace.

She agreed that she could be ready to set out the next day and that she had not the slightest objection to going into Hertfordshire, provided that she returned to her sister in Holborn eventually. 'It must be an object with me,' she announced primly, 'to assist Mrs Gedding in any way within my power.'

I am sure it is, Joanna thought rebelliously, *especially if that involves a comfortable journey in a private chaise with a handsome gentleman to look after all the arrangements, and not a bumpy journey on the public stage!*

The arrangements were finalised and Mrs Gedding took Miss Shaw to the kitchens to collect a recipe she had promised to Mrs Thwaite. Joanna, her vision a blur, got abruptly to her feet and walked out of the room. Giles caught up with her in the garden.

'Are you sulking, Joanna?'

'*Sulking!* No, I am not sulking! I am trying not to cry, if you must know,' she stormed at him, suddenly finding it incomprehensible that she had even liked Giles Gregory, let alone loved him. 'My mother has all but cast me off, my father is unwell and angry with me, my little brother is upset, I am being sent off in disgrace and that horrible woman with a face like a weasel is going to be smug and superior all the way to Hertfordshire.' She took a gulping breath. 'And I will soon be learning all about being the poor spinster relation who is the very person to call in to look after things when one or other of my female relations is confined, or the children have measles or…or…'

'Joanna!' He was laughing at her! The wretched man was actually laughing! 'Calm down, for goodness' sake. I agree Miss Shaw closely resembles a weasel. I agree that your family is distressingly angry with you, but all you need—you and your parents—is a few weeks to get over this. No one, yet, has died of a broken heart and this man who has so cruelly disappointed you is not going to achieve that, or even ruin your life as you are so convinced he has.

'I would be prepared to wager that in six months you will have recovered sufficiently to take an interest in the new Season—and without the impossible task of living up to this paragon you will have much better time of it—' He broke off, looking down into her stormy, upturned face. 'Believe me, Joanna, he is not worth this anguish, whoever he is.'

'I have already come to that conclusion, I thank you,' she snapped, turning on her heel and stalking off into the shrubbery. Giles made no attempt to follow her.

Joanna emerged wan-faced at luncheon and took the opportunity, while Mrs Gedding was out of the room greeting her returning husband, to apologise to Giles. 'I am sorry I snapped at you,' she said stiffly. 'I have everything to thank you for, I should not be so ungrateful.'

He looked up with a smile. 'There is nothing to

thank me for—it was only what anyone would do for a lady in such distress as your mama.' He regarded her downcast, heavy eyes and added, 'And you had a terrifying experience; it is no wonder you are feeling somewhat vapourish just now.'

Well, that has put me firmly in my place, Joanna thought, compressing her lips firmly on a tart retort. *I need not think he had any particular concern for me, only for Mama! And I am suffering from the vapours, am I?*

Her lacerated feelings suffered a further blow after the meal when, returning to the dining room to retrieve her shawl that she had left on her chair, she overheard Mrs Gedding in conversation with Giles. It was apparent at once what they were discussing and Joanna listened with growing indignation from behind the door.

'Miss Shaw is very sensitive, it seems,' her hostess was saying. 'Although I had said nothing to her or Mrs Thwaite of Joanna's true predicament, she appears to have guessed that we are returning a runaway to her home. I suspect that several years as a mistress in a girls' seminary in Bath has given her experience of young ladies overreacting to emotional situations. But she assures me that she will keep a very strict eye upon Joanna, and promises that she will not leave her side, by day or night.'

'I am sure that will not be necessary,' Giles answered. 'Joanna appears resigned to returning home—or at least, to her friends in Hertfordshire.'

'I am sure she has realised the errors of her ways,' Mrs Gedding agreed comfortably. 'But Miss Shaw tells me that she has a number of improving tracts suitable for young ladies and will do her utmost to engage Joanna's interest in them during the journey.'

Joanna did not wait to hear Giles's opinion of improving tracts, but ran out into the sunshine and took refuge in the stables.

'Hateful, hateful woman!' she said vehemently. Moonstone, who had put her head over the half-door at the sound of her approach, shied away with a snort. 'To be dragged back, not just in disgrace, but shut up with her, having to share a bedchamber with her and being lectured morning, noon and night as though I had run away from school with the drawing master!'

She thumped her fist on something, then realised it was the side saddle she had been using with Moonstone, the bridle hanging beside it. Slowly Joanna ran her hands over the hard leather, an idea slowly filling her mind. Dare she? Just how far away was Georgy's house?

The Squire's study was empty and Joanna soon found where he kept his atlases, for one already lay open on a stand. She located Wisbech, then traced the roads back to the village. There were several options, all of them straight, with sharp turns every now and again as they crossed the dykes and canals that drained the flat fenlands. After ten minutes' rapid scribbling on a sheet of notepaper she found on the desk, and some careful measuring with the ruler, Joanna came to the conclusion that even going by the smaller roads, it could not be more than thirty miles to Wisbech. Once she was there, surely everyone would know where to find Lord Brandon's house.

Tactics and strategy, she murmured to herself. Once she was with Georgy, surely Mama would be content to let her stay, for no one could doubt that Lady Brandon, however featherbrained she might be, was not eminently respectable. But with Georgy she would be able to plan and her friend would not be trying to dissuade her from whatever course she decided upon. In fact, now she thought about it, Georgy had been encouraging her husband to take her on a continental tour.

Surely she would want a female companion for
that adventure? And once Joanna had some experience, perhaps she could find a position with
another lady wanting to travel...

Joanna's rosy daydream was clouded somewhat
by the thought of the anxiety this new escape
would provoke, but she knew she would be at the
Brandons' within the day and she could immediately send news of her safe arrival to Mrs
Gedding. It would be far too soon for Mama or
Hebe to be alerted. The only danger would be
capture by Giles.

Tactics, tactics, she murmured, gathering up
pen, ink and paper and retiring to her bedchamber to compose the most reassuring and grateful
note she could to Mrs Gedding. That took some
time and when it was finished there were her
route notes to arrange carefully and to con and a
selection to be made of the absolute essentials to
pack into a small portmanteau.

By dinner time her stomach was full of butter-
flies and she had little appetite, although she
made herself eat as much as possible; it could be
a long and hungry day tomorrow.

The Squire was in excellent spirits and Joanna

was able to keep up the appearance of normality with an odd comment or question while he recounted how he was writing to London magistrates about the Thoroughgoods and their associates and how he had every confidence in them all receiving their just deserts.

After dinner she sat and helped Mrs Gedding with some sewing until the tea tray was brought in, then made her excuses and went up to bed.

'Goodnight, my dear,' Mrs Gedding said placidly. 'It will be as well to get a good night's sleep, for the chaise has been ordered for ten and we must have you all packed and ready before that. I do hope the men will not keep you awake; I believe they are set on a game of billiards tonight, and once the Squire finds a willing opponent he is quite likely to play into the small hours.'

Joanna was delighted with that news, for after a late night she hoped that Giles would sleep in and she would be well on her way before he was awake to miss her. She catnapped restlessly all night, too worried about oversleeping to drop into a deep slumber.

At last she heard the longcase clock strike four and in the grey dawn light scrambled into her habit, pulled on her boots and gloves and picked up the small portmanteau. The note to Mrs Gedding she left on her pillow.

The house was silent and the parlour window opened easily under her nervous hand. She pushed it to and ran across the grass to the stables. The old dog opened an eye as she passed, but he was used to her by now and made no attempt to bark, and then she was inside.

Moonstone stood patiently while she heaved on the saddle and struggled to tighten the girth. The bridle was more difficult, but by dint of standing on a crate she managed it. Then she carefully unbuckled the girth from every saddle in the tack room and the bit from every bridle, dropped them into a sack and hid them under some hay in an unoccupied loose box. That should slow down any pursuit until she was well away and if the hired chaise was not ordered until ten, even that could not hope to catch her.

Joanna walked Moonstone out of the box and across the yard to the mounting block. With a last, anxious, glance up at Giles's chamber window, she turned the mare's head and rode quietly off down the drive into the lifting mist.

Chapter Eleven

Giles woke to a violent pounding on the door. He had swung his legs out of bed and was reaching blindly for where his sabre always used to be before he remembered where he was and that he was not being woken to meet a surprise French dawn attack.

He flung the door open to reveal the Squire clad in a gaudy dressing gown, his nightcap askew on his grey hair and his boots protruding from under the hem. 'She's gone!'

'Who…?' Giles shook the fumes of the Squire's excellent brandy from his head and forced himself to think. 'Joanna? Where?'

'I don't know!' Mrs Gedding appeared from behind the bulk of her husband. 'Look, this was in her room.'

Giles took the note and scanned it rapidly. 'There is only one place she can hope to reach today if we are to take her at her word and believe that she is going to a "respectable friend" and that is Lady Brandon in Wisbech.'

'Oh, I am sure she would not deceive me,' Mrs Gedding said anxiously. 'Poor child, she must have been far more frightened of returning home than I guessed!'

'Poor child!' Giles said grimly. 'I'll give her poor child when I catch her. Have you any idea when she left?'

'It was before five-thirty, for the undergroom went into the stables then,' the Squire said. 'He saw Moonstone was gone, but the fool assumed Rogers had turned her out and it wasn't until I ran out just now that he thought to check.'

'What time is it?'

'Half past seven.'

'I will get dressed immediately,' Giles said. 'Squire, can you get your man to put the greys to? And, if you could give some thought to jotting down the fastest route to Wisbech, I would be grateful. I will be down directly.'

He deliberately kept his anger under control as he pulled on his clothes. There was time for that, and time for the anxiety that was roiling in his stomach, later, after he had found Joanna. That mare was steady, he reassured himself. Joanna was a good rider and the roads were dry and clear. Surely there was nothing that could befall her in a day's ride in the English Fens?

He was met at the bottom of the stairs by the Squire with a sketch map and notes and Mrs Gedding with a bulging napkin and a flask. 'I have no hope of you sitting down to eat your breakfast,' she said resignedly. 'But you can eat this one-handed.'

'Thank you, ma'am…'

'Squire! Squire!' It was Rogers the groom, bursting into the hall without ceremony, a bridle flapping in his hands. 'Every girth's missing from every saddle, sir!'

'Damn it, I'll drive then.'

'No good, sir,' the groom cut in. 'All the bits have gone, too. I've got the lad tearing the place apart now.'

'From my driving harness as well?' Giles demanded before the squire could speak.

'Yes, Colonel.'

'The little witch! I could almost admire her ingenuity if I was not so angry with her. Squire, have you a horse which would tolerate a rope bit? I can ride bareback.'

Followed by Mrs Gedding clutching the food, the men headed for the stables. Ten minutes' careful work with a thin rope and Giles was astride the Squire's raw-boned black hunter, who stood quietly enough, although mumbling his tongue over the unfamiliar feel of rope and not metal in his mouth.

'He'll do you all the way to Wisbech, never fear,' the Squire said, slapping the muscled black neck affectionately. 'Send word as soon as you have news.' He took a satchel from the groom and stuffed the food and flask into it. 'Here. Have you money enough?'

Giles patted his coat pocket. 'More than enough, unless I find she's taken boat for the Low Countries,' he said, with a smile for the look of sudden alarm on Mrs Gedding's face. 'Do not worry, ma'am, I'll have her safe soon enough. In fact, I have no doubt I'll find her snugly ensconced with Lady Brandon drinking tea!'

All she has to worry about, Giles thought grimly as he sent the hunter down the drive at a controlled canter, *is the tanning I'm going to give her backside the minute I lay hands on her.*

* * *

Far from suffering any of the alarms or discomforts that Mrs Gedding feared for her, or which Giles, growing increasingly angry the further he rode, might have wished on her, Joanna had an uneventful journey to Wisbech. The roads were just as she had noted, there were ample finger posts and milestones to reassure her she was on the right route, the sun shone and the only people she encountered were well disposed and friendly to a passing rider.

The last five miles or so were, admittedly, difficult, for Moonstone was tired and Joanna felt it would be a long time before she could sit down again with any degree of comfort. But her flagging spirits lifted at the sight of Lord Brandon's charming house set in its landscaped park and the gatekeeper, respectfully touching his hat, was able to inform her that her ladyship had only returned from a drive a little while before.

She slid stiffly from the saddle at the front door and surrendered the reins to a groom, who was understandably surprised at the absence of an escort. At the front door she was received by a superior butler who regarded her dusty skirts and solitary state with hauteur. 'I could not say whether my lady is at home, Miss.'

'I know she is,' Joanna said wearily. 'Please just tell her that Joanna Fulgrave is here.'

'If you would care to wait in here, Miss, and I—'

'Jo!' With a shriek of delight the lady of the house ran down the stairs and enfolded Joanna in a comprehensive embrace. 'Darling Jo! Where have you sprung from? Did you write and the letter hasn't got here? Rooke, do not stand there like that—refreshments in the Chinese Salon at once! Bring in Miss Fulgrave's luggage.'

Joanna was swept in a swirl of chatter, silks and scent into a pretty room hung with Oriental paper. Her friend pushed the door to with a bang and, seizing Joanna by the hands, stood back to regard her from head to toe.

'Darling, you are covered in dust, your nose is pink and I have to tell you that that habit is quite three Seasons' old, but I am enchanted to see you. Where have you sprung from? How long can you stay?'

Joanna smiled at Georgy, knowing that until she ran out of breath it was hopeless to try and answer her. Lady Brandon was a handsome brunette with a voluptuous figure, wide mouth, endless enthusiasm and rather more kindness than common sense. Her doting husband, a good fifteen years older than she, maintained her in considerable style and indulged her in all her whims except that of living in London or whatever fashionable resort the season of the year demanded. Visits to London certainly, his lordship agreed. Prolonged stays, no.

Georgy, ever optimistic, was convinced that by next Season she would have worn him down; meanwhile she seized upon any diversion from their rural idyll with enthusiasm and the surprise arrival of her dearest friend from their Bath schooldays was a treat indeed.

She finally fell silent and Joanna said simply, 'I've run away.'

'Aah!' Georgy plumped down on the sofa, eyes wide. 'How wonderful! Who is he?'

'Who?' Joanna asked, making rather a business of settling her skirts as she sat opposite.

'The man involved, of course. Is he handsome and dashing and hopelessly ineligible so your cruel papa has forbidden him to offer for you? Or is he taking you for granted, so you have vanished in order to pique his interest? Or…'

'Well, if you must know, he is in love with someone else and is going to marry her.' It was hopeless trying to hide anything from Georgy. She had the instincts of a terrier and the staying power of a running footman.

'That is too bad! You mean the wretch has been flirting with you and then went and offered for someone with a bigger fortune?' her friend demanded indignantly.

'He has not the slightest idea I have any feelings for him at all,' Joanna said drearily, all the exhilaration of escaping falling away and leaving her feeling bereft and anxious. What would Mrs Gedding be thinking now? What was Giles doing? 'Georgy, might I ask you to send a groom with a message? It is all of twenty miles or so, I am afraid, and he must not, on any account, reveal where I am, but my kind hostess will be so worried if I do not write.'

'Yes, of course. Henry is not at home, so half the grooms are sitting around with nothing to do, I dare say. There, use my writing desk.' She managed to contain her questions while Joanna scribbled a note and addressed it, sitting silently until the butler came in with a tea tray.

'Rooke, please see this is taken by one of the

grooms immediately. It is very important it goes at once and he must take a good horse. And, Rooke…'

'Yes, my lady?'

'On no account is he to say where he comes from. He is to leave the note and return at once.'

'As you say, my lady.'

'Oh dear, he will think it very odd,' Joanna said, closing the tambour front of the writing desk and returning to her seat. 'I am afraid he regards me in a very suspicious light altogether.'

'Well, he regards me as being completely unsatisfactory,' Georgy said with a twinkle, 'so he probably expects all my friends to be as well. Now, never mind Rooke, tell me all about this horrid man.'

By the time the ladies went upstairs to dress for dinner Joanna had poured the entire tale into Georgy's receptive ears. At first she kept the identity of the man she loved secret, presenting Colonel Gregory simply as an old family friend who had gallantly come to the rescue, but Lady Brandon knew her far too well.

'It is no good, Jo,' she declared, 'You blush every time you mention him: this Giles Gregory is *him*, is he not?'

'Yes,' Joanna admitted. 'But, please, Georgy, do not breathe a word of it to a soul. He loves someone else and I would die of mortification if he so much as suspected how I feel.'

'I can see that,' Georgy agreed, snuggling back into the sofa cushions. 'It would be the most humiliating thing. But tell me all about him—what does he look like?'

'Tall, very soldier-like, broad shoulders, grey eyes with the most fascinating black flecks, thick hair like dark honey which he should have cut more often...'

'Oh! He sounds *wonderful!*' Georgy's own, much-beloved husband was only a head taller than her, already slightly corpulent and the possessor of a hairline that could only be described as receding. Fond as she was, Georgy could not help but thrill at the description of the gallant Colonel. 'Go on, then...'

She listened with many exclamations and demands for detail to the account of how Joanna had discovered that her love was lost to her, her subsequent misbehaviour, the odious attentions of Lord Clifton and her decision to run away. But when Joanna began to haltingly recount what had befallen her at the Thoroughgoods' hands, the sparkling excitement left her eyes and she stared aghast at her friend.

Only the triumphant rescue restored her spirits. 'Oh, what a hero he is,' she murmured, dabbing her eyes with a fragile scrap of lace. The chiming of the clock recalled her to the time. 'We must dress for dinner in a moment; hurry and tell me how it all fell out.'

Joanna came to the end of her tale as they climbed the stairs. 'Well,' Georgy exclaimed, 'what an adventure! I am sure you have left out lots of important details, but we will have a comfortable coze after dinner. Now, what can we find you to wear? I declare you are more than a head taller than I am. Butterwick! Here is Miss Fulgrave come to stay and hardly a stitch to her back. I rely on you entirely…'

They returned downstairs again half an hour later, Joanna prettily clad in a gown that was somewhat too short but, as Georgy said, 'Who is to see it, my dear? Butterwick can let some things down tomorrow; meanwhile, Rooke and the footmen will have to take a care not to stare at your ankles.'

Joanna was just suppressing a giggle at the

thought of the awe-inspiring butler so far forgetting himself as to ogle her ankles when there was a thunderous knocking at the front door. She gave a squeak of alarm. 'Giles!' and retreated rapidly upstairs to the landing.

Georgy, agog, her heart beating with excitement, continued to descend slowly while Rooke opened the door. Her eyes fell on a tall, travel-stained figure whom she had no difficulty in identifying as Joanna's colonel. Behind him she could see a big hunter, mysteriously saddleless, its head drooping and sweat staining its neck and flanks.

'Sir?'

'I wish to see Lady Brandon.'

Georgy shivered. The voice was deep, perfectly polite and with a bite of utter authority. It was also the voice of a very angry man who was reining in his temper hard.

'I will ascertain whether her ladyship is At Home,' Rooke responded with sublime disregard for the fact that his mistress was in plain view behind him. 'Who should I say is calling, sir?'

'Colonel Gregory. I regret to say I do not have my card case with me.'

Georgy felt it was time to take a hand. The Colonel's patience appeared to be wearing thin, which was understandable if he had just ridden almost thirty miles bare-backed. Although why he should be reduced to such straits…

'Thank you, Rooke. I am Georgiana Brandon.' She held out her hand, tipping her head back to look up at Giles as his large, capable grasp closed around her pampered plump fingers.

'I sincerely trust you know why I am here, ma'am.'

'Really, I cannot—'

'Lady Brandon, I implore you not to play games with me.' The firm grip did not release her. 'If Miss Fulgrave is here safe with you, that is one thing. If she has not arrived, it is most serious and a search must be undertaken immediately.'

Georgy could feel Rooke at her side bridling with indignation that she should be so abruptly addressed, but the look in those dark grey eyes was one of such concern that she could not prevaricate. 'Yes, Colonel. Joanna is here, and quite safe.'

He freed her fingers and for a fleeting moment his eyes closed. His hand reached out for the doorpost and Georgy wondered if he was dizzy with exhaustion, then the grey eyes snapped back to her face and all she could read there was anger.

'Then would you be so good as to allow me to speak to her?'

At the head of the stairs Joanna gripped the banister and strained her ears. Giles's voice came clearly to her and under the controlled cadences of his voice his rage was all too plain for her to hear. She had never heard him speak so levelly. *No, Georgy*, she pleaded inwardly, *do not let him in!*

'I am sorry, Colonel. Joanna is far too tired to receive visitors tonight.'

'Then perhaps you would be so good as to give her a message, Lady Brandon. I will return here the day after tomorrow with a chaise and a chaperon and I expect her to be ready to travel back to Hertfordshire without further prevarication.'

'That is not necessary, Colonel. I have invited Joanna to stay.'

'I am sorry to contradict you, ma'am, but Joanna's parents have charged me with returning her to her home.'

'She does not wish to go.'

'Oh, brave Georgy!' Joanna whispered under her breath.

'What Miss Fulgrave wants is, I regret to say, neither here nor there. She is under age and un-married and therefore under the authority of her father, who has entrusted me with her safe return. I am sure I do not have to tell you what an outrageous risk she took, riding all this way alone?'

'Well, yes, of course, it was most imprudent…'

'And I may rely upon you to ensure she remains here safely until I return for her?'

'I…well…yes, very well, Colonel.'

'Oh, Georgy, how could you?'

'Thank you, Lady Brandon. I wish you good evening, ma'am.'

The door had hardly shut behind him when Joanna came running down the stairs. 'Georgy! I cannot have heard aright! You have never promised to let him take me away?'

'Shh, Jo dear.' Georgy cast a speaking glance at the butler and swept her indignant guest into the dining room. 'Thank you, Rooke, we can serve ourselves, I will ring when I wish the courses removed.'

The butler bowed himself out, followed by both footmen, and Georgy plumped herself down in her chair. 'Don't glare at me so, Jo! What could I do? If I had said no, he would have marched in here and dragged you off, I feel sure of it.' She shivered delicately. 'He was magnificently angry—I am half in love with him myself.'

'Well, you may have him,' Joanna retorted furiously, splashing water into a cut-glass flute with scant regard for its fine rim or the polish on the table. 'He is angry because I defied him and he is used to people obeying his every order.'

'Now, Jo, do calm down and be reasonable. He was angry because he was worried about you, and exhausted. Do you realise he had ridden here bareback? Goodness knows why.'

'I hid all the girths and the bits from the bridles, too.'

'That was clever—although it has done nothing for his temper, I fear. But, Joanna, truly, he was so anxious about you—he only became angry when he was sure you were safe.' She regarded Joanna's stormy face. 'Have some smoked trout, or a little of this chicken; no wonder you are so fractious, you must be starving.'

Joanna reluctantly accepted the food, then began to eat ravenously. 'Oh, I had no idea I was so hungry! But, Georgy, you cannot truly mean to let him take me away when he comes back?'

'I really have no choice, dearest. But Jo, why is that so dreadful? You will have to spend the summer in Hertfordshire with the Tasboroughs—'

'Baby sitting and being disapproved of by Alex.

And that horrible man Clifton will call and try and make me marry him.'

'Then tell him "no". This is not the Middle Ages and your father cannot lock you up in some tower until you relent. And quite frankly—' Georgy helped herself lavishly to spiced prawns '—you could hardly be in any more disgrace than you are already.'

'Georgy.' Joanna put down her knife and fork with some emphasis. 'I am in love with Giles Gregory. You are telling me that I have to spend days in his company and that of a disapproving old puritan with a face like a weasel being sent home in disgrace with nothing to look forward to but the attentions of a loathsome man and the news that Giles's wedding has been announced.

'And when Lord Clifton has finally given up and Giles is safely married to his rich, eligible, lovely wife I will have nothing to do with my life than to dwindle into an old maid.'

'But how would staying here help?' Georgy said imploringly. 'It would save you the journey in the Colonel's company and the stay with the Tasboroughs' but you would still be no better off.'

'You told me that you were going to persuade Lord Brandon to take you abroad. You will need a lady companion. I could perform that role, and when we returned I could find employment with other ladies who wish to travel, for you could recommend me and my languages are excellent. I learned them for Giles,' she added bitterly.

'Oh, Jo, I am so sorry.' Georgy put down the serving spoon, which she had just loaded with yet more spiced prawns. 'I was going to tell you, only your news was so exciting. I am increasing and it will be at least a year, if not more, before I will be travelling on the Continent.'

Chapter Twelve

Giles walked stiffly across the gravel to where the Squire's hunter stood, its head low. 'Come on, boy.' He picked up the reins and started to lead the tired animal down the drive. 'We'll find a good inn in Wisbech with a warm stable for you, a bucket of oats and a good rub down.' The thought of the human equivalent—a hot bath, a thick beefsteak and the depths of a feather bed— were powerfully attractive.

He had been right the other evening to think he was getting middle-aged, he mocked himself grimly. A thirty-mile ride across country, even bareback, was no excuse for the weariness that gripped him. But he had not felt like this until he knew Joanna was safe: then the exhaustion had gripped him.

'Damn it,' he remarked to the horse, which cocked one ear in response, 'she's turned me into a worrier. Do you think I am overreacting?' The horse snorted and butted him gently with its nose. 'Hmm? You are right; I have absolutely no confidence that Lady Brandon could stop Joanna doing precisely what she wants, when she wants to, however good her ladyship's intentions are. Joanna has run away twice now because she thought she was about to be coerced; I am afraid she is quite capable of doing it again.'

With a resigned sigh he veered off the main carriage drive and made for the stables, the low roofs of which were just visible behind a high brick wall. The yard Giles found himself in had a faint air of neglect, then he realised that a larger and more impressive block in bright new brick and stone was visible through an arch. A groom emerged from a doorway, stopped at the sight of a stranger and then came forward knuckling his forehead.

'Can I help you, sir?'

'Yes, you can.' Giles continued forward, ending up leaning on the half-door from which the man had emerged and able to see through it to a line of large loose boxes. All were apparently empty except one where a dappled grey rump could be seen over the door.

'I have called to see my…ward, Miss Fulgrave, who is staying with Lady Brandon. You have her mare safely stabled there, I see.'

'Yes, sir. Were you wanting to look at the animal, sir?'

'No, no. I had not realised Lord Brandon was from home, and obviously it is quite ineligible for me to stay at the house with only the ladies there. Can you recommend an inn in Wisbeach with a good livery stables?'

The man waxed lyrical on the numerous excellent establishments, ending with some skill at the one owned by his uncle. 'Used to be a head groom, sir, your horse couldn't be in better hands. And my aunt cooks a powerful good beefsteak if your fancy was that way, sir.'

Giles noted the name and direction of the inn, gazing round the yard with apparent indifference as he did so. 'Thank you.' A coin changed hands, to the obvious pleasure of the groom. 'Your master has had new yards built?' He nodded towards the archway.

'Yes, sir. And a fine new lodging over the tack room for the grooms, sir,' the man enthused, usefully providing Giles with the information he had been willing to spend another ten minutes in conversation to extract. 'Why, thank you, sir,' he added as another coin exchanged hands and Giles turned to lead the hunter back out of the yard. *Wonder why he don't ride it?* he mused, watching man and horse disappear.

Giles, from years of military service when keeping one's horse in prime condition was both a humane and a possibly life-saving priority, fell into an automatic marching step and applied his mind to strategy. In the big house behind him he was acutely aware that another mind was also setting itself to counter whatever plans he had. The sight of Giles's grim smile might have given Joanna pause if she had chanced to observe it.

Five in the morning dawned clear and chill. Joanna's footsteps sounded hideously loud on the gravel as she hastened around to the old stable block, but she consoled herself that no one was about to hear her. In the quiet house Georgy was sleeping soundly, just as her doctor and doting husband ordered, without a thought that her errant friend was escaping yet again.

She paused in the yard, her eyes flicking over the

empty space, her ears alert for any sound, but it was silent with no sound from the new stables beyond to suggest an early-rising groom was about his business. The double door into the stables with the loose boxes was shut, although above it the door into the hayloft stood open. The interior was in deep shadow and the hoist beam jutted out from it. With its dangling hook and chain it had an unpleasant look of the gallows about it.

Suddenly edgy, Joanna tugged back the bolts and set the door open, hesitating on the threshold at a sudden noise. But it was only the sound of Moonstone shifting round in her box to see who had arrived. The relief at seeing the alert head watching her was so great that the descent of a wisp of hay from above went unnoticed and it was not until a second fell, tickling her nose, that Joanna glanced upwards. And froze.

Giles was looking down at her from the hayloft door overhead. He was sitting with his back against the door frame, one leg dangling over the edge. He appeared relaxed and mildly interested at seeing her. Joanna was not deceived in the slightest. 'Good morning,' he observed pleasantly. 'Somewhat early for a ride, perhaps?'

'I...I...what are you doing here?'

'Waiting for you. I had every confidence that you would come.' Giles got to his feet in a smooth motion that belied the fact that he had been sitting motionless in the cold dawn air since three o'clock. 'No, do not run back to the house,' he ordered sharply as Joanna gathered up the trailing skirts of her habit and turned back the way she had come. 'I have no desire to have this conversation in Lady Brandon's presence, but if you insist, we will.'

With hope draining out of her, Joanna watched as Giles leaned out, caught the trailing chain and hook and swung himself down to the ground. Even in the midst of her mingled humiliation, anger and despair she could not but admire the grace with which he moved. 'You must have been very uncomfortable,' she ventured. He was certainly dusty and, knowing him as she did, she could see the tightness around his eyes from tiredness. But the grey gaze watching her was alert and watchful, not at all the gaze of a tired man.

Giles shrugged. 'One gets used to night watches. A roof over one's head is a luxury.' He glanced around. 'Come, in here. I do not want an early stable boy to see us at this hour of the morning.'

With a sigh Joanna allowed herself to be guided

into the interior of the stables. A textured floor with a drain at its centre ran between two rows of large loose boxes, each surrounded by a high wooden partition topped with iron grilles and with double doors at the front. All of them were closed and apparently empty save for Moonstone's stall at the back, where she still watched them over the half-door, and the box behind Giles, which appeared to be used as a store by the stable boys.

Both its doors were open, a carelessly abandoned pitchfork was propped in the entrance and inside were piled boxes and bales. A sudden glimmer of a plan struck Joanna and she hastily dropped her eyes in case Giles should see either her change of mood or the direction of her interest.

'Just what do you think you are about?' he began, giving Joanna a very fair idea of how he might sound to a subaltern who had been out on the tiles to the neglect of his duty. 'Setting out alone, into God knows what, on a tired horse…'

'Oh, Giles!' she said softly, not having to act in the slightest to produce the quavering note in her voice. She risked a glance upwards from under her lashes and willed the production of two large, glistening tears.

Giles, who was quite used to this sort of outrageous play-acting from Suzanne, entirely failed to recognise it in Joanna. 'Joanna…damn it, there is no need to cry…'

'Oh, Giles,' Joanna said again, on a falling note of despair. Quite unused to this sort of behaviour herself, she was at a loss as to what more to say, but her performance appeared to be working, for a second glance revealed that the Colonel's harsh expression had softened.

She took a stumbling step forward and cast herself with considerable energy on Giles's broad chest, catching him around the neck. Taken by surprise he took a step backwards for, whilst slender, Joanna was tall. Before his arms could close around her to steady her, she thrust out her right foot, catching it neatly between his ankles and threw her weight forward against him.

Off balance, Giles took another unguarded backwards step, the pitchfork caught him behind the knees and he fell back into the loose box.

Joanna was at the door in a second, dragging both top and bottom sections across, bolting them both to the door frame and to each other. Now she must saddle Moonstone up and be away before either Giles managed to scramble up and squeeze through the narrow gap between the top of the railings and the rafters, or his shouts attracted the attention of the grooms.

It was ominously quiet: he must be assessing the best way to climb out. Her heart thudding so loud that it seemed to drown out any other sound, Joanna ran down the aisle and dragged the saddle and bridle off their stand outside Moonstone's box.

'Good girl, steady girl. Stand nicely for me,' she pleaded as the grey sidled and stamped, alarmed by her haste and the urgency of her movements. It seemed to take an hour but, in fact, the horse was saddled in minutes and Joanna led her out into the yard with a scared glance at the box where Giles was imprisoned. There was still no sound: he must be building the boxes and bales into a heap to climb up. He would be so angry… Joanna clutched to herself the memory of that moment when she was in his arms, against his chest. Then she found the mounting block and was up and away, spurring the mare down the carriage drive with scant regard to the noise she made.

It was an hour later when a bemused footman opened the front door to a thunderous knocking and found a large, coldly furious and blood-stained man on the step. A second, incredulous glance identified the gentleman who had called the evening before. 'Sir?'

Giles scrubbed at the trickle of blood that kept blurring the vision in his right eye and snapped, 'Kindly inform Lady Brandon that Colonel Gregory requires urgent speech with her.'

'But, sir…Colonel…it is quarter past six in the morning!'

Giles simply stepped firmly into the doorway and shouldered him aside. At which moment, to the young man's undying gratitude, Rooke appeared. The butler was not best pleased at having had to struggle into his tail coat in haste and had an uneasy suspicion that his neckcloth was well short of his usual standards. His tone as he addressed the importunate visitor was less than subservient.

'Colonel! I really must ask you to withdraw, sir! I will naturally inform her ladyship that you called.'

'When will you do so?' Giles produced a large pocket handkerchief and attempted to staunch the flow of blood from the cut on his forehead. It did nothing to make his appearance any less villainous.

'At her ladyship's normal breakfast hour, naturally.' He took in Giles's expression and added, 'At ten-thirty, sir.'

Giles regarded him with an expression that had routed more strong-willed men than the butler. His voice, however, was pleasant as he remarked, 'You will go to her ladyship now and you will inform her that either she receives me in the room of her choice in fifteen minutes or I will do myself the honour of calling upon her in her bedchamber. Do I make myself plain?'

'Certainly, Colonel.'

'Indeed. Then go and do it—and if you are considering scuttling down the backstairs and summoning support in the shape of a number of grooms or footmen, let me promise you that you will regret it. As they will,' he added thoughtfully.

Rooke eyed the large right fist that was flexing and unflexing and decided that discretion was the better option. 'Philips! Get the Colonel some warm water and a bandage for his head and brush his coat. Her ladyship must not be discommoded—any more than is inevitable.'

It was twenty minutes, not fifteen, before Georgy sent Rooke to say that she would receive Colonel Gregory and his expression as he strode into her boudoir was not conciliatory. Georgy gave a squeak of alarm and shrank back against her maid, but to her relief he merely bowed from the doorway and said, 'My apologies for inconveniencing you at this hour, ma'am. If you will tell me where Miss Fulgrave has gone, I will remove myself immediately.'

'But I have no idea! Surely she is in her chamber?'

'I can assure you, ma'am, that at half past five this morning she was riding away from this house. Are you telling me that you had no idea of what she was planning?'

'No! None at all,' Georgy protested indignantly, pushing back her lace nightcap, which threatened to slip over one eye. 'She was cross with me last night when I promised you I would let her go with you tomorrow, and she was disappointed when I explained that I would not be travelling abroad for some months.'

'Then where will she have gone?'

'I do not know, she has no acquaintance in the area—all I can think of is that she will try and reach her sister, Lady Willington, in Lincoln.' She looked distractedly at Giles, then appeared to notice for the first time the rough bandage around his temples. 'Are you hurt, Colonel? Will you not sit down?'

'Thank you, no, ma'am. A cut and a bruise merely, but head cuts bleed like the dev…very badly. Have you heard of an aunt of Joanna's? A Mrs Faversham?'

'Faversham? No…but how did you come to cut your head, Colonel? And if you knew what Joanna was about at five o'clock, why did you not stop her then?'

'Because,' Giles said grimly, 'she tripped me up with a trick I would have expected—and might have suspected—from a street urchin and locked me in one of your loose boxes. To be fair, I think she had no idea she had knocked me out.'

'Oh, how clever of Jo!' Georgy clapped her hands in delighted admiration, then broke off, biting her lip at his expression. 'I wonder where she learned to do that?'

'I shudder to think. Lady Brandon, I am going to gamble on Joanna attempting to reach her aunt in Norwich. May I ask you to write to Squire and Mrs Gedding—I will give you their direction— reassuring them that she reached you safely and that I am still on her trail? And can I ask you to return Squire Gedding's hunter to him? It is too tired to go on at the pace I must set.'

'Of course. But you cannot waste time hiring another horse in Spalding,' Georgy said. 'Rooke! I know you are out there! Send to the stables and

have them saddle up his lordship's best hunter—
that new one he justified to me by saying it would
go all day.' She turned her brilliant smile on Giles.
'He won't mind, and in any case he is not due
back for two weeks.'

By the time Lady Brandon had seen her
husband's black stallion vanish through the gates
and swing southeast, it was half past seven.
Joanna was already realising that there was all the
difference in the world between setting out on a
fresh horse on a comparatively short journey, well
armed with maps and taking off into the unknown
with only the haziest idea of the distance and direction and with a tired horse under her.

By nine she was weary, hungry and beginning
to doubt her recollection of simple navigation
that her military reading had given her. The sun
rose in the east, she knew that. Norwich was to
the east of Spalding, so she had to travel towards
the sun. But the sun moved. And none of the milestones yet showed Norwich on their carved faces.
Soon she was going to have to ask, and she suspected that it was no use asking a yokel who had
never travelled beyond his nearest market town.
It would have to be someone of more sophistica-

tion—a yeoman farmer, perhaps—and someone of that sort would be very suspicious indeed of a young lady out by herself asking such a question.

Then Moonstone pecked and stumbled. Joanna reined her in and gazed around. Was there anywhere she might safely rest for a while? At least Giles would have no idea where she was going and would probably assume she would be trying to reach Grace in Lincoln.

An open gate slumped on its hinges and gave easy access to a flower-spangled meadow. The tempting expanse of grass sloped to a line of willows, giving the promise of water at their feet. Joanna turned the mare's head into the mead and at the water's edge slipped off her back. It was a perfect spot: the grass was lush and soft, the brook sparkled hardly an inch deep over bright pebbles and the willows cast a welcome shade.

She loosened Moonstone's girths, let her drink then hooked her reins over a branch and left her standing in the shade while she wandered through the long grass to where an old stump made a welcoming seat. An hour would rest Moonstone and give her a chance to think of what she would say to her Aunt Caroline. Would she help her? What would Joanna do if she did not? However uncomfortable, those thoughts were better than the alternative, which was to think about Giles, recall that strong, lithe body swinging down from the hay loft, the anger in his eyes, the feel of his chest under her flattened palms as she fell against him...

Worn out, Joanna dozed where she sat in the meadow, undisturbed by the buzzing bees, bird song and the ripple and plash of the stream as it hastened across the pebbles. Moonstone grazed placidly until the distant sound of hoofbeats made her raise her head.

Joanna smiled in her sleep, for Giles had come and was striding across the field towards her, his arms held out to embrace her, a look of tenderness on his face that made her start to her feet...

Chapter Thirteen

Jerked awake, and finding herself half-slipping from her perch, Joanna blinked in the sunlight, unsure where she was. 'Giles?' He had seemed so real, so close. Moonstone stamped her hoof and Joanna saw that her head was up, her ears pricked and she was watching the far side of the field.

A tall black horse appeared in the gateway, passing at the canter, then it was reined in and the rider pulled its head round to urge it into the field. The horse was unfamiliar, but the tall figure on its back was not. Suddenly filled with unreasoning panic, Joanna picked up the skirts of her habit and began to run, stumbling towards her mare. She glanced back over her shoulder; Giles had spurred the horse into a canter and it was gaining on her. He was riding one-handed, leaning sideways over the pommel, obviously intent on scooping her up as she ran.

Mindlessly, panting with exertion, Joanna dodged to the right, but the great hooves hardly broke stride as he turned the black after her. She twisted round, held up her hands in a futile effort to fend him off and was caught around the waist, dragged off her feet and up against Giles's leg as he fought to bring the animal to a halt.

There was a confused sense of plunging chaos as the horse, resenting the sudden kicking, struggling creature who had seemingly attached itself to its side, fought back against its rider. Giles dragged one-handed on the reins until it stood, then swore as Joanna wriggled out of his grasp and fell to the ground.

Sobbing, she took to her heels again, only to be brought down by a flying body that sent her headlong into the lush grass and landed painfully half on her back, knocking the breath out of her.

Unable to move, unable to do more than fight to regain her breath, Joanna realised that she was pinned down by Giles's body lying along her right flank. His left arm was thrown over her shoulders and his breath was hot on her nape. As rational thought returned to her, she wondered if he had knocked himself out, then realised that the sound she could hear was him swearing, very quietly, under his breath.

'Giles?' she ventured after several seconds when it seemed he was going to make no effort to move. 'Giles!'

'I am trying to decide whether to put you over my knee and give you a well-deserved thrashing and then strangle you,' he remarked conversationally, 'or whether simply to strangle you.'

'Giles!'

Abruptly she found herself turned so that she was on her back and he was over her, pinning her even more effectively than before. His body was hard and heavy and, from where his legs straddled her to the pressure of his elbows, pinioning her own arms as he raised himself to look down at her, she was aware of his every muscle, every breath.

'What the hell do you think you are doing?' he demanded and she realised that he was furiously angry. His eyes seemed almost black as he glared down at her, his breath, for all his control, was short and his mouth was clamped into a hard line.

'I couldn't let you take me back, Giles. I...I will not tell you where I was going, but I did have a plan.'

'You had a plan,' he repeated flatly. 'So you take

off into the wide blue yonder all by yourself. Have you forgotten what happened to you before, damn it? Have you forgotten the Thoroughgoods?'

'No, of course not, how could I? But you told me that very few people were like that, that I shouldn't—'

'Give me strength!' He closed his eyes for a moment, and released from their dominance Joanna noticed the stained bandage around his head and the dried trickle of blood on his temple.

'Are you hurt—?' she began, only to be cut off by the glare of those angry dark eyes as they snapped open again.

'Be quiet and listen to me and try, just try, to behave like the sensible young woman I know you to be. You are unlikely ever to come across anyone like the Thoroughgoods again in your life; agents for specialist breaking-houses are thankfully very rare indeed. But men who would insult, assault or very probably rape some undefended, innocent, empty-headed chit of a girl, wandering around the countryside without the slightest idea of where she was going or how she was going to get there—now I would say that men like that are to be found in every town and many a village.'

'Oh!' Joanna gasped at the stinging frankness

of his words, even as she recoiled from the volume of his voice. She had never heard Giles raise his voice or lose control of his temper, now she was experiencing both at very short range indeed. 'I wouldn't let anyone take liberties,' she began, wincing at the vapid euphemism even as she used it.

'Like you are not letting me take liberties now?' Giles enquired, his voice suddenly silkily quiet. Joanna realised that she could not only feel the weight and lines and heat of his body, but that also the fact that he was powerfully aroused. Without conscious thought her untutored body shifted, accommodating itself more closely to his and instantly he snarled at her, 'Lie still.'

Shaken beyond words by the reality of his arousal, Joanna froze. After her marriage Grace had been asked by Mama to talk to Joanna about married life. She had given some indication of the changes necessary in a man's body to allow lovemaking to take place, but she had been very reticent. Giles was so very…but then he was a big man—obviously everything was in proportion.

Blushing hectically at her own thoughts as much as at the shocking intimacy, she closed her eyes and waited for what would happen next. Then opened them abruptly as she realised just what she was thinking, what she was hoping. Her body was beginning to ache very strangely, not with his weight, but from the inside with an unfamiliar hot yearning. She wanted to move against him, wrap her arms around him, incite him to kiss her again, but the expression in his eyes was so darkly fierce she dared not. 'Giles, you said I could trust you!'

'Damn it, Joanna, if you could not, neither of us would have a stitch of clothing on by now. And stop looking so scandalised. Your dream lover, whoever the bloody man is, is a man too and if you think you can behave with such recklessness with him without provoking a reaction, then you are deluded, my dear.' The hard stare softened. 'If I let you go, will you promise not to run away again?'

'What, not run away now, or not run away again ever?' she temporised, forcing herself to think about anything but the immediacy of his body, of the thin barrier of clothing between them. About the fact that he undeniably desired her and that she wanted nothing more than for him to prove just how much.

'Never again. I warn you, Joanna, you have run the length of my patience. Any more and you will discover exactly what that means. Promise me.'

'No.' She shut her eyes, the only defence against his will, which overwhelmed her, mastered her as surely as his long hard body had subdued hers beneath it.

'Promise me.' He was speaking against her lips, his breath feathering the sensitive flesh like a kiss, his hands cradling her head. She could feel the pulse in his wrists beating strongly and the rhythm of her blood leapt to echo it. 'Promise me.' It was a whisper, soft yet compelling. Her lips parted to deny him, but no words came. There was only the heat of his mouth over hers, the insidiously gentle pressure of his fingertips tangling in her hair, the utterly dominant male weight of him fitting so perfectly to her slender frame stretched beneath him.

Time stopped. Around them the flowers opened to the warm sunlight, to the thrumming bees that pillaged each golden heart for its pollen. Overhead a lark spiralled upwards into a cloudless blue sky, singing as though its heart would break, rising, rising, until the human figures below it were a dot in the green of the meadow.

They breathed with one breath, shared the same heartbeat. Without conscious thought Joanna breathed, 'I love—'

And found herself free of Giles's weight, jerked upright, shaken until her eyes snapped open. *'I know you love him!'* She was kneeling, facing Giles, his hands hard on her shoulders. 'I know you love him,' he repeated quietly. 'But how does running away help? What were you going to do?'

Her breath was coming as though he were still riding her down. His own, despite the control she could feel vibrating through his hands, was short. Shaken out of all attempt at pretence, she gasped, 'I was going to my aunt near Norwich. I knew you would never find me there.'

He smiled at her wryly. 'In fact, I know all about Aunt Caroline; your mama suspected you might go to her. But even without that knowledge, did you think I would give up? Did you really believe I would rest until I had found you again? Joanna, look at me.'

She shook her head, bending her neck until her hair, loosened in the struggle, shielded her expression from his eyes. Giles lifted his hand from her right shoulder, smoothing back the curtain of black silk that slithered over his fingers with its own caress. Joanna found her chin raised inexorably and met his gaze.

The anger had gone, and with it the blackness, leaving once again the cool grey stare that seemed to transfix her. 'You have no hope of eluding me, Joanna. Believe it.' She nodded, resisting the impulse to turn her cheek against the hard, gentle palm with its calluses from years of riding and weapon-handling. 'Promise me you will not try to escape and I will take you to Tasborough and Hebe. No chaperon, no carriage. We will ride, stay at out-of-the-way inns.'

'And…' It was difficult to speak, her voice cracked. Joanna swallowed hard. 'And if I do not promise?'

'I will tie you to the horse and there will be no inns. I will find barns to sleep in.'

She met his eyes, met the implacable resolve in them and believed he would take her back, trussed and thrown over his saddle bow if that was what it took. 'But if we are together for days I will be compromised…'

'I am escorting you with your parents' permission. This is not what they had envisaged, but I can assure you, as I will assure them if necessary, you are going to be delivered into

Hebe's hands in as perfect condition as you left your own home.'

Her gaze shifted under his. 'Being alone is enough. Spending nights alone, however blamelessly, is enough if it is discovered.'

'Then we had better be sure we are not discovered, because believe me, Joanna, I have no wish to find myself married to you.' He smiled grimly at the sudden flare of feeling reflected in her wide green eyes. 'I find myself strangely sentimental: I require love in marriage, Joanna.'

'So do I,' she snapped back, hating herself for the jealousy that flooded through her.

'Then we are agreed.' She stared back into the inimical eyes and nodded. 'You do not try to escape? You give me your word?'

'Yes. I give you my word.' Joanna held his gaze long enough for him to read the truth in what she said, then twisted away to sit with her profile to him.

Giles let out his breath in a long exhalation and let his long body topple back on to the lush grass beside her. Joanna was conscious that he was letting the tension ebb out of him like a big cat relaxing in the sun as he lay on his back at her side, his eyes narrowed against the glare of the summer sky. He turned his head to look at her, crushing buttercups under his cheek. 'Did I frighten you? I am sorry if I did.'

'You meant to frighten me,' Joanna said without rancour. After the almost unbearable closeness and emotion of the past few minutes there was a sense of release. She felt very comfortable with him all of a sudden, just as long as she did not let herself think with her body. 'It worked. I should not have run when you came into the field, but I had been asleep, you see, and you seemed like someone from a dream that had suddenly become a nightmare.'

'You were dreaming about that damn...that man?'

'Yes,' Joanna admitted shortly. 'Oh, look, you like butter—the buttercups are reflecting all gold on your face.' She smiled as he brushed the flowers away, then added, 'But I wish you would tell me about your head. How did you hurt it.'

'Ow! Stop touching it,' Giles protested, pushing her hand away. 'I hope you are proud of the damage you did when you pitched me into that loose box.'

'*I* did that? But how?'

'Well, you tripped me up with a trick I would have expected from any street urchin, but not a young lady—more fool me—and then I fell over a pitchfork, landed on a bale, rolled off it and hit my head on a crate. A most effective attack.' He studied the mingled horror and shameful pride on her face and added, 'You make me feel middle-aged, Joanna Fulgrave.'

'Middle-aged! Oh, no—that is preposterous! How could I make you feel middle-aged?' she protested, laughing at him.

'You and Suzy between you.' Giles sighed, getting to his feet with the careless grace of a youth of sixteen and reaching out hand. 'You make me feel middle-aged and sensible.'

Joanna was very certain that whatever Lady Suzanne made Giles feel, it was not the onset of middle age. The feeling that had swept through her, and which she could only compare to the sensation of having had one glass of champagne too many, left her abruptly. She scrambled to her feet without taking his hand and stalked off towards Moonstone who was making friends with the black hunter.

'Well, if we are to travel in easy stages because of your age, we had better get going again,' she threw over her shoulder, then dodged laughing behind Moonstone's dappled hindquarters as Giles made a mock-threatening grab for her.

Once mounted, Joanna asked, 'How long will it take us?'

'Two days, three possibly.' He squinted up at the sun, appeared to do a rapid mental calculation and turned left out of the gate. 'You really were going to go to your aunt this morning? You did not have some other bolt hole you haven't told me about?'

'No, really,' she admitted ruefully. 'I knew that if she would not take me in I had run out of options, other than to go to my sister Grace. But she would have only sent me home and, in any case, I have no idea how to get there. Not like when I ran away from the Geddings. I had worked out my strategy and made notes from atlases…do not laugh at me!'

Giles was failing to suppress a grin, but he apologised solemnly in the face of her indignation. 'And where did you learn all about strategy, might I ask?'

'Er…I read about it because of William,' she said hastily, crossing her fingers. 'When he was army-mad, you remember. He kept wanting to talk about famous battles and marches and so I read some books so I could talk more sensibly to him.' Well, it was partly the truth, although the person she wanted to have the conversations was not her young brother. 'And I remembered about having an objective and then working out one's strategy for achieving it, and what tactics one needed to employ.'

'I am impressed: most people get in a muddle over the difference between strategy and tactics. Shall we canter? I think we cannot be far from March.'

The long, fine July day passed for Joanna in unalloyed happiness. She was with Giles, riding in easy companionship, and although they spoke little it seemed as though they had no need to and understood each other without words. He would glance at her and she would nod and urge Moonstone into a canter, then just as she was feeling a little tired, he would rein in and they would walk along the quiet lanes, heavily fringed with white clouds of cow parsley, occasionally pointing out to each other a view, a picturesque ruined church or a deer grazing at the edge of a coppice.

They found an inn on the outskirts of Chatteris where the landlady served them thick slices of ham and wickedly vinegary pickled onions with slabs of crusty bread and fresh churned butter. When they had finished Giles pushed aside his tankard and pulled out his notes, gleaned from Lord Brandon's head groom.

'Can you face another twenty miles?' he asked. 'If you cannot, we will stop for the night at Huntingdon, but if we can make it to St Neots we will be that much further on our way tomorrow.'

Joanna was beginning to feel both tired and stiff, but she nodded firmly. 'Of course, that sounds far the best thing to do.'

To her surprise Giles reached out a hand and caught the point of her chin in his fingers. 'Brave Joanna,' he said softly. 'I know you are tired, I know you cannot help but be apprehensive about how all this is going to turn out, and I do believe you when you tell me your heart is broken—even if you don't think I take it seriously. Any other young woman of my acquaintance would be treating me to tears, sulks or tantrums by now.' The strong fingers gently caressed the soft skin of her throat and Joanna swallowed hard at the feeling it evoked.

'Even Lady Suzanne?' she queried tartly in an effort to suppress the desire to turn her cheek into the palm of his hand, to beg for caresses.

'Suzy?' Giles snorted with laughter, the all-too-familiar expression of tender forbearance coming into his eyes. 'Suzy would have decided to run away with her maid, her lapdog, at least two portmanteaux of garments and a courier to enable her to secure the most comfortable accommodation at every stop. Under these conditions she would have burst decoratively into tears fifteen miles ago, called me the greatest beast in nature and insisted on a detour into Huntingdon for some shopping to soothe her fractured nerves. The temptation to elope with Suzy, just to watch the havoc she would wreak along the way, is almost irresistible.'

'But doubtless the thought of your father's disapproval prevents you?' Joanna said sweetly, her nails digging into her palms.

'It would certainly greatly distress him,' Giles agreed. The General would have another seizure, just at the thought of such a scandalous occurrence, Giles reflected with grim humour, although of all the things that he might do to incur his father's wrath, eloping with Lady Suzanne was about the least likely.

As they walked back to the horses, Giles reflected on just why it had never so much as crossed his mind to offer for Suzy until his father had demanded it and why, when the idea was raised, he was so very certain she was entirely wrong for him.

He loved her, faults and all; he admired her beauty and charm and wilful spirit. She made him laugh, she took his breath away when she was attired for a grand ball, he forgave her whatever pranks she played. And yet he could never recall her arousing the slightest desire in his breast, not the faintest stirring of longing to possess her, either for passion or as his wife. He really must love her like the sister he had never had, he realised.

Whereas the young woman beside him was stirring emotions in him that were far from brotherly. She was less pretty than Suzy, she employed none of her ladyship's tricks of flirtation, none of her winsome, charming ploys to attract and amuse. But she had courage far beyond what that shallow, adorable little madam possessed. Courage and an innocent, passionate nature that was making it harder and harder for him to feel towards her as he should.

Giles came to himself with a start to find Joanna waiting patiently for him to give her a leg up into the saddle. He lifted her swiftly, anxious not to linger, aware of a new scent—something of her friend Lady Brandon's, perhaps. He swung up into the saddle and tried to make himself forget the long moments when he had lain across her body in the meadow. The feeling of her trembling, warm form against him, the new scent in her hair as it clouded around his nose and mouth.

And then the even more arousing sensation of her stretched out beneath him, supple and yielding and innocently reacting to the demands of a male body pressing down on hers for the first time. It had taken all his self-control not to lower his mouth to hers, to kiss her until she was dizzy with passion and then…

'Giles?'

'Mmm? Sorry, I was thinking.' *Thinking!* Damn it, he was working himself up into a thoroughly uncomfortable state and he must stop it immediately. Unfortunately Joanna's next hesitant question did nothing to turn his mind from the heated image of what she would look like naked.

'What are we going to do tonight…I mean… when we get to the inn? I have no baggage, and it is going to look very odd, is it not?' She broke off, blushing slightly and Giles administered a sharp mental kick and set himself to reassure her.

'We must agree our story and stick to it. Let's

think: you are my sister. We set out on a foolish whim from St Ives to visit our great-aunt in Sandy, not considering how far it was in this heat. Then Moonstone lost a shoe and we had to find a blacksmith and you are far too tired to ride on to Great-aunt Julia's so we are having to spend the night in St Neots. How is that?'

'That is very convincing,' Joanna agreed approvingly. 'It accounts for everything neatly. What a deplorable turn for invention you have!'

Giles smiled back at her teasing, but his mind was racing. With that story they might find a respectable inn with two bedchambers available and hope their tale would cause no impertinent comment. But he was less sanguine about it than Joanna appeared to be. For a start, they looked not the slightest bit like brother and sister. Even if that went unnoticed, how would she feel when the reality sank in that she was spending a night alone in a strange place with a man? And one who only that morning had tumbled her in the meadow grass and had spoken frankly of male desire to her?

'Yes, quite deplorable,' Joanna continued brightly. Her mind too was racing with thoughts of the night ahead, although she had no intention of insulting Giles by allowing him to think she did not trust him. But his story, ingenious as it was, could perhaps be improved upon. Not for anything would she have him embarrassed by impertinent assumptions about his motives.

'However, it does not account for your bandaged head. How would it be if we say you had a fall—quite early on, to account for it not being fresh blood—and you thought we could carry on, but you had a worse headache than you expected so we have been riding slowly?'

She saw his frown and added, 'I know that you have not regarded it in the slightest, however much it is paining you, but can you not dissemble a little? And we must bicker, too—brothers and sisters do that.'

'Nonsense,' Giles said briskly. 'This is not a dramatic performance. I will deal with the landlord, you remain as unobtrusive as possible and we will brush through this as well as may be.'

Chapter Fourteen

Giles reckoned without an unexpected flair for the dramatic on Joanna's part. From the moment they wearily dismounted in the yard of the Grey Horse in St Neots, she began nagging gently with the air of someone speaking more out of habit than real anger.

'I told you we should have taken the carriage, Giles, now here I am without a hairbrush to my name. What Great-aunt is going to say when we arrive on her doorstep with you looking like a scarecrow, and me hardly any better… Thank you, my man. Where is the landlady to be found, if you please? Giles, stop scowling, you need to see an apothecary with that head, I do not care what you say.

'Ah! Mrs…? Mrs Henderson, good evening to

you. Now, tell me at once, do you have two bed-chambers for my brother and myself? You do? Excellent. Giles! Let the groom help you down, I really think you should go to bed immediately. Perhaps you should be bled as well, but doubtless the apothecary…'

The landlady blinked at the relentless, soft on-slaught as Joanna walked firmly into the inn. 'This seems very pleasant, Mrs Henderson. I will see the rooms directly. Can someone go for the apothecary at once, if you please? My poor brother—such a fall, and of course, a large man like that falls harder—he is my half-brother, as you have no doubt guessed, Mrs Henderson—did you say something, Giles? Ah, this room will be admirable for you, dear, in you go and lie down until the apothecary arrives.

'Now, Mrs Henderson, you are saying to yourself, what are these two people doing de-scending upon my inn without servant or luggage to their name? You may well ask. Our name is Pontefract, Miss and Mr Pontefract, and we are on our way to visit our great Aunt Julia in Sandy. Well, I say our great-aunt, but actually she is my half-brother's great-aunt…'

Joanna's voice continued its penetrating prattle,

clearly audible to Giles through the wall from the bedchamber beyond. He lay down on the bed and gave way to barely suppressed laughter. He was still gasping gently and mopping his eyes when Joanna peered around the door, then came in, eyeing him disapprovingly.

'What *are* you about, Giles? Do pull yourself together. Mrs Henderson is an admirable woman and has entirely believed our story. Oh, stop it, you will set me off! She has sent for the apothecary, and the maid has gone round to knock up Mr Watkins at the haberdashery shop. Apparently he can provide such necessities as hairbrushes, tooth powder and, she gives me to understand, nightgowns. I do hope you have enough money. We must pay Mr Watkins, and our shot here, and the apothecary, and I will have to tip the maid I have engaged.'

Giles sat up against the pillows, sobered at last. 'You have engaged a maid? To sleep in your room?'

'Yes. I hope you do not mind, but it seemed just the sort of thing I should do, and I can't for a moment think Mrs Henderson will suspect anything untoward with me insisting on a girl to sleep on a truckle bed. I have assured her I never sleep alone, but always with my maid, and she appeared to think that showed a refined respectability.'

'Excellent. But why should I mind?'

'Well—' Joanna broke off and blushed. 'I thought you might think I did not trust you.'

'But you do?'

'Of course! Now quiet, here comes the apothecary, if I am not much mistaken. I am afraid you will have to endure my interference, for I am sure Miss Pontefract would want to supervise everything.'

Fortunately the apothecary showed no inclination to bleed Giles, and politely turned his 'sister' out of the room before cleaning up the cut, inserting two stitches and rebandaging it.

To Joanna's indignation, Giles called for supper to be eaten in a private parlour and then sent her up to bed before settling down with a London news sheet and a bottle of the Grey Horse's excellent brandy.

Despite her indignation and the presence in the truckle bed of Polly the maid, Joanna fell into a deep sleep almost immediately.

When she woke with a start it was pitch dark and Polly was snoring loudly in her corner. Muttering, Joanna turned over and pulled a pillow tight around her ears, but the rasping penetrated the goose feathers with an infuriatingly regular rhythm. She found she was lying there listening, counting the seconds until the next predictable snore.

Gradually she became aware of other sounds: the building cooling and settling for the night, the distant sound of a baby crying, a restless sleeper near at hand tossing and turning. It was difficult to orientate herself in the dark, but Joanna realised that it was coming from the room next door and that the sleeper in question was Giles.

Was he just dreaming or had he developed a fever from the blow to his head? Perhaps the cut was inflamed. For perhaps fifteen minutes Joanna lay undecided in the dark, expecting at any moment for the restless sounds to die away as Giles fell into a deep sleep, but they did not. Eventually she slipped out of bed and tiptoed out of the room. Behind her Polly's snores continued unabated, muffled as she cautiously closed the door and cracked open the one to the next room.

The shutter was open, admitting just enough moonlight for her to discern Giles laying on the narrow bed, the sheets tossed and rumpled, one pillow half on the floor. He was muttering; as Joanna hesitated in the doorway, he turned restlessly, flinging out an arm. Despite the nightshirt provided by the shopkeeper, he appeared to be naked under the twisted bed linen.

She should not be there, she knew, and certainly she should not be standing there letting her eyes stray over the muscular planes of his chest as though caressing him with her gaze.

There were so many reasons why she should not be there and only one possible excuse for her presence—that Giles was ill. Joanna inched across the floor, bit back a cry of pain as her bare toes stubbed against a stool leg, and finally reached Giles's bed. She laid the back of one hand on his brow and to her surprise it was as cool as her own, with no hint of fever.

Puzzled, but relieved, Joanna reached down to pull the sheet over the distractingly bare chest and found her wrist gripped suddenly.

'Darling,' Giles said clearly and drew her down on to the bed on top of himself. 'My love.'

For one startled, wonderful moment Joanna thought he was awake and knew her, then she realised he was still deeply asleep, obviously in the toils of a dream into which her fleeting touch had intruded. And it did not take much imagination to guess that Giles was dreaming of Suzanne as his arm tightened around Joanna and his free hand drifted across her breast in a lingering, sensual caress.

Joanna gasped and lay still, her entire body tingling with a surge of heat. His hand flattened against the soft curves of her left breast, stroking until his fingers found the nipple which tautened in response, sending an aching arc of pleasure through her. Her entire body seemed to cry out for his touch as the drifting fingers conjured up sensations not only in her captive breast but, shockingly, down through her belly to her thighs.

Her entire body wanted to move under his hands, stretch itself along the length of his, savour the touch of his bare skin against hers, yet she knew she could not, must not move or she would wake him.

Giles's face was buried in the sweet curve of her neck, his lips tasting the warm skin with tiny kisses, his tongue flickering lines of desire across the pounding pulse at her throat.

Joanna forced back a groan of desire and tried to push back the clamouring demands of her body long enough to think before it was too late. If she stayed where she was, it could only be a matter of moments before she lost all will-power, all self-control and simply allowed herself to be swept along on the tide of sensation his hands and mouth were orchestrating within her inexperienced body.

If she woke him, Giles would be appalled at having compromised her beyond redemption. Somehow she had to free herself from his arms, get away from the bed without rousing him. She caught his roving hand in hers and raised it to her lips, nibbling the fingertips while she slipped from the mattress. Giles reached for her blindly, but she placed his hand lightly on the rumpled sheet and almost ran to the door.

Safely outside, she leant back against the panels and drew a long shuddering breath, willing the cool of the draughty corridor to steady her quivering limbs, calm her ragged breathing. That it could be like that! That she could feel so transported, so utterly possessed when all he had done was to caress her breast, kiss her neck. Why had nobody warned her? Her sister and Hebe both obviously enjoyed the marriage bed, that much was discreetly obvious in the warmth of exchanged looks with their husbands, the fleeting caress in passing. But *this!* What would it be like to make love to completion, to be joined utterly to his strength, to know Giles's as intimately as it was possible to know another human being?

Then the heated fervour began to fade, leaving her shivering and bereft in the bare corridor. She would never know what that ultimate experience was like because all she had done was to steal his kisses and caresses from another woman, one who was so close to him that she haunted his dreams and racked his nights with desire.

On the other side of the panelled door Giles turned his head restlessly on the pillow and murmured, 'Joanna?' then lay still as the dream faded and was gone.

The next morning the landlady was concerned to see that her guests appeared to have slept badly, a worrying matter for a woman who prided herself that her feather beds were the best of any of the town's hostelries.

Giles, who had experienced a torrid night of powerfully erotic dreams, managed to produce a smile and the assurance that it was only the remains of his headache that had disturbed his sleep. Joanna, equally heavy-eyed and subdued, confessed that she had found the church clock disturbing as she was unused to having one so close.

It was true enough. She had lain awake, her mind endlessly recreating those moments in

Giles's arms until her body roused into restless desire again and she was forced to get out of bed and pace up and down the room in the chilly dawn light, willing the chiming hours to move faster and release her from the prison of her memory.

Nor did the fresh air and stimulus of being mounted and on the road again appear to lighten their mood. Giles assumed that Joanna was anxious about the journey and her reception when she reached the Tasboroughs, she that he was missing Suzy. Yesterday's camaraderie had quite vanished and they rode almost as two strangers, forced together by circumstances and awkwardly having to make the best of it.

Joanna let her glance flicker across to Giles, to be met by a guarded look in his grey eyes. *He is tired of having to look after me,* she thought miserably. *He is worried about his father and missing Lady Suzanne. I should never have run from Georgy's house. I should never have entered his bedchamber last night.*

Oh, but her body still vibrated from his touch in the strangest way. Once, she had tried the harp, thinking that she should improve her musical performance, and she could still recall the humming vibration of a plucked string taut under her fingertips. Her body felt like that all through. And worse, she seemed to ache deep inside as though something was missing…

Joanna did not glance at Giles again unless he spoke to her and tried to focus instead on what she could possibly do with her life when the summer was over. Could she face another Season?

After what seemed like an hour of silence Giles said abruptly, 'We can make it to Tasborough by this evening if you feel up to it. I would prefer not to risk another night on the road.'

'I would prefer it, too,' Joanna agreed fervently. She was determined to ride until she dropped if there was the chance that they could spend the night somewhere where they did not have to pretend, watch every word and action. And somewhere where she could sleep in a chamber far from Giles.

'Colonel, sir, and Miss Joanna, good evening.' Starling greeted the pair of them calmly as they stood on the threshold of Tasborough Hall, apparently unconcerned by the unheralded arrival of his lordship's best friend and her ladyship's cousin at ten of the clock, without baggage or attendants and distinctly travel-stained.

'You were expecting us, Starling?'

'Indeed we were, Colonel, although upon which day or time we were not certain. I will inform her ladyship of your arrival immediately, she was about to retire. His lordship is out, but is expected back shortly. Mrs Fitton will show Miss Joanna to her room.'

Joanna was old friends with the housekeeper, who showed not the slightest surprise at her arrival with Giles as she ushered her to her usual chamber. 'There is hot water on its way, Miss Joanna, then I hope you will go down to her ladyship directly. She's been that anxious about you and I have no doubt will not go up to bed as she should until she has seen you with her own eyes.'

'How is her ladyship?' Joanna asked, not a little anxious of the effect her disappearance and the subsequent hue and cry might have had upon a lady so close to her confinement.

'Blooming!' The housekeeper clapped her hands together in barely suppressed excitement. 'Blooming! She says it might be twins, and you only have to look at her to think she might be right.' A cough from the maid bringing the hot water recalled her to the fact that she was speaking to an unmarried girl. 'She's in the Panelled Parlour, Miss.'

Joanna hurried down, not realising, until she pushed open the door and saw her cousin, how much in need of some feminine support and comfort she was. 'Oh, Hebe!' And then she was clasped in her arms on the sofa, being kissed and patted. For almost a minute the two of them clung together, both fighting back tears, then Joanna sat back and managed to produce a watery smile.

'Are you well, Hebe? And Alex and little Hugh?' Reassured on these points, she asked, 'Have you heard from Mama or Papa?'

'At length, dearest, they sound… Oh Giles, how well you look!' She held out her arms as Giles strode into the room and bent to kiss her, then added, half-seriously, 'And if you say one word to Alex about twins I will never speak to you again. He has been intolerable ever since you suggested the possibility to him; I have been fussed to death and it is all your fault, you wretch. But I forgive you everything for rescuing Joanna.'

She glanced at Joanna, taken aback by the bleak look in her cousin's eyes. 'Oh, my dear, I am sorry, I was telling you about what your parents said and now you are worried. There is no need, they sound positively *forgiving*. Yes, I know, I was surprised too, but Aunt Emily has sent all your best clothes over and has begged me to keep you for as long as I wish. All she asks is for me to write the moment you arrive. There is a note for you, and one for Giles. There, on that little table.'

Joanna took the folded paper and regarded it dubiously. That she had been so easily forgiven seemed highly unlikely; no doubt Mama had not wished to sound too angry in her letter to Hebe so as not to worry her. 'I will read it in my room,' she said. 'We must not keep you from your bed, Hebe.'

'No, nor I from yours.' She allowed Giles to help her to her feet and tucked Joanna's hand under her arm as they walked from the room. 'Goodnight, Giles dear.' When they were out of his hearing she remarked rallyingly, 'I have to tell you, Joanna, that not only do you look extremely tired, you are positively brown from the sun. I can see all our cucumber frames being stripped before we can restore your complexion.' This sally produced nothing but a faint smile and she turned to catch her cousin by her forearms, holding her so she could study her face properly. 'Go to bed, Joanna darling, and sleep well. In the morning I can see we are going to have to have a long talk.'

Joanna climbed wearily into bed, the soft imprint of Hebe's kiss on her cheek both a comfort and a reproach. Hebe was obviously concerned for her and would want to help. Yet how could she begin to tell her anything of the truth behind her scandalous escape or Giles's capture of her?

Chapter Fifteen

Joanna slept so deeply that when she finally roused it was several moments before she could recall where she was. When she finally realised that she was safely at Tasborough, she lay rubbing her eyes and watching the play of sunlight through the gap in the drawn curtains. Images and memories of the past few days ran dreamily through her mind. Eventually she roused herself sufficiently to tug the bell-pull beside the bed.

The maid who usually looked after her when she stayed at Tasborough popped her head around the door with a speed that made it obvious that she had been waiting in the dressing room.

'Good morning, Miss Joanna.' She threw back the curtains with both hands, letting in a flood of light and a view across the beech woods towards the Vale. 'I'll have the hot water brought up, miss. The hip bath is all set out in the dressing room. The Colonel said you would be wanting a hot, deep bath.' She whisked out again as rapidly as she had entered, leaving Joanna staring after her.

'*Giles* said I would want a hot bath? Why on earth…ouch!' She struggled to sit up against the pillows, every muscle and joint complaining. 'My word, I am stiff,' she said to Polly as the maid came back, holding out a pale cream wrapper. 'I had forgotten just how far we rode yesterday. What a pretty wrapper, Polly. Is it one of her ladyship's?'

'No, miss. It is one of the new things Mrs Fulgrave sent over for you,' the maid explained, leaning over the bath to check the temperature of the water. 'There are some lovely gowns, Miss Joanna, and a parasol and all sorts.'

New clothes? Joanna's brow furrowed as she shed her nightgown and climbed into the steaming, herb-scented water. She must be well and truly forgiven if Mama had sent what sounded like a complete new wardrobe. The gift itself was wonderful, but she was far more thankful for the forgiveness: being at odds with her family had been one of the hardest things to bear about the entire situation.

'What time is it, Polly?'

'Nine o'clock, miss. Her ladyship said, would you care to take breakfast with her in her room? She usually has it at half past the hour.'

'Please will you send to say I would love to join her. Does anyone go down to the town with post in the morning? I really must write to my parents.'

'John will go down at ten, miss. There'll be just time after your bath.'

Clad in one of three charming new muslin gowns with a pair of wafer-thin kid sandals on her feet, Joanna sat down to pen the second note to her mother since she ran away. This one had just as many tearstains as the first, but they were happy tears. Having seen the wardrobe her mama had sent, Joanna could not be in any doubt she was forgiven, even if she had not read the short affectionate note Hebe had given her.

And please give my most dutiful love to Papa and assure him that I am all too aware of the distress and anxiety I must have caused you. I will do my best to make myself useful here at Tasborough and look forward to seeing you all again very soon. With all my love, your affectionate daughter, Joanna.

She conned the two pages of closely written words and hoped that they conveyed her regrets.

And yet... She folded the pages and wrote the address of the Bath hotel on the front before handing it to Polly to seal. And yet...she would do it again if she had to. She would most certainly not allow herself to be coerced into a loveless marriage, that was for certain, whatever the next Season held for her.

Hebe looked up from the fashion magazine she was scanning as Joanna walked into the room and said immediately, 'My dear! You look so fierce, whatever is the matter?'

'Good morning, Hebe.' Joanna bent to kiss her cousin's cheek and joined her at the little table set in the wide bay window of Hebe's bedchamber. 'I am sorry if I was scowling: it was simply that I am resolved not to allow myself to be pushed into marriage, however grateful I am that I appear to be forgiven.'

'The clothes?' Hebe rang the silver bell beside her plate. 'Yes, I wondered about those. They are a notable peace offering indeed. You may serve breakfast now, Starling, thank you. Has John taken the post? Miss Joanna will have a letter.'

'I have already given it to Polly, thank you,

Starling.' Joanna took ham from the proffered plate and allowed Hebe to pour her a cup of coffee.

When Starling had left the room her cousin asked bluntly, 'Why did you not come to me in the first place, Joanna? You know I will do everything I can to help.'

'I thought…Mama said your confinement was very near, and from something she said it sounded as though you were very tired and perhaps Alex was a little worried about you—' She broke off and eyed Hebe anxiously. 'You are all right, are you not?'

'Absolutely fine,' Hebe assured her, buttering a roll. 'It is just that this seems to be the biggest baby in the world and the weather is so hot. And Alex will fuss so. If only Giles had not put the idea of twins into his head! I am delighted to see you and I want to do everything I can to help.'

'I am not sure anyone else can,' Joanna said ruefully. 'I ran away to think, but all I succeeded in doing was putting Giles to a great deal of trouble, inconveniencing some complete strangers—the Geddings, who are delightful people, by the way—almost ending up in a London brothel and distressing my family.'

'*A brothel?*' Hebe dropped her bread roll and stared aghast at Joanna. 'I wondered what she was so very tactfully avoiding in the letters I had from your mama.'

'I had better explain.' Joanna recounted the tale of her adventures from the moment she crept away from Charles Street in the dawn light to her rescue by Giles and arrival at the Geddings. 'And, Hebe, we must do something about those poor girls who have been already forced into prostitution in those places. I cannot, as an unmarried girl, but you could…'

'Yes, of course, we must discuss it soon, after the baby,' Hebe said distractedly. 'Joanna, I had no idea you had been in so much danger, it must have been terrifying. But why did you run away in the first place? And why did you not come to me from the Geddings? Your mama had agreed to that, after all.'

'I did not come because…because Mrs Gedding had found a horrible chaperon who guessed I was in disgrace and who was going to read me religious tracts all the way here. And I knew Alex would be furious with me for worrying you and I could not bear…' Her voice trailed away as she bit back a sob.

Hebe leaned over and took her hand. 'Could not bear what, darling? Surely you did not think I would lecture you?'

'You and Alex are so…so happy. And there's little Hugh and the baby coming and now I am never…'

Hebe reached for her reticule and passed over a square of fine linen. 'So it is a man? The reason behind all this?'

Joanna nodded, not meeting Hebe's eyes.

'What has he done to you? You can tell me, dearest. I will not be shocked, whatever it is. When you imply that now you cannot have a family of your own…'

'Oh, nothing like *that!* He has done nothing at all, except be in love with someone else.'

'But he made you promises, led you to believe…'

'No. He is quite blameless and he has not the slightest idea I love him. But I do love him, and for ever. And when I found out that it was hopeless, that he loved someone else and wanted to marry her, I just could not think what to do with the rest of my life, and Mama insisted that I marry Rufus Carstairs, whom I hate. So I ran away to think.'

Hebe put down her knife and stared at her cousin. 'But when did you meet this man, Joanna? You have always been so…I mean, we used to joke that you were the perfect débutante.'

'I cannot tell you where I met him. The only

reason I wanted to be "perfect" was for him,' Joanna said bleakly. 'Everything was for him. And, yes, it was a very foolish thing to do, for I never thought about the real man at all, only about my thoughts and my plans and my feelings. He was a dream, an ideal. Nothing you can say will reproach me any more than I reproach myself.'

'Then if you recognise that,' Hebe said, eagerly seizing on Joanna's realism, 'then you know it is not real and you can hope for another person to enter your heart and your life.'

'No.' Joanna shook her head sadly. 'I may have fallen for an ideal, and I know the real man is not a pattern book of virtues. But I still love him. I love him even more for being flesh and blood. And there will never be anyone else. Not while he lives.'

'Who is it, Joanna?'

'I will not tell you.'

'Do I know him?'

'I will not tell you.'

Hebe sat back, one hand on the swell of her stomach and winced. 'Stop kicking, Frederick!'

'Frederick?'

'It is what I call the baby—just in jest, you understand. I am sure he has eight feet, and all of them booted. Joanna, how can I help you if you will not confide in me?'

'You cannot help me, no one can. I must simply find my own way through this. If only I were an heiress, at least I could become an eccentric spinster and do something about those unfortunate women. As it is, I suppose I must become the typical unmarried daughter. I am sorry, Hebe, I cannot expect you to understand.'

'But I do. For several long, horrible weeks I thought that Alex was going to marry someone else. If that had happened, I do not know what I would have done or whether I could ever have contemplated marrying another man. It came right for me, Joanna; we must make it come right, somehow, for you.'

'I wish I had your confidence.' Joanna took a long sip of her coffee. 'But I am not going to repine, for that will not help me. Nor will running away, I know that now. I am here, I have your support, my parents appear to have forgiven me and I hope I can be of some use to you for a while.'

Hebe looked doubtful. 'Promise you will tell me if there is anything, anything at all…'

'I promise. Where is Alex?'

'He rode over to Giles's family home with him first thing. Giles is very worried about his father, as I am sure you know. Alex has promised to support the fiction that Giles is spending a summer of wild indulgence—you know about that as well, I expect?'

'I do. His mother sounds a most unusual lady, does she not?'

'She is charming, but very unconventional. When you get to know Giles really well you can see her in him. But I expect all you saw was the perfect cavalry officer!'

'Er…yes. He is certainly used to his orders being carried out, is he not?'

'Alex says he is the best officer of his acquaintance. It is so sad he is selling out, he would have had a glittering career.'

'He said something about not wishing to be a peacetime officer,' Joanna said indifferently. The pleasure of speaking about Giles was insidious. She was terrified of saying too much, yet to avoid the subject of her rescuer would seem suspicious. Or so she told herself. 'He is going to stay there— his home, I mean?'

'Oh, no. Would you pass the conserve. Thank you.'

'Of course, I was forgetting, he was planning on going to Brighton.'

'No. He is going to stay here—unless he finds things much worse at home with the General. I think he realised I would appreciate him distracting Alex and he said something about buying horses as well. Anyway, he seemed quite content to stay for a few weeks. And it will be company for you.'

'Oh, possibly,' Joanna said forcing an air of vagueness into her voice. 'Although I am sure the poor man has had quite enough of my society to last him a lifetime!'

Inside her heart was beating like a drum. Giles at Tasborough for weeks, Giles at meals, Giles every evening in the relaxed atmosphere of a family home. It had been difficult enough hiding how she felt from him, but now she would not be able to relax for a moment. How was she going to hide her feelings in front of Hebe's anxious, intelligent eyes?

To her relief, Hebe did not appear to want to know the details of their journey. Even the most tolerant cousin was going to baulk at the news of an unchaperoned night in an inn and long rides across country with no escort whatsoever. Joanna caught Hebe easing her position in her chair to give her back more support and guessed that, having got her safe and sound, she was just too preoccupied to think of delving deeper.

Giles and Alex did not arrive back until late afternoon, finding both ladies sitting under the shade of a spreading cedar of Lebanon on the back lawn. To Joanna's loving eye, Giles looked serious but as though a weight had been lifted from him. When Starling brought a tray of lemonade and cakes out, she changed position under the pretext of passing glasses and sat beside him.

'How did you find the General? Is his health still causing Lady Gregory concern?'

'I found him much better. Mama is very pleased with him and I could see the difference immediately. The stiffness has gone from the side of his face and, although he still has a hesitation in his step, it is much improved.'

'I am so glad,' Joanna said warmly, putting out a hand and squeezing Giles's without thinking. 'To be so worried about him at a time when there was an estrangement between you must have been difficult to bear.' She would have been pleased to hear that any person who had been unwell was recovering, but the relief on Giles's face made her feel as though she had received good news of one of her own family.

Giles placed his other hand over hers and smiled at her. 'You are a darling, Joanna.'

Her heart fluttered as though it were a bird he had captured with that strong gentle hand, which held hers within it. He was so large, so masculine close to and yet his voice was tender as he spoke the endearment. Joanna knew she was staring transfixed into his eyes, knew that Hebe and Alex were within feet of them, yet she could not move, could hardly breathe.

Then Giles's gaze shifted and his hand moved and the spell was broken. Joanna tried not to glance round guiltily to see if anyone had observed them. 'And is your father reconciled on the subject of your marriage and you selling out?'

'To the latter, a little perhaps. Not that he will admit it. He lectured me on wasting my substance around town. When I said mildly that on the contrary I had been out of town on an errand for a friend he snorted and said, "Chasing some petticoat, more like!", which was rather too close for comfort and I suspect I may have looked a little conscious of it.'

'And your marriage?'

'Now there, at least, we are now thinking as one. Lord and Lady Olney visited last week, which settled matters and put all misunderstandings to rights. They gave out that they had heard he was unwell, but I suspect Mama had said something to Lady Olney. If he is feeling strong enough, they have invited my parents to visit in August.'

'How wonderful. What good news for you,' Joanna said hollowly. Now every barrier in the way of Giles marrying Lady Suzanne appeared to have been swept away. 'Lord Olney's seat is near Bath, is it not? Will you accompany your parents?' Giles nodded, his expression suddenly unreadable, and Joanna guessed he was thinking about idyllic summer days spent courting the girl he loved.

'Joanna?' It was Hebe calling to her across the grass. 'Should you not move more into the shade? It is very hot and you look quite pale.'

'Thank you, but I am quite comfortable,' she called back, inwardly cursing her own lack of self-control. If she were to change colour every time Giles said something to her, she might as well make a public announcement of her feelings for him here and now.

Beside her Giles was also brooding inwardly although, with more practice than Joanna at concealing his feelings, very little showed on his face. He should never have held her hand like that just now. Certainly he should not have allowed that warmth to creep into his voice when she reacted with such sympathy and understanding to the news of his father. She was sweet and open and had come to be used to him, trust him. And then he did something to remind her of the intimacy she yearned for with that confounded man and she froze and turned from him.

If I knew who he was I would drag him here on his knees and make him beg for her, he thought fiercely. Did Hebe know his identity? How much had Joanna confided in her cousin? Not that he could ask. He watched from under heavy lidded eyes as Joanna got up and ran to met the nursemaid who was bringing young Master Hugh out to his parents. The child saw Joanna and ran to her chuckling with delight, his podgy arms held up for her hug.

Joanna caught him and swung him up into her embrace, teasingly chiding him for being such a big boy. And something inside Giles caught with a sudden stab of pain. It was gone almost as soon as it hit him. With a soft exclamation under his breath he got to his feet and strode over to Joanna, lifting the child from her arms, but holding him close so she could continue the nursery rhyme she was chanting with the child.

'He is too heavy for you,' Giles said.

Hebe, who had turned to watch her son, broke off what she was saying to Alex, an arrested expression on her face as she looked at the little tableau. Then she turned back to her husband and asked urgently in a low voice, 'Is Giles engaged to be married? Or has he his eye on any young lady to ask?'

Alex, inured to his wife's rapid changes of topic, merely raised a dark brow and murmured, 'Doubt it. Hasn't said anything to me, and I think he would. He hasn't been home long enough surely—and most of that time he's been chasing round the countryside after Joanna.'

'That is what I thought,' Hebe replied, a frown marring her forehead. Under her breath she added, 'In which case either I am wrong or what Joanna said makes no sense at all.'

Chapter Sixteen

For the next three days Joanna kept as far out of Giles's way as she could contrive without appearing to avoid him. It proved unexpectedly easy and she found she hardly had to make excuses, for Giles was absent from breakfast to dinner, reappearing only to report visits to local horse breeders and farmers and successful purchases of breeding stock for his new project.

'Have we said anything to upset Giles?' Hebe asked Alex bluntly on the evening of the third day as he stood behind her at the dressing table, fastening a double string of pearls around her neck.

'No. What makes you think that?'

'He is out every day. Are you sure he is buying horses?'

'Well, if the animals occupying the south

paddock are anything to go by, he is. Nice bay hunter he found over Tring way. I'm thinking of making him an offer for it.'

'He isn't courting someone, is he?'

'He's working exceptionally hard if he is managing to do that and visit as many farms as he appears to be doing.' Alex laid his hands lightly on his wife's white shoulders and met her eyes in the mirror. 'What are you thinking?'

Hebe would only shake her head. She wished she knew.

But the next morning it was Alex who left home early to settle some boundary problems on his most distant farm and Giles who was alone at the breakfast table when Starling came in.

'I am sorry to disturb you, Colonel, but Hickling, his lordship's head groom, is outside and wishful to speak to you. I told him to wait until you had finished your meal, sir, but he says it is urgent.'

The problem was apparently his lordship's best mare, who was due to foal any day and who appeared to be in sudden difficulties. 'I daren't leave her until his lordship gets back, but I think the foal's the wrong way round and ought to be turned. None of the lads have any experience of that sort of thing and to tell you the truth, Colonel, sir, I don't like to attempt it on my own. Seeing what an eye you have for horses, sir, and knowing you are a cavalry officer, I thought mayhap...'

'Of course, I'll come and have a look at her, Hickling. Starling, if anyone wants me I will be in the stables. Oh, and, Starling, if her ladyship asks, there is no need to tell her why. Not a subject to worry her with at the moment, I think.'

Half an hour later the two men finished examining the sweating, distressed mare and exchanged grim looks across the loose box where she was circling restlessly. 'You are right, Hickling. The foal's all round the wrong way: I can see we've a long morning ahead of us.' Giles shrugged off his coat and waistcoat and threw them carelessly over the stable door before unbuttoning his shirt. 'No point in ruining good linen either. Now, what do we need? Hot water...'

'Plenty of soap... Ned! Run to the kitchens and ask Cook to put water on the range. Well, sir, are you going to take her head, or shall I?'

Unaware of the drama unfolding in the stables, Joanna finished breakfast with Hebe, who announced that she was going along to the housekeeper's room to discuss the deplorable state of the household linen. 'What are you going to do, dear?'

'I thought I would take my sketch book and go down to the south paddock to try my hand at drawing the horses. I flatter myself that I can draw a bowl of fruit or a landscape with tolerable ease, but I have never tried to draw an animal.'

'Are you sure it is not that you want to have a look at that little mare Giles was so pleased about at dinner last night?' Hebe teased.

'Well…of course, Moonstone is lovely, and Giles is most kind to let me ride her, but the new mare sounds very spirited.'

Hebe laughed. 'Well, try and see if you can wheedle him into letting you try her this evening. If he has another successful day, he will be in a good mood.'

Joanna found her sketch book in the drawer where she had left it on her last visit to Tasborough, picked up a wide straw hat by its almond-green ribbons and ran lightly down the stairs without bothering to set it on her dark hair. Despite everything she could not but feel happy this morning. The sun was shining, Giles seemed content with the way his plans were progressing and she had put on the most becoming of her new muslin gowns. The skirts were simple white fabric with a subtle figuring of white rose buds in the weave. The bodice was the same almond green as her hat ribbons, with puff sleeves and a narrow satin trim around the neck.

Humming quietly to herself and letting her mind wander dangerously towards daydreams of what Giles would think when he saw such a fetching ensemble, Joanna reached the bottom of the front steps and turned away across the lawn towards the corner of the complex of stableyards and the way to the paddocks. Out of the corner of her eye she saw a curricle turn between the high brick pillars of the front gate far off down the drive, but ignored it. A visitor for Alex and Hebe, no doubt.

She reached the entrance to a little yard, unused except for hay and feed storage, and would have walked past but for a pitiful mew from inside. One lost kitten, its eyes just open and its legs scarcely under control, was staggering across the cobbles, squeaking its distress.

'Oh, you poor little thing! Where's your mother?' Joanna dropped hat and book on to a low wall and went to pick up the protesting scrap of fur which immediately attempted to suck her finger.

'What a charming picture,' a voice remarked from the entrance to the yard. 'Quite the subject for a sentimental print.'

'Rufus!' It was Lord Clifton. His driving coat was carelessly open, he carried his gloves in one hand and, as she stared at him, he swept his hat from his blond head and made her an elegant bow. 'What on earth are you doing here? Have you come to visit Lord Tasborough?'

'Joanna, my dear, how low you rate your own attraction. I am here to see you, of course, and to continue the discussions we were having about our impending nuptials before you were so inconveniently summoned to your cousin's bedside. That is the excuse your parents are putting out, is it not? I would not like to get it wrong and cause embarrassment. It is always so difficult to recall in these cases what the story is. Chicken pox? The needs of an aged aunt? How convenient to have a cousin in the country.'

He strolled towards her as he spoke and Joanna backed away, still clutching the kitten which sank needle claws into her unfeeling hand. 'I do not know what you mean. My cousin asked for me to stay, and I am most certainly not going to discuss her health with you. As for our *nuptials*, I have told you before, I would not marry you if you were the last man…'

'On earth, yes, I remember.' His eyes glittered blue. Joanna backed away further then stumbled as her foot found the central drain. She regained her balance, but the few seconds brought him closer. 'But, you see, your parents do want you to marry me, and beside my title and my fortune I have the other inestimable advantage in their eyes of being willing to marry you despite whatever havey-cavey activities you have been up to the past few weeks.'

'If that is what you think of me, I wonder that you care to offer for me.' Joanna continued to back, her eyes never leaving his face. She had been so right to mistrust him on sight, she thought, desperately racking her brains to recall whether this yard was entirely enclosed or whether there was a gate through into one of the others. But the sapphire gaze held hers like a stoat with a rabbit and she could not turn her head to look.

'As I told you before, Joanna, I desire you. You are very beautiful: a collector's piece. And somehow, whatever scrape you have got yourself into, I think you are untouched. Ah, yes, you blush so prettily.'

Another man for whom a virgin was a prerequisite, Joanna thought wildly. 'Perhaps, perhaps not,' she said as casually as she could and saw his eyes narrow.

'I would not joke about it if I were you, Joanna. Now, where was I? Oh yes, the list of your advantages. Respectable breeding, lovely manners when you try and, of course, it would please my mama to have me marry her old friend's daughter.'

She backed into something solid. Looking down, she realised it was the mounting block. Carefully she set the complaining kitten down on the bottom step and straightened up. To either side the walls were uninterrupted by anything but loose-box doors standing open to reveal bales of hay or sacks of feed. No escape that way.

'How did you know I was here now?'

'Why, Mrs Fulgrave told me, of course.' He tossed his gloves onto the mounting block. 'Now, come here, Joanna, let me kiss you and we will discuss plans for our honeymoon. Italy I thought. You will like Italy.'

Mama! How could you? Joanna realised with a burning sense of hurt just why the lovely new clothes had been sent. And she had fallen neatly into the trap by putting on the most becoming gown that morning. Her mother simply could not know what a hateful man her best friend's son had become or she would never have schemed for this meeting.

'Rufus, go away. I have absolutely no intention—' He took one stride forwards and seized her, his hands clamping hard on her upper arms as he jerked her towards him.

'No! Stop it! *Giles!*' The last word was wrenched out of her as Rufus pulled her hard against his chest and fastened his mouth on hers. Joanna struggled wildly, but the folds of his caped riding coat flapped around her, confusing her, his hands were too strong and then the sensation of his open mouth crushing her lips against his was too overwhelming. She was vaguely aware of being pushed backwards, of her heel catching painfully on a threshold and the sense of surrounding walls, then all of her being was concentrated on struggling against the hands that were on her body and the mouth that seemed intent on dragging the breath from her until she surrendered.

Giles exhaled deeply and leaned back against the cobwebbed stable wall. 'We've done it, Hickling!' The groom grinned back, his face as sweat-begrimed as the Colonel's. At their feet a filly foal lay in a wet jumble of legs, the mare already licking and nuzzling it, urging it to stand on its impossibly long limbs for its first suck. Giles dragged his wrist across his forehead and stopped as the groom exclaimed, 'Don't do that, sir! You're a right mess as it is.'

Giles looked down at his filthy torso and then across at Hickling. 'Do I look as bad as you?'

'Worse, Colonel. Better be putting yourself under the yard pump, if I can be so bold. Won't be doing for any of the ladies to be seeing you in that state, sir.'

Giles reached for his shirt, thought better of it and opened the half-door. 'Can you manage now, Hickling?'

'Aye, sir, thank you. I'll find you a bit of towel, sir.'

Giles stretched and strolled across to the pump. The sun was hot on his bare back and the sudden shock of cold well water made him gasp as he stuck his head and upper body under the flow. He emerged running wet with his hair sleeked down dark and scrubbed his head vigorously with the piece of rough linen the groom handed him.

'Thank you. I'll send my valet over to pick up

my clothes, if he ever speaks to me again once he's seen these leathers.' Giles strolled out of the main yard, intending to lean on the paddock rails and admire his new bloodstock. Alex would be pleased with his new addition, and soon the Gregory stables would be full of mares carrying the new lines he hoped to breed.

There was a sound, abruptly cut off from further down the stable range. He raised his head, suddenly alert.

'Giles!'

Joanna wondered hazily how much longer she could struggle, and even if there was any point. Some instinct told her that Rufus was kissing her more out of frustration and anger than desire or even lust. She had spurned him, rejected him and his normally cold and calculating collector's instinct had turned to thwarted fury. If she stopped resisting, he would probably let her go: she had no real fear he was about to rape her. But every nerve in her body refused to submit to him or to let him think even for a moment that he could overcome her.

The violence with which he was wrenched from her sent her staggering against the wall. Dazedly she stared at the figure that appeared to fill the doorway. A figure out of some Norse legend: a tall, hard-muscled, half-naked warrior, the light gleaming off wet shoulders, his face and chest in shadow.

Rufus twisted in the man's grip on his collar then managed to fight his way out of his long coat to stand, fists raised defensively in front of him. There was nowhere else to go, his assailant seemed to block out the light. The man made no move to raise his own hands or to ward off any attack from Lord Clifton. There was contempt in the lack of care he took to watch his opponent as he shifted his attention to search the shadows until he could see Joanna, her dress pale against the brick walls.

Giles. She spread her hands against the rough surface to stay upright. She was not going to let herself collapse in front of him.

'How dare you!' Joanna felt a slight flicker of admiration for Rufus that he could summon up speech in the face of this elemental force. 'How dare you lay a hand on your betters, you clod! I'll have you dismissed.'

'Be quiet. You will apologise to this lady.' The deep, quiet voice neither promised nor threatened. But Joanna saw Rufus take a step back.

'Who…I thought you were a groom…you are mistaken…'

'I told you to be quiet.' Now Joanna could hear the anger beating under Giles's unnaturally calm voice. 'Now, apologise.'

'I'll be damned if I do!' Rufus blustered. 'She led me on, the little hussy. Lures me in here, then screams the place down when I try and take a little kiss…'

The punch was so hard and so fast that Rufus did not even appear to see it coming. It lifted him off his feet and sent him across the box to land sprawled over a hay bale. As he lay there gasping, Giles hauled him to his feet by his collar and spun him round to face Joanna.

'Apologise or I will fetch a horse whip to you.'

She met Rufus's unfocused gaze with contemptuous green eyes.

'I…I'm sorry, Joanna—' He broke off gasping as Giles twisted his grip tighter. 'Miss Fulgrave. I misunderstood…I will not trouble you again.'

She closed her eyes and heard the sounds of Rufus being summarily propelled out of the box and across the yard. Footsteps came back, into the loose box, slowed, halted. Her eyes remained closed, all her concentration seemed to be taken by the friction of her fingertips on the rough brick keeping her upright.

'Joanna?' He seemed to be very close. She could feel the warmth of him in the cool, dim room. What did she look like? Her fingers crept to the torn neck of her gown, then up to her swollen lips. What must he think of her, struggling in the stables with a man? Would he think her a flirt who went too far? Or worse, the hussy Rufus had called her?

The pain in her fingertips was suddenly worse. She was slipping down, the darkness behind her closed lids was full of lights and she was caught up, pressed hard against a chest that was bare and, puzzlingly, wet.

Joanna pressed her cheek against the flat planes, sharply aware through the dizziness of the crisp kiss of hair, the surprising softness of male skin over hard muscle. She turned her face a little and the touch of hair on her sensitised lips forced a gasp from her throat.

The movement stopped. Joanna forced herself to open her eyes a little and discovered that Giles had sat down on a hay bale and had her cradled on his lap, facing the doorway so the light fell on her face. He was studying it with painful intensity, his eyes almost black with the emotion she had seen in them before.

'I am sorry, Giles.'

'You are sorry?' His brows drew together sharply.

'I was not expecting him. I did not realise how foolish it was not to leave the yard immediately. Mama must have told him I was here. That is why she sent me all those new clothes, I expect,' she finished, her voice trailing away. 'I do not think he would have…forced me. I made him angry by rejecting him.' The expression of sudden fury on his face made her gasp.

'Never, *never*, apologise for this! Nothing you could have done justifies the way he behaved to you. Nothing.'

He tightened his arms around her and she flinched as he unwittingly touched the places on her arms where Rufus had gripped her.

'Let me see.' Shakily Joanna stretched out her arms. Already the bruises were darkening on the tender flesh of her inner arm. 'Oh, my God.' Giles closed his arms around her and pulled her gently against him, cradling her so that he did not touch the savage marks, rocking her gently until the pain of his accidental grip ebbed.

Joanna let her body mould to his, reaching around his body as far as she could until her palms were flat on his back, her breasts crushed against his chest. Her head seemed to fit exactly into the angle of his neck so that against her mouth she could feel the hard pulse beat in his neck. Through the thin muslin of her gown, dampened by his wet skin, she could feel the tantalising tickle of chest hair.

Her body, roused into fear by Rufus, changed insidiously until it was desire, not fear, that animated her, sent the blood tingling through her veins, started the deep, mysterious, intimate ache inside her. She wanted to arch into his body, twist in his grasp until she could press her lips to his, fall back on to the soft hay with his hard weight on her.

Her fingers flexed and spread, sensing the matt satin of skin under their pads, exploring the lines of muscle, the hard strength held in check. He was so taut under her palms, so still except for the slow, controlled rhythm of his breathing, the steady beat of his heart and a scarcely discernable vibration that seemed to resonate through her like a note of an organ when it has reached the point beyond hearing.

'Giles,' she murmured against his throat, not knowing whether it was a question or a simple word of thanks. 'Giles.'

Chapter Seventeen

'Giles.' He felt rather than heard the soft whisper against his throat. Could he let her go? He doubted it. He thought about opening his arms, releasing her, gently urging her to her feet and helping her inside to Hebe's care. And could not do it. His arms would not obey, his mind was not ready to exert its will.

She felt so right, curled trustingly against him, as though some sculptor had made a mould of his body and had created this being to fit within the curve of his arm, the shelter of his torso.

He thought about that first glimpse over Clifton's shoulder. Her wide defiant eyes, the bruised mouth, her hands spread against the wall to support her. Those eyes were closed now, he could feel the lashes caressing the tendons of his throat. The slender fingers were spread over his back muscles, unconsciously flexing in a way that made him want to roll her over into the hay, feel her beneath him as he had in the meadow, kiss that bruised delicate mouth into flowering response.

And he could not. He could do none of those things. She was clinging to him out of shock and reaction and because he was familiar and she trusted him. He had to start thinking again with his head, not his body, not with that newly awakened part of him, which was still unsure of what it was feeling but which was intent on turning his will from iron into fragile porcelain.

Joanna felt Giles's grip relax and his arms open. Unsteadily she sat up away from his chest, letting her hands slide round to his sides to steady herself.

'How do you feel now?' he asked, his palm gently cupping her chin so he could tip up her face and look into her eyes.

'Much better, honestly. Oh, Giles, thank you so much. And do not be angry again if I say I am sorry, but I *am* sorry that you have to keep rescuing me.'

She was relieved at his sudden grin and the fleeting caress of his hand as it left her chin. 'No need to worry. Dragon slaying is my speciality.'

Joanna smiled back, then stiffened as her palm

felt a sudden change from the hard muscled smoothness of his side. She twisted in his lap and ducked her head to see better. 'Giles, what a dreadful scar.'

He bent his head to look. 'Oh, that. Shell fragment. They leave very untidy wounds.'

'As opposed to what?' she demanded.

'Lances leave a nice tidy hole, if they don't drag.' He lifted her hand to his shoulder. 'And a sabre—' he moved her fingertips to the long thin scar running down the back of his right arm '—now that can be positively neat.'

Joanna looked at him aghast. 'You might have been killed by any of these!'

'I suppose so. But what did you expect a soldier's body to be like?'

Joanna knew she was blushing furiously, but she was too intrigued to be distracted. 'But this sabre cut—how could you defend yourself afterwards? You are right handed.'

Giles extended both arms, clenching his fists until the muscles stood out. 'You train until you can fight with either hand.' He went still as Joanna put her hands on his forearms.

'Do that again!' Obligingly Giles clenched and unclenched his fists. Joanna gasped, then put her right hand over her own left forearm and made a fist. 'There is hardly anything there and I always thought I was quite strong.'

'You are, look at the way you handle Moonstone. But a woman's muscles are more slender. See.' He traced his index finger down the back of her forearm. It was Joanna's turn to go still. For a long moment they looked at each other, then Giles said lightly, 'As I said before, I appear to be having the most improper conversations with you, Miss Fulgrave.'

'I expect it is because I seem to get myself into such improper situations,' she said with equal lightness. 'Giles, you haven't said why you have no shirt on and are so wet.'

'I was helping Alex's head groom, Hickling, with a mare who has just foaled.'

'Oh, how lovely! May I see?'

Giles stood her on her feet and got up. 'Not today,' he said drily. 'Anyone looking at you would have the impression that you have just been kissed, rolled in the hay and then pressed up against a very wet surface. Somehow I do not think this is a picture Hebe would wish you to present to the outdoor staff. I am afraid that hiding you from all of the indoor staff is going to be impossible. My only hope is that I am going to feature in belowstairs gossip as the rescuer, not the ravisher.'

'You are teasing me,' Joanna said stoutly, well aware that Giles was trying to make light of the possible embarrassment awaiting them. 'I am sure Starling will not permit any gossip.'

Even so, the butler's professional imperturbability was hard pressed by the appearance on the doorstep of Colonel Gregory in a deplorable state of semi-nakedness and grime accompanying Miss Joanna, who appeared to have been…

'Miss Joanna has had a most unfortunate encounter, Starling, although she is thankfully unharmed. If Lord Clifton should call she is not, under any circumstances whatsoever, at home. Regardless of who Lord Clifton is with. Now, if we can just get her upstairs before her ladyship…'

'Starling, what are you whispering about out here?' Hebe emerged from the dining room, a large lace tablecloth in her hands. 'Oh, my goodness!'

'I am absolutely fine, Hebe…'

'No need to worry, I know it looks…'

'I am quite sure, my lady…'

'Oh, be quiet, the three of you.' Hebe regarded them severely. 'We will go upstairs, Joanna, and you can tell me all about it. Giles, put some clothes on, for goodness' sake. You will frighten half the housemaids into hysterics and the rest will fall in love with you. No, Starling, do not fuss, I promise I am quite all right.'

She placed the tablecloth in Starling's hands, linked her arm through Joanna's and proceeded up the shallow stairs. Joanna sent Giles a rueful look and allowed herself to be borne away.

Once away from the men and in the seclusion of her own room, Hebe proved to be far more worried than she had let herself appear. She sat Joanna down and held her hands, gazing anxiously at her bruised mouth.

'Whatever happened, darling? You and Giles have not…?'

'No! Certainly not! As if Giles would do such a thing.'

'Well, no, of course not, although sometimes men just do not know their own strength.' Hebe's voiced trailed into silence in the face of Joanna's furious indignation. She watched her cousin's face for a moment, then added, 'I am sure Giles is always the perfect gentleman,' and hid her own inward enlightenment at the sight of Joanna's rosy blush.

'But if you and Giles have not been, er, romping in a hay stack, what on earth has happened?'

'It was Rufus Carstairs.'

'Lord Clifton? But he has not been here today. Starling would have told me, even if he had told Lord Clifton that we were not receiving.'

'He did not go to the house. I think he must have seen me in the grounds and followed me without announcing himself.'

'Disgraceful! Had you told him you were here?' Hebe was obviously adding general bad manners to Rufus's sins.

'No.' Joanna twisted her handkerchief tight in her lap. 'I think Mama must have done that.'

'Aunt Emily. Of all the misguided things… Try not to be so upset, dearest. He is very eligible and I am sure she thought she was acting for the best.'

'I know. But that is why she sent me all those clothes, you see, Hebe. And I thought it was as a present to show me she had forgiven me.' Joanna tried to stifle her misery, but the tears were running down inside her nose and she ended up producing a pathetic sound between a sniffle and a sob.

Hebe wrapped her arms around her and hugged her tightly. 'I shall write to Aunt Emily today and tell her just how she is deceived in the wretched man. And I shall threaten to keep you here for ever unless she promises never to allow him close to you again.'

She received a watery smile and a murmur of thanks, but Joanna would not meet her eyes and a sudden unpleasant thought hit her. 'Joanna, he did not do anything other than kiss you, did he?'

'No. He hurt my arms holding me so tightly, but all he did was kiss me until I could not breathe. I honestly do not think he would have done anything else, Hebe. He was just so angry with me for not behaving as he thought I should. He is a collector, you see, and he has decided he wants to collect me for some reason. Statues and paintings do not answer back or try and run away, so he is not used to rejection.'

She hesitated, glancing sideways at Hebe. Now was, perhaps, the only opportunity to ask a question that was intriguing her. 'Hebe, why do men set such a store on virginity? He was obviously very concerned that I had not lost mine in the course of whatever scrape I had got myself into. And the horrible couple who kidnapped me were most adamant that that was the most important thing.'

'Joanna! What a question to ask me. Well, I

suppose men want to be certain that their children really are their children—at least the first born,' she added scrupulously with a thought to many a society marriage. 'And those horrible brothels—perhaps that is rarity value, or power, or wanting to hurt someone powerless.'

'And the wedding night, of course, I suppose that is something special,' Joanna mused and was startled at the rosy blush that stained her cousin's cheeks. 'Hebe! You don't mean that you weren't?'

'We were shipwrecked in France,' Hebe said defensively. 'This is thoroughly improper and we are not going to discuss it any more and you are most certainly not going to do what I did.'

'I doubt I would ever be shipwrecked with—' Joanna started with a giggle and suddenly broke off, appalled at how close she had been to saying Giles's name.

'With…?'

'We are definitely not going to discuss this any more,' Joanna said firmly. 'I am quite all right and I will be very grateful if you would write to Mama and tell her about Rufus. Now, are you not going to ask me why Giles had no shirt on?'

Hebe gave up her attempt at luring Joanna into

revealing the name and said with a laugh, 'I am not sure I feel strong enough to know, but you had better tell me. Did it all end with a fight?'

Joanna told her about the foal, which Hebe appeared to find a tame explanation, and then described what had happened when Giles had burst into the loose box.

'He only hit him once? I find that very disappointing. I was hoping that you would say he had knocked out his front teeth and broken his handsome nose for him.'

'How bloodthirsty you are.'

'Only when wretches like that hurt my family. Now, I am going to ring for my maid, have my stays unlaced, put on a wrapper and take a light luncheon up here. Why do you not do the same?'

In the event the cousins spent an indolent afternoon in a state of *déshabillé* in Hebe's room, glancing at fashion plates, gossiping, discussing whether the latest hair styles could possibly flatter anyone under the age of thirty and catnapping.

It was therefore two well-rested, enchantingly gowned and frivolous young women who came downstairs when the dinner gong was rung and it was quite twenty minutes into the meal before they realised that they were sharing the table with two unusually silent men.

Hebe broke off an amusing tale concerning a neighbour and her trials with an unsatisfactory governess and regarded her husband, her head on one side. 'What is the matter, Alex? I declare you are positively dour and you have not touched that terrine, which is usually your favourite. Are you not pleased about the new foal?'

'Nothing is the matter, my dear. I have just got rather a lot on my mind. The new foal? Yes, excellent news, she is one of the Starlight line so I have high hopes of her. I must see about a bonus for Hickling.'

'And for Giles,' Hebe teased.

'Nonsense. He is eating us out of house and home, it was time he earned his keep.'

Giles, who was making substantial inroads into the roast goose, raised a quizzical eyebrow at his friend but did not say anything.

Hebe rolled her eyes expressively at Joanna and announced, 'Well, coz, I can see we must bear all the burden of the conversation ourselves. Let us discuss hemlines.'

Even this dire threat did not appear to register with the men who spoke when spoken to, assisted the ladies punctiliously to whichever dish they required and otherwise remained silent.

'They are communicating with each other, you know,' Hebe said in exasperation as she and Joanna retired to the panelled chamber, leaving Giles and Alex to their port.

'I have seen them do it before,' she continued, sinking on to a *chaise longue* and thankfully putting her feet up on the footstool which Joanna fetched. 'They lapse into long silences, occasionally make eye contact and grunt. Then the next day they have apparently planned a journey, or decided what to do about poachers or announce they are going to a prize fight. I challenged Alex about it once. He just said that when men know each other really well, as he and Giles got to do in the army, then they don't need to talk. Or prattle, as he rather unkindly put it.'

'Then what are they planning now?' Joanna asked.

'I do not know. I just hope it isn't—'

The door opened and the men walked in. 'Would you mind if we play billiards?' Alex said.

'No, of course not.'

Alex got as far as the door before turning. 'Oh,

yes, I almost forgot. I will have to go up to town tomorrow. Some slight matter of business.'

'I thought I would go with him,' Giles added. 'We will be back on Wednesday.'

'No!' Hebe said with such emphasis that Joanna jumped. 'No, you will not do anything so foolish, either of you.'

'What?'

Hebe turned to her, anger sparkling in her eyes. 'Ask them why they are going.'

'But Alex said, a matter of business.'

'Ask them what business.'

Joanna had never seen Hebe so furious. More out of anxiety to keep her calm than a desire to interrogate her host, she said, 'Please explain, Alex. Hebe seems rather upset.'

Alex's face wore the darkly severe expression that had led others to describe him as looking like a member of the Spanish Inquisition. 'We have to talk to a man, that is all.'

'Which man?' Hebe asked Joanna between gritted teeth.

Feeling as though she was caught up in the midst of a farce, Joanna dutifully repeated, 'Which man?' and was met by two equally stony and uncommunicative faces.

'Nothing you need worry about,' Alex said, fatally misjudging his wife for once.

'In that case, Joanna and I are coming with you.'

'I forbid it.' A shiver of awed excitement ran down Joanna's back. Alex in a towering rage was a force to be reckoned with.

'And I forbid you to fight duels,' Hebe snapped back.

'I am not…'

'But Giles is, is he not? And you are going to stand his second. And, if he kills that wretched Carstairs, the pair of you will have to leave the country. And if you think I am going to have a baby all by myself, Alex Beresford…'

'I am not going to kill him,' Giles said, managing to get a word in between the furious married pair.

'But you are going to fight him,' Joanna stated, cold gripping her heart.

'Yes.'

'And if he kills you? Do you think I want that on my conscience, Giles Gregory?' She found she was standing toe to toe with him, glaring up into his face. Behind her Alex and Hebe had fallen silent.

Giles laughed contemptuously. 'Kill me? I hardly think so.'

'Oh, you arrogant, infuriating, pig-headed...' Joanna struggled to find a bad enough word and finished '...*man!*'

Giles's laugh turned into one of pure amusement. 'I will admit to the last charge. Ouch! Stop that!'

Joanna, infuriated beyond words, had begun to hit his broad chest with her clenched fists, ignoring the tears running down her face. 'Please, Giles, do not do it. He isn't worth it...'

Giles caught her pummelling fists in one hand and held them just tight enough to stop the blows. 'Shh, little one. There is nothing to worry about.' Joanna blinked back her tears and looked up at him through soaked lashes. His expression was so gentle the breath caught in her throat.

'Please,' she whispered.

As he bent his head to catch the word, Hebe said sharply, 'The risk to Joanna's reputation is too great. There is no saying who he has told he was coming here. He reappears in town with, I presume, a bruised face and the next day her cousin's husband and his friend descend and call him out. Do you think the gossips will have no difficulty putting that puzzle together and making a very pretty picture of it?'

Giles raised his head and looked across to Alex,

then at Hebe. His grasp remained tight around Joanna's trembling hands. At last he said, 'You may be right. I just hate to think of him getting away with this.'

'He has not,' Hebe said with conviction. 'The word will go round that he is not to be trusted with young ladies. Soon he will find that he is not welcome to pay his addresses when he seeks a wife of the eligibility his pride demands. No one will know quite why, just that his perfect reputation will be ever so slightly tarnished. He will hate that.'

'Good,' Joanna said, her voice sounding distant even to her own ears. Something very odd was happening. Surely she was not going to faint? She never fainted. Even that dreadful night at the Duchess of Bridlington's ball she had not fainted. Even this afternoon in the stableblock she had only been dizzy....

She came back to consciousness to find herself being carried in Giles's arms. He seemed to be climbing. 'Where am I?'

'On your way up to bed.' He glanced down at her and his arms tightened. Joanna fought the instinct to wrap her arms around his neck and bury her face in his chest. 'You fainted.'

'I never faint. Where is Hebe?'

'Downstairs making up with Alex. She sent Starling for your maid to meet you in your chamber, so there is no need to worry about the proprieties.'

'I was not,' she protested. 'Giles, please promise me not to fight Rufus.'

'Very well, I promise. Why are you so against it? Surely you don't think I would either kill that fool or let him kill me, do you?'

'I have caused you more than enough trouble,' she mumbled against his shirt front.

'You have certainly caused me trouble,' he agreed. 'Can you stand? I had better set you down here.' Then, to her amazement, as he put her on her feet outside her chamber door he bent and kissed her forehead lightly. 'Whether it is more than enough trouble remains to be seen.' On which enigmatic note he strode off down the corridor.

Chapter Eighteen

For three of the residents of Tasborough Hall breakfast the next morning was an uncomfortable meal. Hebe was pale with dark shadows under her eyes, but although Alex tried to insist she go back to her room she protested that she was too restless to settle.

Alex ate with a darkly severe eye on Joanna, who was convinced he blamed her for the previous day's alarms and arguments and therefore for Hebe's discomfort. Uncomfortably torn between meeting his judgmental gaze, flustering Hebe by looking at her and appearing to fuss and catching Giles's eye, which for various reasons she was reluctant to do, Joanna kept her eyes on her plate.

Only Giles appeared to be in good humour. Seeing the reddened and grazed knuckles of his right hand, Joanna assumed he was pleasurably satisfied at having delivered such a devastating blow to Rufus Carstairs. Men, she gathered, set a lot of store by that kind of thing. At least he did not appear to be repining at not challenging him to a duel.

Joanna had lain awake half the night worrying that Giles might slip away up to London, even if Alex could not for fear of upsetting Hebe. He had promised not to call Lord Clifton out, but she was certain there were ways in which he could turn the tables and publicly provoke Rufus into issuing a challenge.

And during those long, restless hours Joanna had found her memory was all too vivid and awake. Rufus's assault troubled her not at all. What kept her tossing and turning was the memory of Giles's body sheltering hers, his anger for her, the tenderness in his eyes as he looked at her cradled in his arms. And that enigmatic remark as he had left her outside her room; almost as though he *wanted* her to cause him more trouble. But that was absurd.

Hebe crumbled a roll and said, 'That is a very fetching habit, Joanna. I like the pale revers.'

Thankful for something to talk about, she replied eagerly, 'Yes, it is nice, is it not? Mama sent it. The skirt is lined with the same colour as the revers so it shows a little when I am mounted and the hat and veil are *very* dashing.'

'Is it not too hot to ride?'

'I was going to go after breakfast. I was only going to get a little fresh air in the paddock. Unless you would like me to stay?'

'No, dear, you go out, the fresh air will do you good.'

That appeared to exhaust everyone's capacity for conversation. Joanna glanced round the table and saw Giles was smiling at her. He raised one eyebrow and glanced sideways at Alex and Hebe with a rueful expression. She could not help but smile back, wondering if she dared give into temptation and ask if he would ride with her.

No, it was not safe. It was so wonderful to be alone with him, so painful when they parted or something reminded her that he could never be hers. And it was increasingly difficult to keep her feelings from showing. She kept catching herself looking at him, then did not know whether to look away rapidly which might look self-conscious or risk being seen staring.

He was getting to know her too well, that was the trouble. It was the only explanation for the oddly tender look in his eyes sometimes and the almost possessive way he protected her. Giles was obviously a man who was fiercely protective of 'his' people, whether they were his family, his men or, in her case, a stray young woman he had offered to help. It must be one of the characteristics that made him such a good officer: his men would sense his concern and interest, even if he never allowed it to show in the way he did with Hebe, or his father, or herself. How was she going to cope with this ache inside once he was no longer with her?

'A penny for your thoughts,' he said suddenly, startling her into unwary speech.

'I was just wondering how on earth you are going to fill your time now you can stop rescuing me.'

Giles grinned. 'I do not anticipate being bored. Quite the contrary. I have…plans.' There was a note in his voice of mischief, and something else that Joanna did not recognise, but which caught Alex's brooding attention.

'Indeed? And what is her name?'

Before Giles could reply Hebe said, 'Alex!' sharply and Starling came in with a silver salver.

'The post, my lady.'

'Give it to his lordship, please, Starling. My goodness, what a pile of letters. All our acquaintance no doubt telling us how much happier we would be in Brighton or Bath, I expect. I hope they have some interesting gossip. Oh, how I wish I could go sea bathing right this minute.'

'Really?' Joanna was startled.

'Yes, truly. I do not understand it. I feel so restless, as though I could walk for miles.'

'You'll do no such thing my darling, but if you are good and rest I will take you to Brighton the moment the doctor says you may go. Here you are, three letters for you, that should keep you occupied.' Alex passed them across and tossed one letter to Giles. 'One for you, Joanna.'

Joanna slit the seal on her missive, which by the handwriting was from her sister Grace. No doubt she was now fully informed by their mama of her younger sister's shocking behaviour, dangerous adventures and also Mama's hopes of a proposal from Lord Clifton despite all this.

She skimmed the letter but it was exactly as she feared—shock, surprise, gentle chiding and a strong hint that good fortune was going to smile upon her despite it all. Joanna folded it crisply and set it down beside her plate. She was in no mood for lectures or sermons, however softly delivered.

Giles had unfolded the wrapper on his letter to

reveal what appeared to be at least three sheets of expensive paper covered in a swirling hand. A cloud of attar of roses' scent wafted across the table, making Hebe cough.

He was reading with some difficulty but with an all-too-familiar expression on his face of loving amusement.

'A letter from Lady Suzanne, I collect,' Joanna enquired, attempting to keep the sharp note out of her voice.

'Yes. I have not written for *an age*, so she says, and she is taking the opportunity to chide me for that and to remind me, with very little subtlety, that it is her birthday in ten days. I suspect that all this hinting is because she knows I am buying horses and she would like a showy hack to ride in town.'

'How old will she be?' Hebe asked.

'Twenty.'

'And no offers yet? I am surprised. Surely she is an exceptionally eligible young lady.'

'Exceptionally,' Giles agreed. He hesitated, then added, 'It is not yet spoken of, so I am sure you will not say anything, but there will be an announcement very soon.'

'A lucky man,' Hebe said.

No one except possibly Alex noted the sharp

tone of Hebe's comment. Joanna stopped breathing, her every nerve seemed to be alive and shuddering with pain. She was unaware that she had gone white, was unaware that she had put her cup of tea down so sharply that it slopped into the saucer. All she was aware of was the loving expression in Giles's grey eyes as he looked at the letter in his hand.

Suddenly she found she could move. In fact, it was almost more than she could do to control her instinct to spring to her feet and run. She stood up abruptly, causing both men to rise rapidly also. 'Please, don't.' She gestured for them to sit. 'I think I will go for my ride now.' She was at the door before Starling could collect himself to open it and there was an awkward shuffle as they both reached for the handle, then she was out and the door closed behind her.

In the long silence that followed Hebe watched Giles with such concentration that his eyes dropped from hers. He sat looking at the fallen sheets of paper in front of him, then got to his feet. 'Excuse me, Hebe.'

Left alone in the dining room with only the discreet figure of Starling moving chafing-dishes on the sideboard, Alex said with an air of sudden discovery, 'Hebe, are Giles and Joanna…?'

'Yes,' she said tightly. 'The trouble is, I don't think they both know it yet.' She broke off, an arrested expression on her face. 'Oh! Oh, Alex, I do believe the baby has started.'

At which point the question of his friends' relationships suddenly ceased to interest Lord Tasborough in the slightest.

Joanna arrived somewhat precipitously in the stableyard to find Hickling in earnest discussion with an undergroom who was just tightening the girths on Moonstone's saddle. She set her hat rather more firmly on her head and pushed in the pins.

'Miss Joanna, Robbins says you sent to have the grey saddled this morning.'

'Yes, Hickling. Is there a problem? She isn't lame, is she?'

'No, miss, nothing like that. It s just that the Colonel ordered her rested and to have extra oats because of the long journey when you arrived here.'

'Yes?'

'Well, miss, now she's as fresh as paint and ready to jump out of her skin, I don't know as how you really ought to be riding her, miss. Perhaps I ought to send one of the lads out on her today, shake some of the mischief out.'

'Nonsense, I can manage her,' Joanna said, walking firmly up to the mare and pulling on her gloves. 'I am only going to ride in the paddock.'

She gathered up the reins and stood waiting for Hickling to give her a leg up. 'Thank you.'

Giles arrived in the yard just as she was hooking her right knee over the pommel and flicking her skirts into order. Apparently he had come straight from the breakfast table for he was hatless and appeared to have been running. Joanna pulled down her veil and made a business out of gathering her reins.

'Hickling, is that mare fit to be ridden?'

'Fit? Yes, Colonel. I was just saying to Miss Joanna, she's jumping out of her skin after all that rest and oats.'

'Jo…Miss Fulgrave, I think you had better dismount. Perhaps we can find another horse for you this morning.'

'You think I am an incompetent rider?'

'You know I do not, but Moonstone…'

'But Moonstone is about to become a birthday— or is it a bride-gift—is she not? Surely you would not deny me one last ride on her, Colonel?'

'I am not giving Moonstone to Suzanne, if that is what you mean.'

'No? Then you will have no objection to me riding her, will you?'

'Joanna…'

But as she spoke Joanna dug her heel into Moonstone's side. The mare needed no encouragement. From a standing start she was cantering as they reached the stableyard arch. Joanna took her under it in a sweeping turn towards the front drive and disappeared.

'She said she was going to ride in the paddock, Colonel,' Hickling said, 'I'd never have got her mounted if I'd known.'

'She was going to, until I interfered,' Giles responded grimly. 'What have you got in the stables? I don't want to waste time having something fetched up from the paddocks.'

'Just Black Cat, sir. I'll get him saddled up.'

Hickling ran for the box and dragged back the bolts. Giles joined him inside, pulling the saddle off its tree as Hickling reached down the bridle. An intelligent Roman-nosed head swung round to regard them with mild interest.

'Damn it, he's big!'

'Up to your weight, Colonel. He'll go all day,

agile as the cat he's called for over wall and ditch, but he's got no great turn of speed. Long stride, though. Coom up, Cat!'

Thus encouraged, the big horse allowed himself to be led out into the yard where he stood placidly while Giles swung himself up into the saddle. He broke into a steady canter as they left the yard, but to Giles's grim amusement his ear flicked back as though in amazement as he was asked to gallop. 'Come on, Cat,' he encouraged him. 'We've got a little grey mouse for you to catch.'

Luckily the fine weather had given way to showers during the night and had softened the ground just enough for the marks of Moonstone's passing to be visible. Giles checked as three long rides split off from the carriage drive. Each headed deep into the dense beech woods, but only one showed the cut turf left by elegant sharp hooves. Cat wheeled neatly and followed Giles's guiding hand down the left-hand ride, the one which followed the very scarp edge of the Chilterns before they plunged down into the Vale below.

As she rode Joanna caught glimpses through the trees of the fields and hedges, the curls of smoke over the villages, but her attention was far too concentrated on Moonstone to admire the view. The mare was proving just as much a handful as Hickling had warned and Joanna was aware that she was riding at the very limit of her skill and strength.

Not that there was any spite in the mare, but she had been bored standing in a strange paddock and the sensation of a familiar rider and wide open rides stretching before her was too much to resist. Joanna sensed that if she was allowed her head she would calm down of her own accord after a mile or two and there was no point in indulging in a fight.

The concentration needed to keep balanced and maintain at least the illusion of control helped blot out the memory of Giles's face as he read Lady Suzanne's letter, but try as she might Joanna could not stop the words *announcement...very soon* repeating themselves over and over again to the rhythm of the hoofbeats.

Then Moonstone burst out of the ride into a small clearing where four ways met and straight into a herd of fallow deer that had been grazing on the clipped turf. The hinds bounded away but the stag, his spread of antlers broad and menacing, stood his ground, head lowered.

Moonstone stopped so abruptly that Joanna

almost went over her head. Somehow she scrambled back into the saddle, groped for the reins and thrust her foot back into the wildly swinging stirrup. The mare tossed her head, allowing Joanna to grab a handful of mane and rein, then took off down a ride at a flat-out gallop.

Joanna had never ridden so fast. Hauling on the reins did nothing to stop the panicked animal and only threatened to unseat her. At this speed a fall could be fatal. She gave up and clung to mane and pommel and prepared to hold on until Moonstone calmed down.

Behind her Giles was making ground, for although Black Cat had no great turn of speed his stride was immense and his steady canter ate up the distance. Then they reached the clearing and Giles reined in hard at the sight of the welter of hoofprints dug deep into the ground. For a moment he circled, his face set, then leaning over he tore a hazel switch from a bush and applied it to the black horse's flank. 'Come *on*, Cat, gallop!'

With an indignant snort the big animal gathered his hindquarters under him and took off. Giles's mouth twitched in a humourless smile. Now he had her.

The chase took longer than he imagined. By the

time he caught a glimpse of dappled grey hind-quarters ahead of him, the Cat's neck was flecked with foam. Joanna and her mount had reached a point where the ride curved in to skirt the edge of a deep dell. At some time long ago the farmers far below had hauled chalk from it for their heavy clay soils, now it was simply a deep depression lined with years of fallen beech leaves, crisp and tan in the sunshine.

Joanna had regained the reins as Moonstone slowed and had begun to pull on them, talking to the mare as she did so, 'Come on, girl, steady, steady now, that's enough.' Moonstone slowed, halted, then, hearing the hoofbeats behind her, put back her ears and reared. They were on the edge of the dell. Under her hooves the chalky soil crumbled. The mare slipped, recovered, twisted and Joanna went over her shoulder, tumbling head over heels through the thick leaf mould to the bottom as Moonstone bolted into the depths of the wood.

Black Cat was coming on so fast that he reached the point where Moonstone had reared before Giles could pull him up. Despite his legendary nimble-ness the big horse stumbled, pecked and stopped with a suddenness that jolted Giles in the saddle.

Joanna looked up from where she lay flat on her back in a deep mattress of leaves and saw the plunging animal and then Giles swinging down from its back. 'I am all right!' she called. 'Just give me a moment to get my breath, there's no need…'

But Giles was already over the side of the dell and half-sliding, half-jumping down towards her. He reached a shelf in the slope where grass grew thick and checked the slope for a moment, then stepped forward again.

The sound—a crack, then a thud—was so strange that it made no sense to Joanna. Then with a gasp that she realised with horror was a choked-off cry, Giles fell sideways on to the ledge, clutching at his leg.

She got to her feet, scrambling frantically up the slope, clawing at roots and scrubby branches until she reached the ledge. 'Giles?'

He was lying awkwardly and for a long moment Joanna could not understand what was wrong. Then she saw the cruel iron jaws clamped around his right calf and realised that he had stepped on a mantrap.

'Giles!' She fell on her knees beside him, ineffectually trying to find a point where she could grip the trap to pull it apart, but it bit tight into the leather of his boot cutting deep into the flesh beneath and the gap either side of his leg was too close to the hinges for her to be able to exert any leverage.

Joanna stopped her frantic, futile efforts. Her gloves were torn and stained red with blood and rust. She wrenched her gaze from them and forced herself to look at Giles. He was white, his mouth a tight line and his eyes dark. How he was conscious Joanna had no idea: the sight of his leg was enough to make her feel sick and dizzy; she could not begin to imagine the pain.

'I will go for help,' she said as steadily as she could manage with tears trickling down the inside of her nose. *I will not cry, I will not!* 'Moonstone has bolted, but your horse is still here.'

Giles focussed his eyes on her with an effort. The first stunning blow as the jagged teeth closed around his leg had been replaced by a burning agony that seemed to fill his consciousness. He could not tell whether any bones were broken, all he was aware of was a sensation as though something was gnawing the flesh from them.

The image of Joanna blurred and then cleared. She was sheet white, her eyes filled with tears, but there was a fierce determination about her from the set of her jaw to her clenched, stained fists.

'Black Cat,' he managed to say. 'He's steady, he'll know his way home.' He saw her look at his leg and wondered with a strange sense of detachment if he was going to lose it. 'Is it bleeding much?'

'Oozing,' Joanna replied, bending over to look closely. Her hat had come off in her fall and her hair was loose. He half-lifted a hand to touch it, then let it fall back again. 'I think the trap is so tight around it that it is stopping much blood.'

And stopping much blood going to his lower leg and foot, Giles realised grimly. 'Do not try and hurry,' he said as she got to her feet. 'Get there safely. Alex will know what is needed.'

'I cannot believe he would be so barbarous as to allow these things,' she said, her voice shaking with anger.

'Not his land,' Giles managed to grind out. He was damned if he was going to pass out in front of her.

Joanna turned to clamber up the slope, stopped, turned back suddenly and stooped to drop a kiss on his forehead. 'Lie still, I will be as quick as I can.' Then she was gone. He could hear her scrambling progress, then, 'Here boy, here, Black Cat.' Silence. A gasp. 'Oh…oh…hell!'

Giles twisted awkwardly in an attempt to see up the slope behind him, failed and fell back sweating. There was the sound of someone slipping and sliding down again and Joanna re-appeared in front of him, a saddle over her arm.

'He is dead lame,' she said furiously, falling to her knees and turning the saddle over.

Giles felt a flicker of amusement run through him. 'Your language, Miss Fulgrave!' he murmured.

'Do not joke,' she retorted. 'I can't…can't…just don't, that's all.' She broke off and swallowed. 'I thought that if I could get the saddle under your thigh and knee it would support it and take some of the strain off the muscles.'

Giles watched her from between eyelids that felt dangerously close to closing. She was so shocked and frightened, yet so determined to cope that her own weaknesses were making her furious.

She got the saddle into position and began to slip it underneath, breaking off to take his thigh between both hands in an attempt to straighten the angle. He bit back a gasp of pain and saw her anguished face as she glanced at him, then she set her lips tight and carried on. The relief as the padded lining of the saddle took the strain from his leg was so immense that it almost undid his resolve to stay quiet and stay conscious.

'I am sorry I hurt you,' she said stiffly and he

realised with a twist of his heart that tears were running unchecked down her cheeks now. 'But I think it will help.'

'So much courage,' he whispered but she did not react and he realised that his voice was so quiet she had not heard him.

'Right, now then, I will start.' Joanna said with brisk determination. 'It will take longer, of course, on foot, but I will go as fast as I can.'

She scrambled to her feet again and Giles saw with a pang that she was scrubbing the tears from her face with the back of her hand like a tired child.

'No.' His voice sounded oddly remote and he cleared his throat and concentrated on making her attend to him.

'What did you say?'

'I said no. You are not travelling through these woods alone on foot.'

'Giles, I cannot just sit here and do nothing! It is broad daylight, I am unhurt and it is all my fault that you are—' Her voice cracked and she stumbled to a halt.

'You do not win battles by sitting around apportioning blame,' Giles snapped. He hated speaking to her like that, but her chin came up again and he saw she was listening to him. 'You lost your temper and I...I realised I hadn't been looking beyond the end of my nose,' he finished. Joanna looked mystified, but he knew what he meant and he was not about to explain it now.

'Well, I am going anyway,' she retorted defiantly, turning on her heel.

'Stop!' It was the voice he used in the heat of battle to reach troops around him and it halted her in her tracks. 'I *order* you to come back here.'

Their eyes met: implacable pain-filled grey clashed with tear-soaked, anguished hazel. Giles put every ounce of authority he possessed into that look, knowing that he had no hold over her whatsoever beyond that which she chose to let him have. Their eyes clung for a long minute, then,

'Yes, Giles,' Joanna said, and came back to sit beside him.

Chapter Nineteen

Joanna sank down beside Giles, feeling as though she had fought a battle, and in some obscure way had managed to both win and lose it. Her every instinct screamed at her to go for help, but the part of her she had tried to train to be the perfect wife for a soldier told her that this was a dangerous situation and that Giles knew what to do far better than she.

The struggle of wills seemed to have exhausted him and he lay back awkwardly, his eyes closed. Joanna wriggled round until she could take his head and shoulders into her lap and cradle them in the deep folds of her habit.

Giles's eyes opened with a hint of his wicked twinkle in their depths. 'Now that is nice,' he remarked.

'Giles, is there anything I can do?' she asked, trying to sound practical and down to earth. The last thing he needed to be coping with was a watering pot of a female.

'No. Hickling saw us leave and he will be on the watch for us returning. If Moonstone gets back to the stables he will be alerted at once, if not, I am sure he will go to Alex by midday.'

'How will they find us?'

'The ground is soft—I was able to track you easily. Given the size of Cat's feet, they will have no trouble following us.' He was speaking calmly to her and she recognised that he was deliberately pitching his tone to reassure her. How many frightened young subalterns had he spoken to in just such tones before now?

He moved slightly and Joanna felt the shock of pain that went through his body. Her hands tightened on his shoulders and she bent over him, desperate to do something, anything to stop this torture. Watching his pain, his efforts not to show it, was an agony in itself and one she suddenly felt she could not bear. Then the vein of reality and self-knowledge that ran deep through her came to her aid. *If he can bear it, and he has no choice, then I can certainly bear it*, she told herself grimly.

'Talk to me,' he said, eyes closed.

'Of course. What about?'

'Tell me about this man you love so much that losing him has left you with nowhere to go, no direction to take.'

Joanna hesitated, her heart thudding. The need to talk, to confide, was an almost physical thing. Yet how could she do so to the very man concerned? 'I will not tell you his name,' she said at last.

'Very well.' Giles's eyes were shut. She could sense through every quivering nerve in her body responding to his that he was husbanding his energy to withstand what was happening.

'I…met him when I was…before I came out. I fell in love with him almost at once.'

'Why?'

The stark question took her aback. Why did she love Giles? Had she ever thought about it, analysed it?

'Because he has the power to inspire devotion,' she managed at last.

'Hmm.' Giles murmured. 'I distrust that.'

'What? An officer distrust leadership?'

'Ah, now that is different. You do not have to inspire devotion in order to lead. Sometimes you have to be hated, but they must still follow you.'

Joanna pondered this. Was what she felt for Giles devotion, or a response to a natural power to lead? Just now she had subdued every instinct in order to obey him. No, she had done as he had asked—as he had commanded—because deep down she trusted him.

'Trust then,' she amended. 'He inspires trust.'

'Very well, I will accept trustworthiness. But was that all?'

'He is very good looking, very…male,' she confessed, blushing.

'So, what then?'

'I knew he would not think twice about me,' she said ruefully. 'I was a harum-scarum schoolroom miss. But I knew what I had to do if I was to be the perfect wife for him. I applied myself to every lesson in manners and deportment, I practised my languages, I studied to please anyone of any rank and influence. I read everything I could about…about his profession.' She paused to pull a handkerchief from her pocket and gently wiped the sweat from his forehead.

'He was destined for very great things, all I could do was to make sure I was as fitted as possible to support him.'

Giles stiffened in her arms. 'Listen!'

Joanna strained her ears to catch the distant sounds. 'Deer, perhaps, not horses, I think.'

'Go on.'

'I was such an innocent fool,' Joanna said abruptly. 'He was gone for thr…years. Every day I studied the announcements and felt myself safe because there was no notice of his engagement. It never occurred to me that he was living his own life, finding his own love.'

'When *did* you realise it?' Giles was sounding increasingly distant. Joanna willed him to give up and to slip into merciful unconsciousness until rescue came.

'I realised when I saw him with the woman he loves at the Duchess of Bridlington's ball. I did not face up to just what an idiot I had been all that time until after I had run away and had time to think about it.'

'Tell me about the ball…what…?' Joanna felt Giles's tense body relax into her arms and let out a deep, answering, sigh of relief. He had gone at last. But now she had begun to talk it was difficult to stop. Anxiously she studied his unconscious face. The traces of pain still marked it, a thin line of blood at the corner of his mouth marked where his teeth had closed in agony on his lip. But his breathing was deep and regular and the strong torso in her arms had the weight of oblivion.

Reassured she continued speaking as though by telling herself the story she could staunch the wounds that evening had left.

'I went to the Duchess's ball, even though I was in disgrace with Mama and Papa for not receiving Lord Clifton. I had no expectation of seeing… seeing *him* there: after all, I had looked for him night after night, day after day for three years.

'But he *was* there, like some wonderful, in-evitable miracle and I started to make my way up the ballroom to meet him. It was going to be perfect, I knew it. Then he went into a retiring room. I never even thought to wonder why, I simply followed him and there she was in his arms, that beautiful, eligible young lady. And he was telling her he was going to speak to her father, telling her she was his first and only love. I saw his face: I could not doubt him. His eyes betrayed just what he felt.'

Joanna was hardly aware she was speaking aloud. Her arms cradled Giles, rocking his body against herself in a gesture as old as time. 'I got away somehow, and then you came and looked after me. Nothing mattered after that. What was I to do? Not marry some man I detested, that was all I was certain of. I had to get away, and you know the rest.'

The soft sigh of his breathing was all the answer she received. Joanna bent her head silently to study every line of Giles's face and set herself to wait.

How much later it was before she heard the sounds of hooves approaching, then the blessed sound of voices raised and calling, Joanna had no idea. The sun had moved almost overhead, her mouth was dry and her stomach grumbled at her.

'Giles! Giles, they are here!' She shook him gently by the shoulder, then raised her voice and shouted, 'Here! Help! Help, down here!'

It seemed like dozens of men who came crashing down the slope as she arched protectively over Giles's body. Then it resolved itself into Alex, his face like thunder, Hickling and three grooms.

Alex fell to his knees beside Giles, his eyes appalled as they took in the bloodied and mangled leg and the cruel trap around it. He reached out one hand and pressed his friend's shoulder, then snapped at Joanna, 'Get away from here.'

'No! Why…?' She was hauled to her feet and dragged to one side, still protesting. 'Giles needs…'

'Giles would not be in this state if it were not for you.' Alex's face was drawn and furious. 'When we release the pressure of those jaws the pain is going to be infinitely worse than it is now as the blood begins to flow again. He is going to want to swear or throw up or faint—or all three— and he does not need to have you hovering around clucking and making him feel he cannot do any of those things in front of a lady.

'Now get out of here and find Peter. He'll take you up and you can ride with him back to the Hall. Tell the doctor what has happened and get Giles's room ready.'

'The doctor? The doctor is at Tasborough?' Joanna pushed Alex's angry, hurtful words to the back of her mind and clutched at the one thing that mattered.

'Hebe went into labour after breakfast,' Alex said grimly.

'She is all right?'

'How the hell would I know? The last person they tell is the father. It all seems to be taking a damn long time.'

No wonder he was so angry with her! Joanna

reached out and gave Alex a swift, hard hug. 'She will be fine, Alex. Now, look after Giles. I will go and do just as you say.'

Resolutely she pushed the thought of what was happening in the dell out of her mind and ran to the ride where one of the undergrooms was waiting with a farm cart and three horses. Black Cat, his off-hind cocked up, was standing dolefully, nose to nose with one of his stablemates.

'Peter? His lordship said that you are to take me up and we are to return to the hall to alert the doctor. The Colonel has been hurt.'

The ride back, clinging to Peter's rough jacket, was little more than a lurching blur. As they reached the steps Joanna slid from the horse and ran for the front door which opened as she reached it.

'Miss Joanna! What has happened?' It was Starling, shaken right out of his usual imperturbability.

The ride back had given her enough time to order her story and what she must do. 'The Colonel has been caught by a mantrap and his leg is badly injured. His lordship is bringing him back in the wagon. We must tell the doctor and make the Colonel's room ready.' She was already running up the stairs towards Hebe's chamber. 'We will need hot water and bandages,' she tossed back over her shoulder.

She got no further than the dressing room before being firmly turned away by the housekeeper. 'You cannot go in there, Miss Joanna!' she said, scandalised.

'I do not want to,' Joanna managed to pant out. 'I need the doctor for Colonel Gregory. How is her ladyship?'

'As well as might be expected, considering, miss.'

Considering what? No wonder Alex was getting so agitated! 'May I speak to the doctor?'

Eventually that harassed gentleman put his head round the door long enough to listen to Joanna's tale. 'Hmm. Let me know when the Colonel arrives: it will definitely need seeing to at once and nothing is moving at any speed here, that is for sure.'

Joanna retreated to hover at the head of the stairs, giving orders to a distracted butler and harassing the maids who she sent scurrying for bandages, basilicum powder and extra pillows. At the sound of the arriving wagon she hastened for the doctor, only to find herself put very firmly outside the door as Giles was carried in on a hurdle.

Starling appeared with a sandwich and a glass of wine, which he insisted she ate. It tasted of straw, but she sensed that looking after her was all that Starling was able to do at the moment and so she ate it to please him.

It seemed an age before the doctor reappeared, wiping his hands on a towel. After a sharp look at her white face he took pity on her and stopped long enough for a rapid bulletin. 'He won't lose the leg and nothing's broken. But the muscle is severely crushed and bruised: he'll be in a lot of pain for some days and then will need careful exercise to get the strength back in it.'

He strode off to his other patient, leaving Joanna leaning against the panelling too relieved even to cry. Eventually she pulled herself together sufficiently to open the bedchamber door and look in.

Giles was alone in the room, stretched out on the big bed under a single sheet. He looked alarmingly still, but as Joanna tiptoed forward he opened his eyes and smiled at her. She smiled back, opened her mouth to speak, then found her throat was too tight.

'Stay with me?' He turned his head on the pillow and glanced towards the armchair standing beside the empty grate. Joanna went to pull it over to the bedside, but when she had it in position and looked back to the bed he was asleep again.

It was a big old leather-covered chair, deep and sagging comfortably. Joanna curled up in its depths and settled down to watch Giles. At first she was inclined to be anxious that he slept so deeply, then she recognised it for what it was: the utterly relaxed reaction of a strong, fit man whose body knew what it had to do to heal itself.

She closed her eyes, and against the lids saw again his warm, sleepy smile as she had entered the room. *Stay with me.* That spoke volumes for his trust in her that he should want her with him while he was vulnerable, unconscious. They had become very close over these past days: perhaps these few hours alone with him were all that were left to her of that intimacy before the demands of marriage and Lady Suzanne and his family took him away from her.

Joanna opened her eyes and simply sat looking at him, letting her gaze rove slowly over the long form outlined by the thin sheet, the breadth of his shoulders, bare where the linen folded down, the stubble golden on his skin, the fading scar on his forehead.

She catalogued each characteristic in her

memory to last forever. The fact that his hair needed cutting and that where it was overlong at his nape it was beginning to curl. The sweep of his eyelashes, darker than his hair, ridiculously long for such a masculine man. The precise, complex, curl of his ear. The way his neck was strapped with muscle, the firm line of his jaw, determined even in sleep.

And his mouth. Expressive, flexible lips that she knew could firm into anger, part in uninhibited laughter, soften, then harden into a demanding, thrilling kiss. Her fingers curled and flexed with her longing to touch his mouth, to trace the sculpted upper line, the fuller, sensual lower swell.

Time passed and Joanna did not move as the clock in the hall below struck the hour. When it struck again Giles opened his eyes and looked directly into hers. Time stood still as grey met hazel gaze and locked in wordless communication in a language that she did not have the key to.

Then Giles moved slightly and caught his breath at the pain in his leg and the moment shattered.

'Damn it,' he muttered, raising himself on his elbows in an effort to sit up. Joanna jumped to her feet and shook the pillows behind him into a pile to support him, stepping back sharply to avoid touching him as he managed to draw himself up the bed and lay back.

'How does it feel?' What a stupid question!

'Sore,' Giles admitted in what she felt must be a massive understatement. He saw her face and grinned at her expression. 'Truly, not that bad, I've had far worse, and far worse conditions to recover in, let me tell you.'

Joanna, reassured, stopped hovering at the bedside and resumed her seat. 'That wound in your side?'

'Hmm? I had forgotten you had seen that. Yes, they picked me up, tied my sash round it tightly, slung me over an army mule and carted me back to camp like a sack of potatoes. I then spent two weeks in a flea-infested barn. And no beautiful nurse, only my batman, whose ideas of medical care were, to put it mildly, rough and ready.'

Beautiful. Joanna hugged the word to herself and asked, 'Is there anything you need? Something to drink?'

'Yes, please.' He ran his tongue over his lips. 'Would you ring for a footman?'

'I can get what you need.'

Giles cocked an eyebrow. 'I think I would prefer a footman.'

Joanna opened her mouth to protest, then realised that there might indeed be reasons why he would prefer to be attended by a footman. 'Oh, yes, of course. I'll send someone up.'

Starling was pacing distractedly in the hall. Joanna felt a pang of sympathy: he was probably unconsciously echoing the Earl's own restlessness on the floor above.

'Could you send a footman to the Colonel, please, Starling? He has woken up and says he is feeling much better.'

Starling hurried off and Joanna was about to go upstairs to see if Alex had any news when she glimpsed the fine array of walking canes in the hall stand. She selected one which looked long enough for Giles and went to find Alex.

To her relief he was at least sitting down and demolishing a pile of sandwiches and a tankard of ale. He gestured Joanna to a chair and pushed the plate towards her.

'Is there anything to drink?'

In answer he poured ale into a spare tankard and Joanna cautiously tried it. To her surprise it was surprisingly good and she also found her appetite had returned. Goodness knows what Hebe would say if she saw her cousin sitting quaffing ale out of a tankard, elbows on table and ham sandwich in hand.

'Is there any news yet?'

'The doctor emerged about fifteen minutes ago, told me not to be such a damn fool and stop worrying and went back in again. How is Giles?'

'He's been sleeping and has woken up saying he feels better and asking for a footman. I'll go back in a while if there is nothing I can do here.'

Alex's mouth twisted into a rueful smile. 'Unmarried girls and husbands are apparently of no use whatsoever at a childbed, so I suggest you go back to Giles. I am sorry I shouted at you, Joanna. By the way, Moonstone is quite unharmed and Black Cat will be fine—Hickling sent to tell me a while back.'

'I do not blame you for being angry,' Joanna said. 'You must have hated to leave Hebe and to find Giles like that…'

They sat in companionable silence for a while, then Joanna went back to her room, washed and changed. The clock was just striking five as she tapped on the panels of Giles's chamber and heard him call, 'Come in.'

Chapter Twenty

Giles was sitting up in bed, looking so much better that she could hardly believe it. Her surprise must have shown on her face for he remarked, 'Shave, wash, clean shirt, ale and a sandwich.'

'Me, too—all except the shave, of course.'

'Ale?'

'I know, Hebe would be shocked. I have been keeping Alex company for a while. I think everything is all right, he is just finding the waiting, and the fact that no one will tell him anything, very trying.' She recalled the walking stick and held it up. 'See what I found for you.'

'Thank you! Do not tell me this means you are not going to cluck over me?'

'Of course,' Joanna said briskly. 'If you were William I would be clucking like a flock of hens, but you are far too old to need that. Besides, you have been wounded enough to know exactly what rest you need and when you should exercise.'

Giles regarded her, a quizzical look in his eyes. 'Tell me, this man you love…'

'Yes?' Joanna felt instantly defensive. Now what was he going to ask her?

'Would you do whatever he told you to?'

'Yes…no. No, I would not, only if I agreed with him.'

'Good. Would you mind locking the door?'

Joanna looked at him, realised that her mouth had dropped unbecomingly open and shut it with a snap. To be in a man's bedroom was shocking enough, though probably even her mama would approve of her being with Giles in view of his injury. But a locked door was enough to compromise her utterly.

She turned the key. 'Why?'

'Because I need to talk to you and I do not want to be interrupted. You locked it before asking why.'

Joanna ignored that observation and went towards her chair.

'Would you mind moving this pillow for me?' It seemed perfectly well positioned to her, but she went to do as he asked, was caught neatly round the waist and swung on to the bed beside him.

'Giles!' She wriggled but found herself firmly held.

'I want to talk to you, and I do not want you to interrupt…'

'I do not interrupt!'

'…interrupt me. Now, sit there where I can see you and I will tell you the story of *my* evening at the Duchess of Bridlington's ball in return for your tale this morning.'

'The Duchess's…' *No! He couldn't have heard what she'd said in the woods, he was asleep, unconscious…*

'Shh.' Giles placed one finger fleetingly on her lips. 'No interruptions, remember?

'I had hardly been back in London two days, but I met the Duchess in Piccadilly and she invited me. So I went: it was as good a way of taking my mind off what I knew was going to be a difficult interview with my father as any other.

'I was not expecting to see her, but before I knew it Suzy had lured me into a retiring room and was wheedling me into teaching her to drive.'

'To drive?'

Giles's finger pressed on her lips again and this time lingered for a moment. 'To drive—which her father was adamantly opposed to because a female relative had been injured in a carriage accident. However, as Suzy knows only too well, she has been able to wind me round her little finger since I was ten years old. Like a fool I agreed to ask the Marquis and, of course, the little madam was instantly immensely grateful—as only Suzy can be.

'So there I am, faced with the unenviable task of persuading her father to let me teach her to drive. I only agreed because if I hadn't she would have prevailed on someone else to teach her and at least her parents trust me to keep her out of trouble.'

Complete confusion was blurring every certainty in Joanna's mind. He was speaking of Lady Suzanne with deep affection, but in the most un-loverlike terms. He had known her since he was ten, her parents trusted him to keep her out of trouble…

'She…'

'Shh. At least the minx has good hands—you saw her in the Park. But as you may have gathered when we met at the masquerade, she also uses me to rescue her from the endless pranks she gets up to. She went to that romp with a quite ineligible party and made sure I got the message about where she was in sufficient time to come and remove her before things became too hot.'

Joanna ducked away from under his hand and demanded, 'But you love her!'

'Like a sister,' Giles agreed amiably. 'But I am most certainly not in love with her. I would as soon marry a cageful of monkeys and I have only the deepest sympathy for Lord Keswick. You will not repeat that yet, please, it will not be announced until the new Season.'

'But…'

'Anyway, as I said, no sooner had I arrived back in England than Suzy had embroiled me in her usual battle of wits with her father. Off she flits and I emerge from the retiring room to find you…'

Joanna twisted right away until she was crouched on the furthest side of the bed. 'You were not unconscious in the woods, you heard me and now you are saying that because I… Oh!' She buried her face in her hands, too humiliated to continue.

'Joanna.' She remained huddled, her face hidden. 'Joanna!' She looked up, white-faced, and saw Giles was regarding her patiently. 'Did you believe I was asleep?'

'Of course I did! Do you think I would have said what I did otherwise?'

'Exactly. I congratulate myself it was as good a bit of acting as the time I had to pretend to be dead while being prodded by a French bayonet. So, if I was in love with darling Suzy, there was not the slightest reason for me to tell you this, was there? I could just have tactfully removed myself.'

'Even so, I have embarrassed both myself and you.' Joanna forced herself to speak calmly, although she could not meet his eyes. Somehow she had to get out of this room before the floor opened up and swallowed her. 'I am sorry, I will go away now and go back to Mama and Papa tomorrow.'

'You know very well that you cannot run away from me, Joanna. I have captured you before, I will have no difficulty doing so again.'

'Why do you want to humiliate me like this?' she whispered, swallowing back the tears.

'Joanna, darling, come back over here.'

'No. And do not call me that. Just because you feel sorry for me because I have made a complete fool of myself, there is no need to patronise me.'

'Joanna, at least look at me.'

Reluctantly her head came up and she met his eyes. He was regarding her ruefully. 'I am making a compete mull of this. Joanna, *I love you*. I thought you were in love with someone else: so in love that you would defy your family, risk ruin rather than compromise that love. How could I even admit to myself how I was beginning to feel about you?'

'You love me?' she whispered. This was not real, it must be some dream, some hallucination. Perhaps she had struck her head when she fell and had not realised. 'How? When?'

'I think, looking back, from the moment I came out of that room and you looked up at me with huge, pain-filled eyes. You were beautiful, brave and I wanted to hit the man who had made you feel like that.

'Then when I found you at the Thoroughgoods something should have told me. I have never felt such killing rage before; I knew I was not safe to be alone with them, I just did not realise why.' He regarded her, his face more calmly serious than she had ever seen it. 'I told myself it was simply what I would feel about any young woman trapped like that and I told myself that the way I found myself thinking about you, the effort it took not to touch you, kiss you—I told myself that was desire, impure, but simple.

'When I kissed you that evening after I had talked to you about life in camp, I should have known then but I kept denying it to myself. How could I fall in love with you when all you thought about was that man? God, but I wanted you. When you ran away from me and I caught you in that field it was all I could do not to take you there and then on the grass amidst those flowers, under the sun.'

'When did you realise?' Joanna could not make herself believe this was happening.

'When I found that lout Clifton mauling you. I held you afterwards and you fitted—not just fitted into my arms and against my body, you fitted my heart and my soul. I told myself it was hopeless, but something, some instinct gave me hope. I do not know what.'

'Perhaps the shameless way I kissed you, the way I clung to you,' Joanna said shakily. Feeling was beginning to come back to her limbs, she was conscious of breathing again. This was not a dream. Giles was saying these things to her. *He loved her.*

'I thought you were lonely, that you were innocent and curious and trusted me. I hated that. I would have rather you thought of me as dangerous than as safe.' He laughed harshly. 'Male pride. Then I got that letter from Suzy this morning. I was a fool, I had no idea that I was hurting you, I was just so relieved that everything had been agreed about her marriage, for there is some history between the two families and for a while it looked as though it might not happen.

'Then you swept out of the room and Hebe was looking at me as though I had just sworn at you and suddenly I realised what she had seen. *I* was the one you loved and you thought I loved Suzy. Such a coil and such an easy one to resolve, I thought—until I saw your hurt and anger.'

He lay back against the pillows, his grey eyes steady on hers, waiting for her to speak. Joanna drew a long shaking breath and stared back, reading his soul in his eyes, reading the truth. Against all the odds, despite her foolish, romantic, unrealistic dreams, the lengths she had gone to to try his patience, Giles loved her.

Carefully avoiding his injured leg Joanna returned to kneel beside him and reached out her hand. Her fingertips grazed down the side of his face and he turned into the caress until his cheek lay against her palm. 'I love you,' he murmured against the delicate skin.

'Oh, Giles!' Joanna hesitated no longer. Somehow she was in his arms, cradled across his knees and his mouth was hard on hers, possessive, demanding, rough with an urgency she returned as she curved her arm around his neck and kissed him back.

They fell apart breathless, laughing with relief. 'Oh, Giles, what will the General say? He wanted you to marry the daughter of a marquis.'

'He wanted me to be a Field Marshall as well. He won't ever have that, but he is going to have a daughter-in-law he and my mother will adore. And what about your parents? They wanted you to marry an earl.'

'They already know and love you—and from what Hebe tells me she wrote to them, they will be so thankful you saved me from him they will fall upon your neck.'

They sat there handfast, too overwhelmed to even want to kiss for the moment. Then Giles said, 'They are going to want a big wedding, you know. After all the risk of scandal with you running away, they are going to expect banns and weeks of planning. There will be hoards of guests, a magnificent wedding breakfast… I will not see you for weeks because you will be buying your wedding clothes—' He broke off to caress her face. 'I am going to miss you so much. Still, it will give me time to sort out where we are going to live.'

Before she thought Joanna said, 'I do not want to wait,' then blushed crimson.

'We have waited a few weeks, sweetheart, a few more...'

'You might have waited a few weeks, Giles Gregory—I have been waiting for you for three years.'

A wicked sparkle came into his eyes. 'You want to make love?'

Joanna tried to drop her gaze, found she could not and admitted bluntly, 'Yes. Giles, I am sorry if that makes me sound wanton and shocks you, but I thought I had lost you for ever and it has been torture being so close to you every day and when we touch—' She broke off in confusion, only to be caught hard against his chest.

'Are you sure?' he said harshly.

'Yes. I want to be yours. I do not want to wait for weeks and have Mama explaining things to me the night before. I do not want to worry that I will not be perfect on our wedding night.'

Giles laughed, a suppressed chuckle against her hair. 'I rather think you are going to have to endure the pre-wedding talk from your mama, unless you want to explain it is rather late.' He tipped her head back and looked down at her.

'Nothing would give me more pleasure than to make love to you now, my darling. I cannot help feeling this is all a dream and I need to have you in my arms to make it real. But only if you are quite sure.'

He sounded very calm, very controlled, very reassuring. Then Joanna saw the banked fires burning in his eyes, felt the tension in his body and knew he was far from calm and the control was achieved only by exerting his will to the utmost.

'Make it real, Giles,' she murmured, letting her fingers tangle in his hair, pulling him down towards her. He shifted to hold her more easily and she felt rather than saw the stab of pain that ran through him. 'Oh, your leg, I am so sorry, I had forgotten.'

'To hell with my leg,' he said. His lips were nuzzling down the sensitive line of her neck until they found the edge of her dress where it touched her collarbone. His hands came up and searched for the fastening even as his mouth continued to explore the area where lace and skin met. Joanna wriggled round to let his questing fingers find the buttons then, overcome by shyness, hid her face against his neck as he slid the bodice from her shoulders. Somehow the dress was off before she realised it, leaving her clad only in her thin summer cambric shift and petticoat and her silk stockings.

She was still curled on his lap and his fingers seemed to find their way to her garters and be rolling down her stockings before she could have time to wriggle away. He rolled each one down, taking his time, letting his fingers linger on the soft skin behind each knee, the sharp point of her ankle bones, the arch of her foot. As he pulled off the second stocking he tickled her instep, making her giggle despite her tension.

'Giles! That tickles,' she protested, trying to evade his fingers and was silenced with a kiss.

'Making love can be fun, you know,' he remarked. He released her lips and bent his head to wrestle with a bow fastening her chemise, which had pulled tight.

'Fun?' Joanna was feeling so taut with nerves and desire that it was difficult to speak.

'It isn't all high passion and intense, serious pleasure.' He moved on to another bow without Joanna realising that the chemise was slipping from her shoulders. 'Can you remember that meadow where I found you after you had run away from Lady Brandon's?' She nodded, intent on his words, on watching his face. 'Can you imagine making love naked in that long grass, tickled by those flowers, seeing just where buttercups would reflect gold on each other's body? Then bathing in that shallow stream afterwards, splashing in cold, clean water?'

'Oh, yes! I see what you mean about fun: Giles, can we find a meadow and…oh!' She fell silent, blushing as the chemise slipped off, leaving her breasts bared. Her hands went up to shield herself and were caught in one of Giles's, held while he bent his head and kissed the tip of one nipple. The sensation seemed to flow through her body from the gentle touch of his lips, down to become a unfamiliar ache low in her belly.

She closed her eyes as his lips were replaced with his tongue tip, then a gentle teasing nibble that made her gasp and arch against him. Giles bent her backwards to lie beside him and began to stroke the fullness of her other breast as his mouth continued to play havoc with the first.

Joanna shifted restlessly, her feet tangled in petticoats and the sheet, trying with what rational thought was left to her to recall which of Giles's legs was injured so she did not knock against it.

'This is like trying to make love in a laundry basket,' Giles remarked, his mouth still against her breast. He raised his head and smiled wickedly at her and she found she could breathe again. This was not at all how she imagined losing her virginity. Grace's careful description of the process had sounded embarrassing, alarming and downright painful— 'But no worse than having a tooth pulled, and it is never as bad as that again.' It had definitely seemed to be something that should be got over with and then one could hope for some pleasure from the marriage bed. But Giles's love-making was leisurely and, while startling in the effects it was producing, certainly not alarming.

She smiled back at him, suddenly realising that she was no longer embarrassed and that he was right, this was *fun. So far*, a cautious inner voice warned her.

'I think we are getting rather tangled up,' she observed. 'If we get rid of the sheet—'

'And all our clothes,' he finished for her, dragging his shirt over his head and tugging at the edge of the sheet. As he was under half of it and Joanna was on top of the other half, removing it involved her getting off the bed before she could turn back. The sight of Giles stretched out completely naked stopped her in her tracks, the colour mounting hectically into her cheeks.

She had seen him stripped to the waist in bed at the inn, had been held against his bare chest after he had hit Lord Clifton, she had been aware of his body as he had trapped her in the meadow. But the naked reality of a man in the throes of lovemaking was still a shock.

Giles lay there unselfconsciously while she swallowed hard and climbed back on to the bed. 'It is all right, you know. Everything is designed to work together.'

This insight into her thoughts made her blush more deeply. Giles caught her round the waist and pulled her down against him again and kissed her with such thoroughness that she stopped thinking again and simply clung to him, drinking in the scent of him, letting the heat of his mouth envelop her as his tongue teased hers and his teeth caught at the sensitive fullness of her underlip.

Somehow he had managed to undo the tapes at the waist of her petticoat and Joanna found herself as naked as he was. Her immediate instinct was to curl against his flank, hiding herself against him, but he stopped her, easing her back against the pillows and raising himself on his elbow to look down at her.

'You are so lovely.' He reached out a hand and

freed her hair from the pins that held it and it tumbled down, black against her white skin. Giles caught up one lock and used the ends to caress her breast, his eyes never leaving hers as he did so.

She saw his pupils widen as he watched her, knew hers were dilating too, feeling that if the subtle caress did not stop soon she must seize his hand and press it to the flesh that seemed to be becoming heavier, tauter with every whispering stroke of the fine hair over it.

He bent his head to recapture the nipple and with a gasp she closed her eyes, reaching blindly to caress his hair, hold him closer to her. His hand slid down her side, paused at the point where her hip curved, then ran over the gentle swell of her stomach. The warm palm spread and flattened over soft skin that seemed to quiver under the pressure.

Joanna moaned softly, her head moving restlessly on the pillow, her hands tangled in Giles's hair. His mouth on her breast was creating strange feelings deep inside her close to where his palm stroked across her stomach.

'Giles, I don't…I don't know what…'

'I know, sweetheart, I know. Just trust me.' His fingers slid lower into the triangle of black curls and she stiffened, her thighs tight together in instant rejection. Giles's mouth left her breast and she almost sobbed, convinced she had displeased him. Then his lips found hers again and he murmured, 'Shh, my darling, just relax, let me love you.'

His fingers moved down, parted her, slipped gently into secret, sensitive places that made her gasp against his mouth. Then the ball of his thumb found and caressed her in a way that stopped the breath in her throat. Without conscious thought her body arched to press against his hand. The amazing sensation went on, on, until she thought she could not bear it any longer, then his finger slipped into the moist centre of her and through her delirium she heard him whisper, 'Open your eyes, Joanna, look at me.'

Her lids fluttered open. Her eyes widened, found his tender, watchful gaze on her. 'I love you,' he said as everything gathered inside her into one imploding firework that burst through her veins and nerves, made her cry out with amazed joy, then fall trembling back against the pillows.

Giles caught her against him and held her until the trembling stopped. Gradually some sort of coherent thought came back and she found herself resting against his chest, hearing the re-assuring beat of his heart under her ear. 'Giles?'

'Yes, sweetheart?'

'That was…that was wonderful.'

'Good.' He sounded gently amused.

'But that wasn't…I mean, you didn't…'

'No, you are still a virgin. I just wanted to give you pleasure, that is all.'

'You succeeded,' she said shakily, wondering if she had the courage to lie back and look at him. 'But what about you? I mean, don't you want to…?'

'We do not have to take this to its conclusion Joanna, not unless you are sure. You can give me pleasure, just as I pleasured you. Look.'

Shyly she lifted her head from his chest and watched as he guided her hand on to him. For a moment she kept it still, then the heat and hardness under her fingers, the sensation of soft skin, fascinated her and she closed her grasp. 'Oh!' To find that she could provoke a reaction just by a touch was a revelation. Biting her lip in concentration, she tentatively moved her hand and was rewarded by a soft groan from Giles. She glanced up at him, saw he had closed his eyes and let her hand move again.

'Giles, am I doing this right?'

He caught her caressing hand in his and opened his eyes. 'You are doing it so right that I think you had better stop.' He hesitated, his eyes dark with passion. 'Joanna, do you still want to do this? Do you still want me to make love to you?'

'Please, Giles.' She slid her hands up across his chest, pausing to savour the unfamiliar feeling of his nipples hardening against her palms, then cradling his face between her hands. 'Please love me.' This time it was she who bent to kiss him, discovering the intriguing difference of being the one on top, of being able to vary pressure and contact. Greatly daring, she let her tongue flicker out to trace the line of his upper lip then caught his lower lip in sharp teeth, teasingly threatening to bite.

For a few seconds he let her lead, then with an easy strength rolled her over until his weight lay on her, his knee pushing hers gently but inexorably apart.

Joanna struggled against the desire to surrender utterly to the sensations flooding through her and managed to gasp, 'Your leg?'

'Just give me a moment,' Giles shifted his position, winced, then smiled down into her wide, anxious eyes. 'Provided you don't kick it we will be fine.'

She fitted against him so well, Joanna realised hazily, burying her face against his neck, feeling the reassuring strength of his shoulders under her hands, which were trembling with nerves. Lower, where she still tingled from the pleasures his fingers had wrought, she was overwhelmingly conscious of his aroused body and tried desperately not to think, simply to trust Giles and endure the next few minutes.

He nudged against her and she found with a shock that he had already entered her a little. It felt strange but good and she let herself relax. Then he stopped and she was aware of a tightness, a constriction, as though her own body was barring the way. Giles bent his head to whisper against her lips, 'Trust me, sweetheart', then he thrust into her. There was a fleeting sensation of pain, more of discomfort and tightness, then he was lodged deep within her and she realised that they were joined, that this was Giles whose body was cradled within hers and that her own body was opening around him, caressing him, holding him.

Her eyes fluttered open and she found his, a mixture of awe and anxiety in them. 'Giles.' Her voice was an unsteady whisper.

'Sweetheart, are you all right? Did I hurt you?'

'No, yes—just a little. Oh, Giles, I do love you.' Her body was telling her to move so she tried, tentatively. In answer Giles began to move too, the rhythm of his passion overtaking her caution, sweeping her along on a building crescendo of sensation that she recognised from his earlier lovemaking. But this was fuelled, driven, by his body, too. She was part of it, swept up in it, unaware that her head was moving restlessly on the pillows, her fists were clenched against Giles's chest or that she was crying out with pleasure. It reached a point where she could not withstand the tension any longer, her body arched into his, driving him deeper, convulsing around him as he cried out and the two of them collapsed back on the bed in a tangle of entwined limbs, their mouths locked in a final, desperate kiss.

Chapter Twenty-One

Joanna came to herself to find that Giles was still lying above her, his weight on his elbows, his forehead resting against hers. Her wide open eyes were so close to his that their eyelashes tangled and he smiled and raised his head to look at her better.

'Thank you,' he said simply.

'It was all right? I…'

'You were perfect. I could not have dreamed of anything more perfect. That you want me, that you trust me—I cannot imagine a more wonderful gift.'

'I loved it, too,' Joanna said, uncaring how brazen that sounded. 'Giles, I had no idea it would be like that. I thought perhaps you would find me clumsy: everything I did was just instinct.'

'Mmm.' He bent his head to kiss her slowly along the line of her collarbone. 'Your skin is like silk.

Instinct? You have the most wonderful, sensual, loving, natural instincts, Joanna. Just think how good we are going to be together the more we practise. I foresee the need for a lot of practice.'

He rolled carefully over on to his back and stretched like a cat. 'I feel so good.'

'Even your leg?' Joanna sat up rather unsteadily and looked at the bandage that appeared, by some miracle, to still be in place.

'I wouldn't want to go on a route march,' Giles admitted, cautiously flexing the foot and grimacing as the damaged tendons stretched. 'I am going to have to make love to you at least three times a day simply to get enough exercise.'

'Oh,' Joanna feigned a pout. 'Only three times?'

'Minx,' Giles said appreciatively. 'If you carry on sitting there looking so utterly delectable I will just have to…'

He broke off at the sound of the door handle being rattled. Then they heard Alex's voice on the other side raised in what Hebe always referred to as his 'parade-ground shout'. 'Giles! This door is jammed.'

Giles shouted back at the same volume. 'It's locked, you idiot.'

'Then open it!'

Joanna pressed her hands over her mouth to suppress the giggles.

'How can I?' Giles demanded. 'I can't walk.'

Joanna hissed, 'Ask him if everything is all right. He sounds drunk.'

'Lord, Hebe! I had forgotten.' Giles raised his voice again. 'Is everything all right? How is Hebe?'

'Couldn't be better!'

'He *is* drunk,' Giles commented, grinning. 'The baby has come?' he shouted back. 'Really,' he added, dropping his voice again, 'this is a ludicrous way to have a conversation.'

'Then make him go away and I'll open the door,' Joanna said, hopping out of bed and searching frantically for her stockings. 'I can hardly let him in now, can I? Look at this room.'

'Indeed,' Giles drawled, regarding the havoc from under sensual, hooded lids.

'Of course the baby's come! We want you to come and see. I'll get Starling to fetch the spare key and a couple of footmen with a chair.'

On this threat he appeared to leave. Joanna gave a muffled shriek, scrambled all her clothes together and bolted into the dressing room, only to be recalled by Giles.

'Unlock the door, quickly, and throw that sheet back on the bed!'

Joanna closed the door of the dressing room and pulled on her clothes with as much calm as she could manage given a mixture of giggles over their predicament, joy at hearing that Hebe and the baby were both well and a complete sensual daze engendered by Giles's lovemaking.

At the sound of Starling and what sounded like at least four footmen arriving in the bedroom, she sat down at the dressing table and regarded her image in the glass. Dragging Giles's comb through her hair restored some order to her appearance but did little for the flush in her cheeks or the crimson swell of fiercely kissed lips.

'He loves me,' she whispered. *'He loves me.'* It was a miracle, but it was no dream, not with her body throbbing with the knowledge of his, not with the proof of his love in every tender word, every skilful caress.

When the room outside fell silent she risked a peep around the edge of the door to find Giles sitting in the chair clad in a gorgeous Oriental silk dressing gown, the walking cane she had fetched him by his side.

Giles grinned. 'Starling says that he trusts that his lordship's natural joy at the "Happy Event" did not disturb my rest, but he fears that his lordship cannot have tried the door handle properly in his "understandable excitement". He quite understands that I do not wish to be carried through the halls of Tasborough in the manner of a Roman emperor and will make my own way to her ladyship's suite when Miss Fulgrave returns from her own room.'

'Thank goodness. Giles, have you any idea where my hair pins ended up?'

'All over the bed, I imagine. That *will* cause the chambermaid to speculate in the morning.'

'No, it won't,' Joanna was determinedly shaking out pillows and smoothing the under sheet. 'Six, seven…eight. That's all of them. Now I'll just put my hair up and we'll go and see Hebe.'

With the aid of her arm and the stick, Giles managed to get to his feet and hobble painfully along the corridor. 'Can't put any weight on it, otherwise it's fine,' he ground out in answer to Joanna's attempt at a calm enquiry as to how his leg felt, but the beads of sweat on his forehead said rather more than he was willing to reveal and Joanna could only be thankful that there were no stairs to negotiate.

To Joanna's anxious gaze Hebe seemed very small and far away in the big bed, but although her voice was tired it sounded strong as she cried, 'Joanna, Giles! Come in. Giles, sit down at once—Joanna, why did you let him walk?'

Joanna pressed Giles firmly into the nearest chair and ran to Hebe's bedside. 'How on earth do you expect me to stop him? He is as stubborn as a mule. Oh, Hebe, how lovely! Is it another little boy?'

'Meet young Giles,' Hebe said with a smile which lit up her tired, pale face. 'Here, take him.'

'Oh, may I? He is so tiny! Giles, look…'

She turned to find Giles still sitting in the chair, an identical shawl-wrapped bundle in his arms and Alex by his side looking not drunk, just utterly dazed and happy.

'Twins! Giles, you were right!'

'This one is little Joanna,' Alex said, smiling as Joanna had never seen him smile. 'We thought you both might be willing to be godparents.'

Giles looked up at his friend. 'Very happily, on one condition: you stand as my groomsman.'

'Joanna!' Hebe threw her arms wide and, handing little Giles to his father, Joanna went and cast herself into her cousin's embrace. 'Thank goodness, I was beginning to think the pair of you would never work it out.' She looked closely at Joanna and said, low voiced, 'If there is anything you want to talk to me about, you only have to say.' Joanna blushed hotly and Hebe's eyebrows rose. 'I see, perhaps I am a little late. *What* a bad chaperon I am.'

'Dreadful,' Joanna agreed solemnly, 'but a very good friend. Oh, Hebe,' she whispered, 'I love him so much it hurts.'

'I know,' Hebe agreed. 'And it never gets any better, thank goodness.'

They were interrupted by Nurse bringing Hugh down to meet his new brother and sister and Joanna helped Giles to his feet and out of the room.

'This is a truly wonderful day,' Giles said, gathering Joanna against his side and hugging her tight. 'Shall we go back to my room and discuss exactly how many children we plan to have?'

'It is very tempting,' Joanna smiled up at him, 'but first I must write to Mama and the Geddings and Georgy, and you must write to your father.'

'No, that is the second thing,' Giles said, seeing Starling advancing in a stately manner down the corridor. 'Starling! Break out his lordship's best champagne and find me those footmen and their chair. I intend to be carried in state to the dining room and there to consume lobster and champagne with my affianced bride.'

Starling rose to the occasion. 'Congratulations, Colonel. I will place the wine on ice at once and set out the very best crystal. As to the lobster, I will ascertain whether one is to be found upon the premises.'

As the butler swept down the staircase, summoning minions to his side, Joanna rested her cheek against the heavy silk of Giles's sleeve. 'I do not think I would ever have had the courage to rebel as I did if it were not for that champagne you gave me at the Duchess's ball. Do you remember? I had a dreadful hangover the next day and as far as Mama was concerned that started my disgrace.'

Giles pulled her tight against him. 'I just want to see your eyes turn green and sparkle with that same fire I saw in them that night. I want to kiss your lips to taste the wine on them as I could not then. And I never, ever want to part from you again as long as I live.'

'You want to hold me captive?'

'Chained to my heart and my soul for ever.'

At the head of the stairs Starling held up a restraining hand to four stalwart footmen who were carrying a chair between them. They obediently turned their backs and waited patiently while Colonel Gregory satisfied himself that his runaway love perfectly understood the terms of her surrender.

'For ever,' Joanna whispered against his lips. 'For ever.'

* * * * *